YEAGER'S LAW

A THRILLER

SCOTT BELL

Unlocking New Worlds

Yeager's Law
Copyright © 2014 by Scott Bell. All rights reserved.
First Print Edition: May 2015

ISBN-13: 978-1-940215-48-8
ISBN-10: 194021548X

Red Adept Publishing, LLC
104 Bugenfield Court
Garner, NC 27529
http://RedAdeptPublishing.com/

Cover and Formatting: Streetlight Graphics

*For my parents, who read my early stuff and pretended to like it,
and for my wife, who suffered through too many drafts to count.*

CHAPTER 1

Highway 67
Near Judsonia, NE Arkansas

Two hours after dawn, at the wheel of his Peterbilt, Abel Yeager glanced at the fuel gauge. His frown turned into a deep scowl. *Maybe it's just kidding.* He tapped the gauge with a blunt finger, as if he thumped it hard enough, fifty gallons of diesel would reappear. Instead, the needle sank closer to E.

He shook the last two antacid tablets from the family-sized bottle he kept in the center console and crunched the cherry-flavored chalk. If Tums had nutritional value, he would never have to stop for food again.

Yeager did the math. Again. He would need to refuel before Chicago. After that, he could either hang around the terminal looking for a load, or dead-head back to McAllen, making at least one more fuel stop along the way. Another chance at plasticide, playing Russian roulette with Visa, MasterCard, and American Express. He maybe had one more attempt at a balance transfer before they caught on to his bill shuffling.

Traffic had thinned the farther he got from Little Rock. A black Lexus was pacing him in his rearview mirror. The driver hung back at a steady half-mile distance, not passing, not pulling off, and not falling back. It itched like a bug bite that was just out of reach. Probably nothing more than a civilian who happened to be going the same way. That happened sometimes on long stretches of Interstate.

1

Nothing to get your panties in a bunch over. Yeager twisted his neck, making it crackle, and decided it was time for a pit stop.

He pulled his rig into a rest area on US Highway 67 outside of Judsonia, Arkansas. A block building stuck on the edge of a soybean field, with state-maintained toilets and concrete picnic benches, was flanked by parking lots for trucks on one side, cars on the other. He had the place to himself at eight o'clock on a Monday morning.

He grabbed a dog-eared copy of *Field & Stream*, locked the cab, and headed for the john. A mild June breeze ruffled the soybean fields that stretched as far as a rifle shot across the red clay soil to a distant tree line. A rabbit bolted from the mown grass of the rest area and bounded into the field, white tail flashing.

Yeager paused to watch it. *We're hunting wabbits.* A kid in his old platoon, Sonny, could imitate Elmer Fudd as if channeling the spirit of Mel Blanc. Platoon C, sweating, tired, and edgy, would be on the trail of some Taliban bad guys deep in Indian country, then Sonny would turn around and whisper, "Be vewy, vewy quiet. We're hunting Tawwiban. Heheheheheh." The guys would crack up.

The New Jersey boy had stayed in Southern California after mustering out. He, his wife, and two kids shared a three-bedroom bungalow with his brother.

Sonny had called him last week and said, "Yo, Staff Sergeant, you'll never guess. I got a job."

"What? Hey, that's great."

"Yeah, I'm a route man for the Bud distributor. I drive around with cases and cases of beer, man. Can you believe it? Beer, beer everywhere and I don't even drink."

"That's good news, Sonny. Glad to hear it. Don't make the mistake I did and buy your own truck, amigo. It ain't worth the hassle."

After a long pause, Sonny cleared his throat. "Ah..."

"Spit it out, Private."

"It's about the money, Staff Sergeant."

"What money?"

"Yeah, funny. Look, man, I'll pay you back."

"Bullshit you will," Yeager said. "What you're gonna do is go into HR tomorrow and start taking out ten percent—not five, not eight, but *ten* percent—of your pay, and you're gonna put that in a college fund for your yard monkeys."

"But—"

"Did you just use the word 'but' with me, Private? Did I hear that come out of your mouth? Because if I did, you know I'll reach through this phone and rip your lungs out through your mouth. You feelin' me, Marine?"

"Yes, Staff Sergeant."

"Good. Now give Maria a kiss from me, and go do what I say."

"Aye-aye, Staff Sergeant."

Pushing open the door to the restroom, Yeager cracked a tiny smile and sent Sonny a silent prayer of goodwill.

The black Lexus glided into the rest area and purred to a stop behind the dumpsters, concealed from the big rig.

"Now?"

"Yes, Jaime, *mi hijo*," Humberto Cruz said. "You know what to do?"

"Of course."

"Julio, back him up. Hector, stay here and keep an eye out. You have your tire iron?"

Hector nodded and slapped the length of iron bar into one hand. Cruz had seen him use it once. From what he could tell, Hector had enjoyed the experience.

Car doors thudded, and Cruz watched the team go to work. Several times, he had considered telling them his real objective, but in the end, he'd decided to keep that to himself. Sharing family business with a bunch of kids seemed... unworthy.

Those three were all he had available. Talent was hard to find with the cartels ratcheting up the pressure for shooters. Getting men who wanted to train for something as simple as hijacking wasn't easy.

Jaime practically skipped toward the target.

Cruz smiled. *To be so young...* He shut off the engine, climbed out of the car, and stretched his aching back.

Jaime went to work on the truck's door while Julio kept watch.

They moved quickly, and Cruz nodded in approval. In a minute, maybe less, they would have the truck, leaving Señor Yeager without a livelihood.

Cruz sneered as an American phrase popped into his head. *Payback's a bitch.*

⟫❖⟪

Yeager washed his hands and face with the pinkish soap from the dispenser. In the mirror over the sink, he saw a man he hardly recognized. Tiny crow's feet attacked the corners of his eyes. Sad eyes, women said, on those rare occasions when a woman had gotten close enough to comment on them. To him, they simply looked bloodshot and tired, more defeated than sad.

He dried off with a wad of paper towels, headed outside, and followed the concrete path back to his truck. A slim Hispanic kid was leaning against the fender.

Where'd he come from? Yeager spared a quick glance around. The parking area remained vacant, aside from his truck. A sparkling green quilt backdrop lay across the surrounding fields, the dew not yet burned off.

The guy wore jeans, cowboy boots, and an untucked Western shirt. Though his hair was cut high in the back, a long chunk of it fell over his forehead. The boy had to keep flipping it out of his eyes with a head toss.

He's gonna ask for a handout. One of those come-ons like: Hey, can you lend me a dollar for the bus, so I can get back home. A scam. It's always a scam. Yeager sighed and patted his pockets to see if he had any change.

Hairflip whistled through his teeth, and another Mexican kid barely old enough to shave popped his head up from behind the rig's steering wheel.

What the hell? I locked the cab. Yeager stalked closer, throttling his temper. Maybe they weren't trying to steal his truck. Maybe it was all a big mistake. *Sure. And chocolate milk comes from brown cows.*

Too often lately, anger simmered near the surface. Not much feeling remained in the black hole where his heart had once lived,

4

other than a pulsar of annoyance and bitterness that flared when he was upset. Like matter collapsing into the gravity well of a dead star, every other emotion had been crushed, condensed, and compressed by an unending implosion of bad luck and trouble. Divorce. The wreck. Six months of physical therapy. One damn thing after another.

Law Number Eight: Never fight angry.

Well. Fuck that. "You boys lost?" Yeager smiled, jaw clenched. "You needing a ride?"

A growling rig climbed the rise on US 67, downshifted, and rattled off into the distance. The breeze carried the scent of compost and diesel.

Hairflip held up his hand in a stop gesture. He strutted over and jabbed that hand into Yeager's chest, fingers spread. A lava flow of irritation bubbled from Yeager's belly.

The one in the cab had a ragged caterpillar of a mustache, and his gelled hair made him look like a teenage maître d'. His eyes peeping over the top of the steering wheel were as big as hubcaps.

Hairflip shook his head. "*Señor*, is best you go."

"Can't do that, amigo."

The puffed-up little delinquent tried a tough look, but his response came out petulant. "Go! We are taking this truck, *Señor*. Go away, and you will not get hurt."

Yeager snapped the boy's hand into a wristlock and took him down to one knee. "Now, son, I need this here truck. I borrow it every month from the bank, and they'd be upset, I was to lose it. You boys can walk away from this. Just nod your head if you understand."

The kid's mouth opened, and his eyes widened as he squirmed, trying to ease the pressure on his wrist, but Yeager had a solid grip. Yeager twisted the thief's hand back until the wrist turned white. He let out a breath and held short of the breaking point. Another half-ounce would do it. A tweak, really. Yeager grimaced and eased the pressure, gaining control of the bubbling little flare of hot violence.

The young hijacker in the cab scrambled down like a kid on a jungle gym. He hit the ground and dug into his waistband.

Law Number Six. Do something. Right or wrong, do something, and do it fast.

Yeager hit Hairflip with the force of a diesel piston firing, clubbing him with an iron fist framed by heavy bone and ridged with calluses. Something cracked in the punk's face, and he tumbled down, eyes rolling back in his head.

Yeager stepped over him and closed on the other kid, bull fast. He had another gear when it came to hand-to-hand combat. He shifted from DEFCON 2 to Wrath of God mode.

The boy's mouth flew open with a startled squawk. He scrambled back, whipping out a lock-blade knife with four inches of wicked-sharp steel. He flashed the blade—a poor man's Zorro sword—and rattled off something in Spanish. The kid lunged, stabbing at Yeager's belly. Yeager deflected the blade and snared the kid's wrist, inverting the knife-arm. Using his right hand like an ax, he chopped the back of the kid's elbow.

The arm made a wet, popping sound, like a turkey being torn up at Thanksgiving dinner. Screaming, the kid dropped the knife. He folded over, cradling his broken arm, and yammered away in Spanish, bawling and screeching.

Sounds a lot like my ex-wife. Knows some of the same words, too. Yeager kicked the knife, sending it skittering under the truck.

Footsteps scuffed behind him, and he pivoted. A third guy rushed around the front of the Peterbilt, a tire iron cocked, set to take off Yeager's head. Older and bigger, the new attacker had deep-set eyes and a mat of black hair cropped tight to his skull.

The pure, blazing-hot joy of action flared in Yeager's belly. Like the cool crust over a lake of boiling magma, his shell of indifference cracked, and golden warmth poured out. Fighting was something he could do. *That,* he understood.

Yeager ducked, and the metal bar *whooshed* past his ear. He came up into the big guy's middle with an uppercut that took the wind out of his attacker. Bad breath exploded in a huff, and the bigger thief staggered, face already turning red.

Yeager stepped back and measured off a right cross that rocked the guy back on his heels, sending the tire iron ringing off the pavement. The thief shook his head like a wounded bull. Yeager kicked him in the crotch then slammed both palms over the big man's ears. The guy dropped to the ground, one hand over an ear, the other cupping his balls.

Yeager sucked in a deep breath. Not many years ago, a fight like this would have been a good warm-up. Not anymore. He felt as if he'd run up a hill at Camp Pendleton with a full rucksack. He threw the tire iron into the field and stepped toward his truck to retrieve his cell phone. Calling the cops would result in a monumental loss of road time, but hijackers were bad for business. Getting those guys locked up might make the road safer for another trucker.

Pay it forward: Beat the crap out of hijackers.

With a screech of brakes, a shiny black Lexus slammed to a stop one space away from Yeager's vehicle. A guy hopped out of the driver's side and made his way around the front of the car. He was an older man, maybe in his sixties, with a shock of thick white hair gelled back. The guy wore a white Guayabera shirt with black slacks and shiny black shoes.

He also held a blue-steel semiautomatic pistol pointed right at Yeager.

CHAPTER 2

Highway 67
Near Judsonia, NE Arkansas

C HARLOTTE BUCHANAN MISSED THE RACE Street off-ramp before she realized there were no more exits for Searcy, Arkansas. No more chances for a decent bathroom from here to Canada. Or at least Missouri. And suddenly, the need to pee turned from urgent to critical.

She hunted for an exit with an overpass, but instead a Rest Area ½ Mile Ahead sign flashed by. *There. Problem solved.*

She flicked the BMW's turn signal and coasted into the parking lot, passing a black Lexus parked under the trees. She found a spot near the cube-shaped building and climbed out, stretching and holding her lower back.

Both restroom doors opened on a common breezeway, with caged vending machines standing in lockdown along one wall. She used the toilet and washed her hands. The facilities were surprisingly clean for a roadside stop in Arkansas. Charlie smiled at her Texas snobbery. *You're in Arkansas, not Somalia.*

She shouldered open the door rather than touch it with her freshly washed hands. Somebody screamed from the truckers' side of the rest stop, freezing her in place, halfway through the doorway.

What the hell? Forcing her feet to move, she crept to the end of the breezeway, peeked around the corner, and blinked in surprise. Three guys were on the ground, and a stocky man in a tan work shirt and jeans stood with one foot on the steps to a big rig. He was built like a Hummer, jeans one thread away from a patch and a

John Deere cap shading his eyes. Her first thought was that he was stealing the truck.

A black Lexus slammed to a stop next to the truck. A swarthy man in a white shirt climbed out of the car, his back to her. Clean shaven and almost aristocratic in appearance, the old man could have passed for a wealthy banker or a politician, except for the pistol he was pointing at Mr. John Deere Cap.

"*Pendejo*," the gunman said. "I was gonna let you live a little longer but not now."

Charlie hesitated. John Deere Cap looked like the good guy, but looks could be deceiving. If what she was seeing was just a falling-out among thieves, the wise thing to do would be to tiptoe away and leave them to it. But her feet wouldn't move. If John Deere Cap was the victim, she couldn't simply stand by and watch him get shot.

She stuck her hand into her shoulder bag and touched the butt of the revolver she carried while traveling. It had been her daddy's gun, and he'd taught her to shoot it. *A woman alone needs protection*, he used to say. She'd never pointed it at anybody in her life. A bass drum beat in her chest, hard enough to make her ribs hurt. From the heat in her cheeks, a flush was certainly turning her face scarlet.

I hate confrontation. The wrong move could get somebody killed—maybe *her. Then where would my son be?* A cold hand gripped her stomach, icy fingers digging in and making it hard to breathe. She needed to pee again.

It would be best if she backed away. If she left, no one would see her. She could call the cops once she was a few miles down the road. That would be the safe thing to do, the *smart* thing. Stepping into the situation and trying to play negotiator would be dangerous.

"Hey, *el jefe*," John Deere Cap said. "Sorry I broke your guys." He was poised, predator-still, only his head moving as he tracked the Lexus driver around the front of the car. Something about the way he stood plucked at her conscience. Leaving him to be killed would haunt her for a long time.

"You had to be a hero, hey?" Lexus raised the pistol, leveling it at John Deere's head. The gunman's voice rang out clear and loud in the morning stillness, and Charlie could make out every word, despite his accent. "Well, now you are to be a dead truck driver."

Charlie dithered, fear warring with her conscience. *I have to do something.*

━━━━━◆◆◆━━━━━

Yeager froze when the white-haired gunman squinted over the pistol's sights. The guy held the weapon properly, not sideways like the idiots in the movies. His stance, his eyes, and his utter calmness marked him as a pro, not some amateur hijacker.

Yeager calculated his odds at minus zero and falling. *I need him within six feet—even ten would do—so I have a chance to make a play.* He might take a bullet. He was prepared for that; he'd been shot before. It sucked then and it would suck now, but if the wound wasn't immediately fatal, he could come to grips, deflect the pistol, and break the guy's neck. *Simple as nuclear fission.*

"Are you the boss of this outfit of would-be badasses?" Yeager asked. If the guy was talking, he wasn't shooting. If he wasn't shooting, Yeager had a chance.

The older man glared. "It is my responsibility."

"To do what?"

"To take care of my family's business." He cocked his head a tiny bit to the right to focus over the sights. He appeared to be savoring the moment.

Yeager slid his foot forward, edging toward the Lexus and trying to close the distance a bit. If he couldn't make a play for the gun, maybe he could use the car as a shield. To rush him, Yeager would have to jump over one unconscious body, cross twelve feet of pavement, maneuver around the front of the car, and then disarm his attacker. *And maybe pigs will buy first-class airline tickets to Hawaii for their own cookout.*

El Jefe's black eyes were ice cold, surrounded by darkened sockets, as if the skin around them had been freezer burned. He stood at the front bumper of the Lexus and pointed the pistol directly at Yeager's forehead.

The guy could shoot me forty-seven times, go for coffee, come back, and shoot me some more before I covered that much distance. He snorted quietly. *Maybe that would be for the better. No bad dreams in Hell.*

El Jefe's finger tightened on the trigger. Yeager tensed to jump and roll behind the Lexus.

"Freeze!" a woman barked.

The hijacker jerked. Yeager let out a shallow breath when the white-haired killer didn't shoot him in surprise.

A redhead marched from the restroom breezeway, carrying a nickel-plated, large-frame revolver. She walked with a loose, rolling gait that covered ground fast and swished her skirt around her calves. Yeager blinked, and she didn't go away, so she had to be real. She held the weapon as though she knew how to use it, too.

She stopped close enough to not miss if she fired and too far away to be rushed. She assumed a letter-perfect shooter's stance, big gun braced with both hands, legs positioned to absorb the recoil. "Drop the gun!" she ordered. Her hands trembled slightly, the knuckles gone as white as her face. She was obviously scared spitless, but she was holding it together.

El Jefe lowered his pistol and looked at the woman with an expression that would have been funny had Yeager seen it in a movie. The triple click of the redhead cocking her massive revolver made Yeager's butt squeeze. A tiny bit of trigger pull and that hand-cannon would go off, flattening trees and knocking down telephone poles. It was at least a .41 Magnum if not a .44.

Time stretched, seconds thudding in a delayed beat. The gang leader—more like the gang's schoolmaster—tensed as if he might go for it. He probably thought the redhead was some white suburban housewife playing with a big firearm that would knock her on her ass the first shot. His face remained inscrutable, except for the eyes. Yeager sensed a reptilian soul living in those dark pits. The guy would be a tough read across a poker table. *The question is, will he call or fold?*

One eye squinted, El Jefe took a deep breath and let it out, still holding a murderous frown. He lowered his handgun and engaged the safety. "Is okay," he muttered. Then louder, he called to her,

"See? We are going." He turned to the older hijacker, the one still holding his balls, and spoke in Spanish. "Get your brother into the car. Everyone. In the car."

Yeager's border Spanish was good enough to keep up with El Jefe's instructions. Like an angry father herding his children into the family vehicle to go on vacation, El Jefe watched his flock of would-be gangsters slink away. The limping guy helped Zorro into the backseat. The boy cradled his arm like a baby, and his brother took care not to jostle it. The first guy Yeager had decked, the one with the flopping hair, slid into the passenger seat, glaring in capital letters at Yeager as he passed within arm's length.

"See, *mi hermosa*, we are going." El Jefe stalked, stiff-legged and angry, to the door of the Lexus. Yeager noted that he tucked the automatic under his shirt at his back as he climbed into the driver's seat.

The redhead tracked the driver the entire way, laser focused. She swallowed hard enough that her throat moved. It took strong arms to hold a gun as heavy as her Smith & Wesson on target, yet she managed to keep her aim as steady as a marble statue.

Yeager didn't breathe again until the Lexus zoomed away and headed up the entrance ramp, turn signal flashing. *How courteous. He'll jack your truck and threaten to shoot you, but he practices defensive driving.*

The sedan accelerated onto the highway and disappeared from view, carrying away the load of juvenile crooks and the old killer with the ice-cold eyes. Yeager frowned. That meant the hijackers were ahead of him, somewhere on the road. And they were pissed.

CHAPTER 3

Highway 67
Near Judsonia, NE Arkansas

"THANKS FOR THE RESCUE," YEAGER said. Oddly, he found he was feeling pretty good for having had a close brush with death. Better than he'd felt in days. "It wasn't your fight, but I'm glad you got involved."

Slumped as if all the air had leaked out of her, the woman held the revolver loose, down by her side. "Well, I didn't have anything else to do this morning." She laughed, but it sounded shaky.

"You look a mite pale. Why don't you sit down for a minute?"

The taller-than-average, lean, and long-limbed woman wore a sleeveless shirt-dress that she filled out nicely. Her thick mane of coppery-red hair, the color of last year's pennies, flared as a gust of wind stirred across the soybean fields. "Good idea. I think I'm going to throw up."

Yeager touched her gently on the elbow and led her to one of the concrete picnic tables, where she sagged more than sat. He took the bench across from her and gestured at the shiny Smith & Wesson she laid on the table.

"May I?" He pointed at the gun.

She hesitated a second but nodded. He picked it up and broke open the cylinder. Six fat .41 Magnum cartridges rested in their chambers. He plucked one out. *Hollowpoint. Holy cow.*

He snapped the cylinder closed and laid the weapon back on the table. "You plannin' on killin' a bear today?"

"Daddy told me that if I didn't hit 'em, at least I'd scare 'em to death." She flashed a weak smile. Red blotches colored her neck and the exposed skin at the open collar of her dress. She had clear sky-blue eyes, direct as sunlight, and a delicate face with high cheekbones and a slim nose.

"Muzzle blast alone ought to do it. You handled that situation like a pro. Are you a cop?"

"No, not even close." She tried out another shaky laugh. "My first showdown."

"Will you be okay here? I need to go call the cops. I've got a CB in my truck, and that'll be faster than using a phone."

"Sure."

Yeager walked to his truck and fired it up to start the power going. He reported on the emergency channel, giving his location and a description of the Lexus. By the time he signed off and returned to the picnic table, the lady seemed composed. The gun had disappeared, presumably back into her purse. At a distance, she appeared to be the type of lady he'd see coming out of a Nordstrom's or sipping iced tea on the porch of a mansion. Upon closer inspection, the laugh lines and the dusting of freckles said *tomboy*.

Yeager pushed his cap back on his head, acutely aware of his underarm sweat, worn clothes, and bristly face. "So what do I call you? Besides my hero, I mean." Something stirred south of his belly that hadn't been heard from in a while. Not since the wreck, anyway. It wasn't much more than a twinge, but he crushed it quick. *No use letting wild thoughts of happiness take root.* That road led to nowhere but the town of Disappointment, population *him. Anyway, she's way out of your league, Abel. You can't even buy a ticket to a game in her league, let alone play there.*

She extended one slim hand. "Charlotte. Charlotte Buchanan. But my friends call me Charlie. And you? Are you Abel Yeager?"

Yeager stiffened. "How'd you know that?"

"That's what it says on the door of your truck. Abel Yeager Trucking, McAllen, Texas."

"Ah." Yeager glanced at his truck. "I'm a genius."

"So what was all that about?"

14

"Hijackers. I suspect they were after the copper."

She cocked a questioning eyebrow. A breeze blew a red ribbon of hair across her face, and she pushed it back over her ear.

"Copper wire," he explained. "Street value's damn near as high as cocaine. And it's easier to sell."

She nodded. "That happen a lot? Hijackers?"

"Not to me, but yeah, especially since the cartels started fighting it out down in Mexico. Lots of bad guys these days, looking for new ways to make money." He looked away—Charlotte Buchanan's eyes had hit him with an almost physical force—and studied the parking area. "You handled yourself pretty well there. You always that cool under pressure?"

"No, never. I don't know what I was thinking. I can't even return something to a store, I hate confrontation so bad. I'm like the UN because I'm always the peacemaker." Charlie smiled and shook her head. "How'd they know what you were carrying?"

"I imagine they followed me from the wire factory down in Benton."

An eighteen-wheeler with a PetSmart trailer rolled into the rest area and came to a stop at the far end of the parking lot. The parking brakes hissed. Yeager waited for the driver to come out so he could warn him about the hijackers, but the truck door remained closed. The diesel idled, sending vibrations through the ground to his feet.

"What happens now?" she asked.

"Well, if I'm lucky, they'll catch them old boys somewhere down the road and send 'em all to jail. If I'm really lucky, those guys'll run off the road and all die in a fiery crash." An image of the young hot-wire kid came to mind, and he winced. *That boy ought to still be in high school, not out boosting trucks.* "Ah hell. I don't really mean that. I don't think they ought to die, but I hate the idea of wasting time testifying in court. Or worse..."

A crow cawed from the far side of the soybean field, and another answered from near the picnic bench.

"Or worse what?" Charlie prompted.

"Or worse, they'll be laying for me somewhere down the road, and the next time I won't see 'em coming."

The state cops were efficient but in no particular hurry. They listened to Yeager's account of the attempted hijacking, took notes and digital pictures, looked in the cab of his truck, and then made him go through it again. They turned serious and a little tense when they discovered Charlotte Buchanan carried a whopper of a gun in her oversized shoulder bag. She let them take it out and unload it before she put it back in her purse. The cartridges disappeared in a pocket of her dress.

A slim, black cop with a dusting of snowy white in his hair filled out a form on a metal clipboard. He stood eye-to-eye with Yeager, at about six feet tall. "Did you get a tag number?"

"No, they had one of those paper tags that car dealers use, had a date instead of numbers."

"Got it. Well, maybe we can pull something from the video."

"What video?"

They were obvious once the trooper pointed them out. A brace of cameras covered the parking lot and the vending machine area.

"The state installed security systems at these rest stops a couple of years ago. Somebody got raped in one down south of here and sued the state for lack of security. We'll get the Highway Department out here to open the door so we can pull the recording." The trooper dug out a blank form from the back of his box-like clipboard and turned to Charlie. After the basics of name and address, he asked where she worked.

"I own a bookstore in Austin and an online book business," she said.

Abel watched her while she answered the questions. A pulse beat steadily in her throat.

She held her hair back with one hand. "My store is called Book Finders. You know, like book binders? But with an F? I was on my way to St. Louis to buy a bulk load of mass market remainder books for my online division."

She produced a business card and handed it to the trooper. He clamped it under the clip and copied information from the card onto the form.

The other trooper returned from the patrol car and led Yeager over into the shade of another picnic area canopy. An SUV pulled into the rest stop. It slowed, the family inside staring at the police activity. They must have decided they didn't need to stop after all because they drove back out onto the highway. Yeager didn't blame them.

"So where'd you learn to fight like that?" The cop took off his Smoky Bear hat; the strap left a mark across the back of his scalp. "Taking out three guys, I mean."

"Marines. I spent some time in the sandbox."

"Iraq or Afghanistan?"

"The Stan."

The officer nodded. "I was in Iraq. Logistics battalion."

Yeager looked across the green soybean fields bordering the rest stop. A hawk turned in the air, wings spread to catch the breeze. The PetSmart truck still idled at the far end of the lot. The driver was probably in the sleeper, catching a nap.

"How long will this take?" Yeager asked. "Not to sound like I'm bitchin', but I'm losing time here."

"Should be about done." The trooper glanced back at where his partner was talking to Charlie. "She's a looker, huh? Classy, too."

"Yes, she is that."

Charlie must have sensed their gaze. She looked up and smiled at them.

"That's a woman would make a potato sack look like a prom dress," Yeager added.

"You gonna ask her out?"

Yeager croaked a startled laugh. "You see that gun she carries? Besides, I'm a truck driver, made it through high school thanks to kindhearted teachers. I got no business thinking about a woman like that."

The state troopers took another half hour completing their paperwork before releasing Yeager and Charlie. While the cops climbed in their patrol car, Charlie glided over to Yeager with that fluid, rolling gait of hers and extended her hand for a shake. She had a firm grip.

"Well, until the next time you meet some hijackers..." she said.

"I'll be sure to call you." Yeager twisted his lips in a strained smile. The muscles around his mouth weren't used to the expression.

She dug out another business card, prompting Yeager to go into his wallet and find one of his. His card looked as though it had seen better days, coming out of his wallet like a homeless guy from a shelter.

"Thanks," Charlie said, with no apparent disdain for the tattered card. "I'd say let's do this again, but I don't want to tempt fate."

"No problem. And thank you for saving my ass."

Charlie smiled, said goodbye, and headed for her car with brisk, businesslike strides. Yeager stood for a moment and enjoyed the sway of her skirt and the way her hair bounced on her shoulders. *Better get back in the truck, Abel. Got miles to go.*

CHAPTER 4

HUMBERTO SANTIAGO CRUZ GUIDED THE black Lexus off the highway at the first exit past the rest stop. He took the two-lane country road for about a mile before he found a spot wide enough to pull over.

"Shut the fuck up," he told the moaning Jaime. "You cry like a woman."

Hector, Jaime's brother, huddled in the back seat with one arm around the injured kid. "His arm is broken. We need to get him to a doctor."

"What do I look like to you? Blue Cross Blue Shield?" Cruz yanked out his cell phone and stabbed at the buttons. "We should maybe go to a hospital and say please fix my friend's arm? Huh? How did he break it? Well, we were stealing this truck, and some gringo, some motherfucking truck driver, kung fucked the shit out of us. Now shut up." Cruz put the phone to his ear and barked, "Chupa? We have a problem."

A dusty red tractor puttered toward them. The farmer jouncing in the seat gave a lazy wave as he passed. Cruz sneered and didn't wave back.

"Where are you?"

"Searcy. At the Carl Jr's."

"Yes, good, you're close. I need you to find the rest stop on 67 outside Judsonia."

"*Donde*?"

"Judsonia, *cabrone*! Look it up on the fucking map. Find the copper wire truck—"

"The Yeager hombre's truck?"

"Yes, that one. It's a long story. Now shut up, and do what I tell you. Follow the truck. Don't let the guy see you. Soon as you can, put a tracker on the cab. I want to be able to find him again, *comprende? Bueno.* I have to dump this car and somehow steal another one here in Dog Tick, Arkansas."

Jaime moaned again.

"And I got to find a doctor for your *puta* friend, Jaime."

"What's up with Jaime?"

"No, never mind. I tell you later. Do what I say." He ended the call and took stock of his sorry crew.

Julio glanced up through one eye, the other swollen shut. Jaime rocked back and forth, pale and sweaty. So close. Cruz'd had the killer in his sights, looked directly into the man's eyes. *I will see that* pendejo *truck driver again. And the next time, won't be some bitch with a gun around to save his ass.*

Scattering gravel, Cruz pulled back onto the highway. He made a U-turn and gunned the engine.

<hr/>

Sullivan's Steakhouse
Austin, Texas

Dr. Steven Buchanan's cell phone vibrated right at the crucial moment of his pitch. The downtown steakhouse buzzed with lunchtime traffic, waiters in white shirts pinballing from table to table. His pair of fish—Dr. and Mrs. Dodson—diddled over their Irish coffee while he checked the display.

Charlie. His ex. She was probably letting him know she'd made it to St. Louis.

Good. Convincing her to go had been easier than he thought. Steven mentally crossed his fingers. *Please, Lord, don't fuck things up now.* If Charlie figured out what he was doing, she'd...

Steven tapped Ignore with his thumb and kept the rhythm of his patter going, using the potential distraction to sweeten the pot. "Sorry, that was my research lead texting me. We've gotten a really good response on the NOX4 inhibitors."

"NOX4?" Mrs. Dodson, gray hair piled in a beauty-shop perm and fixed in place with a spray-on lacquer, blinked wet eyes then fixed her doughy husband with a befuddled look. After two pre-lunch gin and tonics, red wine with her meal, and a second Irish coffee, the woman was listing slightly to one side.

"It's an oxygen-sensing enzyme that plays a role in inhibiting reactive oxygen species, or ROS," Steven explained. "Usually... well, let me say it this way: limiting ROS is a good thing, and our NOX inhibitors are going to do exactly that."

"All the more reason," Dr. Dodson rumbled, "you should let me in on this deal, Stevie."

Steven leaned back in his seat and picked up his cup of coffee—regular, not Irish. It was time to play hard to get. But not *too* hard. The patter never varied. He could practically turn on a mental tape recorder, hit Play, and not even have to think about what came out next. "I don't know, Gene..." Steve grimaced and rubbed his chin, staring at the table. "The pot's pretty full already. I mean, look at it this way: My investors are expecting to hit it big. The more money in the pool, the lower everybody's dividend when the FDA approval hits. We go public with Phase One trials, and—*boom!*—stock will skyrocket."

"So you're thinking what, six hundred percent return?" Dr. Gene Dodson had a beefy face and a triple-bypass body. When they played golf, the man had to stop for a breather—and a beer—after nine holes. "My little bitty chunka change can't make *that* much difference."

"Gene—"

"I mean, make it easy on yourself. How much can I buy in for and not rock the boat? Fifty K? A hundred?"

And there it was. Every time a fish bit the hook and jerked the float underwater, a zinger of electricity shot through Steven's chest. Better than sex. Better than a perfect tee shot. Better than when he made his first legit million. Or mostly legit.

"All right, Gene. You win." Steven sighed and signaled the waiter for another round. "Looks like we may be here awhile. Let me call my office and have 'em courier over some paperwork."

Dodson slapped the table. "There you go! That's what I wanted to hear."

"Congratulations, Mrs. Dodson," Steven told the owl-eyed woman. "Your husband has bought you a piece of a medical miracle."

<hr>

Dallas, Texas

Harlan King picked up Warren "Skeeter" Davis at the corner of Commerce and Industrial, outside the Lew Sterrett Justice Center. Downtown Dallas jutted up on the other side of the freeway, glass buildings baking in the afternoon sun. Diesel fumes and the toxic smell of the Trinity River drifted on the air.

Skeeter wasn't hard to spot, standing on the corner like a piece of chewed-up beef jerky that had been left to dry on the sidewalk. After half his life in prison, he stood slightly stooped, like a human praying mantis.

"Yo, dog," Harlan said when the mantis dropped into the Challenger's passenger seat.

"Yo, dawg?" Skeeter's Alabama drawl came with a coating of tar and nicotine. "What's 'is 'yo, dawg' shit? You ain't no gang-bangin' asshole. You're a goddamn ghost-white surfer from goddamn Anaheim."

"I'm still a stone killah. Shit sounds cool, dude. Y'hear what I'm sayin'?"

"Shee-it." Skeeter hit the switch that put down the window and lit a cigarette.

"Want something to eat?" Harlan asked.

"Sure." He drew it out, so it sounded like *shore*.

Harlan cut a U-turn and headed to the McDonalds a block away. After they ordered burgers from the drive-thru, Harlan wheeled around to I-35, got confused by the street signs, and headed north, away from Dallas, toward Denton. He took the next exit and turned around. The smell of cheeseburgers and ketchup filled the car.

Harlan ate one-handed, trying to keep from spilling hamburger gunk while he weaved through the stinking afternoon traffic.

Sunlight hammered the bright orange Dodge, reflecting off concrete and chrome, sparkling and hot.

March in Texas and already nine thousand degrees. Climate somewhere between Vegas and Hell.

"So, how was your last day, Junior?" Harlan asked. "Teacher give you a good grade?" He steered around a lawn care truck, Mexicans in the back staring at the tinted glass of his windshield. "Look at these fucking dipshits. No more brains than to ride around in the heat and do shit work for no pay."

"Huh?" A sharp-faced man, leathery-skinned, with one eye cocked off in a different direction, Skeeter was all planes, angles, and jagged edges.

"Last day in jail, dude. Did they give you a gold star for good behavior?" Harlan bit off a chunk of McBurger, ketchup dribbling down his palm. His light blond hair ruffled in the breeze from the hard-blowing air conditioning vent.

Skeeter chewed for a bit then sucked down some soda. "Yeah, they give me a get-outta-jail-today card, that's what they done. Three weeks was all they could keep me this time. Overcrowding."

"I'll bet."

Stalled in traffic, Harlan revved the engine, enjoying the rumble of the big Challenger. The new retro models didn't rock like the original version, but the throaty sound could still give a man a woody. Skeeter rolled down the window again, letting a hot, dry wind blow into the car, and tossed his takeout bag out the window.

"Jeez, dude," Harland said. "Don't be a litter bug."

"Fuck you. Didn't know you was the Enron-mental Pollution Agency." Skeeter lit another cigarette and blew smoke out the window. "So where we goin'?"

"St. Louis."

"Stoney's St. Louis deal going down? Whoo-wee. That right there's retirement money."

Harlan gave him a lopsided smile. "Everything's set. Just waiting for the last piece. We're going to see Dmitri, make sure he does his part. We have to stop in Texarkana along the way, squeeze the nuts of one of Stone's pet doctors. The guy's all of a sudden got a conscience, and we need to correct that little defect."

"You brought guns?"

"Dawg." Harlan tried out his ghetto voice. "Who you talking to? I gots me 'nough hardware, brotha, we's could take off da Pentagon."

Skeeter nodded, eyes crinkling as he squinted into the glare. "Good, cuz I feel like shootin' somebody."

━━━━➤◆◄━━━━

Big River Wholesale
St. Louis, Missouri

Charlie Buchanan had known Dareas Thompson for less than twenty minutes, and she already loathed him. He was fat enough to use a freight scale to weigh himself, and his body odor reminded her of rancid cheese. His teeth, when he leered at her, were stained as dark as tea. And the strawberries in her cream? He exuded a self-satisfied arrogance that made her dig her nails into her palms to keep from screaming.

Sweat beaded on the back of his neck and stained the collar of his Kobe jersey—size Huge?—as he led her into the Big River warehouse. She tried to breathe through her mouth in small sips as they went down a narrow hall and entered the warehouse proper. Once out of the confined space, she discreetly moved a few steps away. The warehouse was a cavern with metal racking to her right, open bay doors on her left, and a staging area in front of her. A forklift dropped a shrink-wrapped pallet at the opening of one of the bays and backed away, beeping a warning signal.

"You wanted the Wiley and the Harper nonfiction stuff?" Coupled with his careless attention to personal hygiene, Thompson possessed the customer service skills of a Russian waiter. "Mostly it's in them racks there." He pointed down an aisle, the flesh under his arm sagging. "Go'wan and take a look, see what you want. Write down the skid number."

"Thanks," she said, grateful to get away from him.

But he trailed after her, no doubt eyeing her ass as she walked where he pointed. Knowing she would be digging around in a warehouse, she had put on jeans and an SMU T-shirt, a relic from her college days, along with her New Balance running shoes. Not an outfit designed to attract men, but Mr. Thompson seemed undeterred.

Charlie had learned to ignore a man's sexual interest before she graduated high school, but Thompson was the type who wouldn't be deflected by subtlety. A ribbon-thin band of fear clamped her throat, making it hard to breathe. She would have to get her nerve up and somehow manage to shut him down.

Pull a gun on him, she thought. *Just like at the rest stop.*

That experience seemed so surreal. *Why did I do that?* She'd asked herself that a thousand times since, and no good answer had come to her. She was a conciliator, a facilitator, the one who settled arguments with cool words and a quick joke. So why had she acted all Chuck Norris and stuck her nose into that situation?

She dug into the skids, which were pallet-loads of books dumped haphazardly, chest high, into a cardboard box held together with shrink wrap and hope. The books were remainders, overstocks, and returns from major bookstores or publishing houses. Charlie bought an average of five tractor-trailer loads of remainders per year, from a variety of suppliers. Her current trip was her first, and probably last, visit to Big River.

"That's a good skid, right there," Thompson said, leaning on a rack, bald head gleaming in the yellowish overhead lights.

"Mm-hmm." Maybe he would get bored and leave if she didn't interact.

Charlie used a miniature barcode scanner attached to a PDA to check the current online price of each title. In every skid, some would be crap, and some would be gold, the trick being to find more gold than crap.

"Be a lotta fast movers in there."

Charlie ignored him and moved to the next skid.

"How'd you come to find us?" Thompson asked.

"My ex-husband, the doctor, believe it or not." She regretted using the term *ex* as soon as it left her mouth. "He met the owner somewhere and said I really should check you guys out."

"Where ya staying?" Thompson waddled a little closer. "You in a hotel?"

"No, heading out today." Charlie fought hard not to wrinkle her nose, but her eyes watered.

"Hey, Mr. D!" Saved by a scrawny worker with a Slavic accent. Thompson turned to see the guy on the forklift idling at the end of the aisle. "Where you want I put this?"

"I done tol' you, dumbass!" Turning back to Charlie, Thompson said, "Man, the guys I have to put up with. 'Scuse me jus' a minute."

"Sure," Charlie said. "No problem. Please. Take your time."

As she dug through the skids, she knew some of the books would end up in her retail shop, while the rest would go through her online division. In her retail store, a customer could find anything from the latest Nora Roberts to first-edition Hemingways and Faulkners, titles that had long since glutted the online marketplace. Her warehouse operation sold through sites like Amazon, eBay, Alibris, and her own website. Online sales demanded a keen eye for value, for prices fell quickly as dealers undermined each other for the lowest price.

Unbelievable. Steven was right, for once. There really is a lot of good stuff in these pallets. I may be forced to buy from Thompson, after all. How lucky can a girl be?

Interstate 57
60 miles south of Chicago, Illinois

Yeager didn't see the black Lexus, El Jefe, or any other potential troublemakers, which meant absolutely nothing. A tail on the Interstate could be pretty hard to spot. Drivers often saw the same cars for miles, sometimes leapfrogging each other as one or the other stopped for fuel, food, or facilities.

The PetSmart trailer from the rest area had followed him for the first hundred miles or so. Mr. PetSmart even pulled into the same fuel stop where Yeager stopped to top off his tanks, hit the john, and refill his thermos. The entire time Yeager was in the restroom, he tried to hurry, conscious of what had happened the last time he took a pee break. He didn't need another confrontation with hijackers. When Yeager pulled out, the PetSmart driver stayed behind, and Yeager saw nothing more of him.

Still, as he rode the concrete ribbon of Interstate through the heartland of the country, uneasiness settled in his stomach and wouldn't go away. He spent Monday night in the sleeper behind his cab, snoozing with one eye open.

Late Tuesday morning, hitting the thickening network of towns outside of Chicago, Yeager finally gave in to paranoia. He dug his cell phone out of the clutter on the seat beside him, powered it up, and hit the speed dial for Victor Ruiz. It rang a half dozen times before a familiar voice answered.

"My favorite gringo! Wassup, my truck drivin' frien'?"

"Hey, Por Que." Yeager had anointed Victor with the nickname long ago, because every time someone told young Victor that he was not allowed to do something, Victor would look at Yeager and say *"Por que no?"* Why not? "All the parts of your Huey still flying more or less in the same direction these days?"

"What?" Victor sounded hurt. He could sound hurt better than anyone Yeager knew, including his own mother. "No small talk? No how you doin', my best friend, since forever? I not only nurture you and protect you from all the evil bullies at McAllen High School and drag your sorry ass out of the brush in Afghanistan, but I also give you my sister in marriage?"

"Yeah, let's not bring that last one up, okay?"

"Okay. Good point."

"Listen, buddy, I need some help." Yeager related the hijacking attempt in rapid-fire bursts of words, as if giving a military briefing. "I have a bad feeling about these assholes. Nothing I can place, but I'm getting the willies."

"Oh no!" Victor could also sound dramatic better than anyone Yeager knew. "I know jus' wha' happens, you get the willies. It means some bad shit's about to rain down."

"So can you glue the rotor back on your antique helicopter and bring me some stuff?"

"*Por que no*, eh?"

That simple phrase had landed them in hot water more times than Yeager cared to count. Rumor had it that teachers, principals, and local law enforcement held a secret celebration party on the day Yeager and Ruiz graduated high school. When they returned to McAllen after their stints in the military, there was talk of holding a prayer vigil.

"For you, not only will I glue the rotor back on," Victor continued, "I will also go buy a compass from the Walmart. I think I can get one for two, three dollars, maybe."

"Yeah, spare no expense. Can you find Chicago with it?"

"No problem! Is that somewhere near Matamoros?"

"Yeah, that's the one."

Victor could wear him out, playing the dumb Mexican. About the only time he had ever been serious was on the day Yeager married Martina Ruiz, Victor's sister. Victor stood next to him, swaying slightly, monstrously hung over, and dug in his pocket for the ring while the guests watched from the pews. He looked as though he wanted to die or fall down, and it didn't matter which. He stayed serious the entire ceremony. At least until the reception.

"Listen, *mi amigo*. You want me to get to Chicago in a Huey, you know I'll have to fuel like a hundred times. I'll get Cujo to fly me up there."

"Does Cujo still have a pilot's license?"

"Yeah. Sure. Kind of." After a moment of silence, Victor added, "Don' worry. We'll fly very quietly."

"I need some stuff from my house," Yeager said. "Get a crayon and write this down."

CHAPTER 5

Big River Wholesale
St. Louis, Missouri

DAREAS THOMPSON TOLD THE BONEHEADED forklift driver, Dmitri, where to put the pallet. Again. The skinny Russian annoyed the crap out of him, always underfoot, asking stupid questions, getting in the way. At least the dimwit brought coffee every day.

Thompson mopped sweat from his forehead with the back of one hand and flicked it off, spattering the warehouse floor. He was wet as hell but still chilly. *Hope it's not a damn cold.* Being sick would really screw up his chance to talk that fine-looking redhead into staying in town and maybe having a little lunch with him. *Or some afternoon delight?*

His cell phone rang, not his regular one, but the special one. *The fucking Mexicans.* Thompson answered. He *always* answered.

"We want to place an order." No small talk, no jokes, no how's the weather bullshit. Which was fine with Thompson.

"Sure," Thompson said. "I got six skids of books, wrapped and ready. Usual place?"

"*Sí.*"

"Okay, when?"

"The truck will be there Thursday."

Two days away. "Got it."

The phone went dead. He watched the redhead bend over, digging through a skid. *Tasty. Skinny, moderate rack, but a fine, fine ass.*

Thompson shivered and wiped more sweat off his forehead, then massaged his left arm, which had started to ache.

<hr />

Austin, Texas

A guy in a Cadillac, on his cell phone, camped in the passing lane of I-35, his cruise set on fifty-eight miles per hour. Steven Buchanan rode the guy's bumper until he had a clear opening to pass on the right, then cut across the Caddy's nose, missing the slower car by the width of a sheet of paper. He shot the guy the finger and took the Infinity up to Mach 1.4.

His Bluetooth earpiece played a tone, and he tapped it on. "Go for Buchanan."

"Steven, ol' boy! How y'all doin'?"

"Danny Ebsen," he replied, injecting cheeriness into his tone. He made a mental note: *Next time, by God, check the caller ID before answering.* "Right as rain and fine as frog hair. What about you?"

"Howzat miracle cure comin' along?"

"Makin' progress, Danny, makin' progress. In fact, I got a text from the attorney, Rusty. He said the FDA has all but signed off to go to Phase One."

"Rusty? I thought you said the attorney's name was Tony-something."

Fucking accountants. They never forget anything. "Tony Wasserman's the top guy. Rusty's a junior partner, y'know?"

"Gotcha. So when are we gonna get out there to this lab? I'd like to get a look at this thing I sunk a half-mil into."

Shit. I should have stayed away from the nosy bastard. "Damn, Danny, wish I could, but I'm flying out to DC tomorrow to kiss ass at the FDA some more, make sure they don't get cold feet. Don't know when I'll be back."

"Well, all right, bud." Ebsen paused for several seconds. "Let's catch up soon, y'hear? Play us a few rounds."

"You betcha." Steven tapped off the connection.

Past time to move on and get the hell out of Dodge. The biotech thing wouldn't stretch much longer, and if the St. Louis deal played out the way they hoped, then nothing else would matter.

Thinking of St. Louis made him think of Charlie. Stephen took a couple of deep breaths then hit the speed dial for his ex-wife.

⟴

Big River
St. Louis, Missouri

Charlie perched on one of the two visitor chairs in Thompson's meager office, on the guest side of his chipped and stained wood-veneer desk. All the available shelves and surfaces were covered with die-cast metal cars on stands. She leaned back until her chair hit the wall, but her knees still rubbed the underside of the desk. Thompson pecked at his calculator while referring to her list of skids. Her phone buzzed, but she ignored it when she saw Steven's name on the screen.

"Here ya go." Thompson slid a piece of paper across the desk.

She read the itemized pricing, confirmed it matched the total in her head, then looked at the shipping total. "*How* much for shipping?" In the past, she had paid less than half what Thompson had written on that paper. No wonder his price for the books was so low—he made it up on the shipping charges.

"Rates is high these days. Price of gas, you know?"

She shook her head. "No. I *don't* know. I pay for shipping all the time, and this is... a lot."

Thompson seemed unperturbed. "You're welcome to arrange your own. Do you have a trucking company?"

"Yeah." She dug in her bag and found the worn business card. "I think I do."

⟴

Comfort Inn
Wheeling, Illinois

Yeager delivered his load of copper wire, got his paperwork signed, and drove his rig to the Wheeling Comfort Inn close to the Chicago Executive Airport. He winced when he thought of the cost of Avgas for the spit-and-baling-wire machine Victor's friend was using these days.

Cujo ran contraband across the border in whatever cheap, partially airworthy craft he could find. "If I have to ditch the plane," he once told Yeager, "I'm only out a few grand. If I bought, like, a real plane... well, shit, I'd be out a fortune if I had to dump it and run."

Three cards short of a full deck, Cujo reminded Yeager of the Muppet drummer, Animal. No one knew the man's real name. He had followed Victor back from Afghanistan like a lost puppy, a rabid, insane lost puppy, but still... Victor treated Cujo like the idiot brother-in-law in the family, the guy who showed up at Christmas, got drunk, and threw up in the kitchen sink. He had taken Cujo under his wing and mentored him, teaching him Victor's Rules of Good Crime.

"Good crime," Victor once told Yeager, "fucks over the Man. It's like Robin Hood, you know? Bad crime fucks over regular people, like you and me."

"I'll stick to legal trucking," Yeager had responded. "I may go broke, but I won't go to jail for fuckin' over the Man."

"Is okay for you. You a gringo, have all the advantages in a society designed to repress the Mexican."

"So what's Cujo? He's as white as I am."

"Cujo, he a Mexican at heart."

Yeager didn't want to spend the money on a hotel, even a cheap dive, but he needed a shower and a few hours of sleep in a real bed. Since the truck was empty, maybe the danger of theft had passed, and he could relax a little. *So why is the itch still there between my shoulder blades? And why did I drag Por Que up here, riding shotgun in a plane with a maniac?*

When he checked in, Yeager handed over his Visa card and studied the desk clerk's face while the man swiped it through the reader. Not seeing the frown he expected, Yeager released his pent-up breath. His cell rang as he took the card back from the clerk. Yeager answered without looking at the caller ID.

"Mr. Yeager. This is Charlie Buchanan. Remember me?"

He had expected it to be Por Que calling with an ETA, so the woman's voice threw him off kilter for a moment. Over-tired and groggy, Yeager's mind went blank. *Who?*

"The rest stop?" she said. "Monday? Hijackers?"

The name finally clicked. "Yeah, sorry, Charlie." *God, that sounded stupid.* "I didn't expect to hear from you again—I mean, so soon."

"I have a favor to ask."

"A favor? Sure, anything." He tucked the phone tighter to his ear, wondering why his heart had started thumping like a teenager's when asking for a prom date.

Charlie told him about some shipping issues she was having with Big River and asked him for a quote to move her skids from St. Louis to Austin. "I'll pay you a fair price for it. No obligation on your part."

Anything beat running empty back to McAllen. He asked some questions about the load, gross weight, and number of pallets, then quoted her a price that would at least help him pay for diesel on the way back.

"That's more than fair, Mr. Yeager," Charlie replied. "Are you sure it's not too low? I don't want any special deals because..."

"Because you saved my ass?" Yeager laughed. "I should be doing this for free. Wasn't for you, I'd be driving a truck full of coal down to Hell about now."

"I hardly believe that, Mr. Yeager." Her smile came through in her voice. "I was going to say because we fought bandits together."

"That we did. And please call me Abel."

"Abel. Will do. And thanks again, you've saved *my* butt this time."

"No problem," Abel said, finding it hard to end the conversation. "I don't see any problem at all getting your books down to you. Should be a piece of cake. I'll pick 'em up Thursday and have 'em down to you probably late Friday, early Saturday."

"Perfect. See you then."

CHAPTER 6

Little Rock, Arkansas

HUMBERTO CRUZ PAID HIS TAB at the Ruby Tuesday off I-30 on the outskirts of Little Rock and left the air-conditioned restaurant for the muggy parking lot. Streetlights were coming on, encouraging an onslaught of flying bugs. Highway traffic droned in the background.

He dropped into the driver's seat of his fresh wheels—a Ford Taurus—and started the engine to get the cool air blowing. He dialed a number on his prepaid cell.

"Si?"

"Get me my brother," Cruz said.

Muffled sounds and a voice he couldn't make out came through the earpiece. The restaurant doors opened, and a family of six trickled out and piled into a nearby minivan.

"Humberto?" Oscar asked.

"A little setback." Cruz explained about the hijacking attempt and the woman with the gun. "I had Chupa plant a tracker. He said the big trucker never even looked twice at the PetSmart truck. He planted the device clean. I sent Hector and Julio ahead to keep an eye on the trucker."

Oscar sighed. "I told you the plan was ridiculous. You should have driven up and killed him, right there when he got out of the truck."

"You are such an old woman sometimes. I told you, simply killing him is not enough. He must suffer more."

"How? By stealing his truck?" Oscar's voice pitched up a notch.

34

"He is nearly bankrupt. What more do you want? Just kill him. Or shoot him in the kneecaps, so he never walks again. Then we will have our revenge."

Cruz lit a cigarette. The lighter flame flickered as his hand trembled. "It is not enough," he finally said, blowing smoke through his nostrils.

"Fine," Oscar snapped. "Do it your way. I'm tired of arguing. Do you need more men?"

"No, I have Juan and Fidel on standby in San Antonio. I have a little surprise planned that should slow the trucker down long enough to get us all together."

"Fine." His brother hung up.

Cruz keyed in another number.

"Si?" Hector said.

"Where is he?" Cruz asked.

Comfort Inn
Wheeling, Illinois

Yeager parked his rig in the hotel's back lot, lengthwise across the lines. It took twenty minutes to disconnect two cell bridges from the battery bank and stow them in his toolbox. Any would-be thief would have a hard time hot-wiring the ignition without a spark. The evening was unseasonably warm and humid for June, and sweat patches soaked his shirt by the time he finished.

He lugged the toolbox and duffel bag through the side door of the hotel, doing an awkward shuffle to get his room keycard into the slot with his hands full. The hotel, built like a tall shoebox, boasted all inside rooms—with their doors opening to an interior hall for greater security, as opposed to those facing a parking lot—and a free continental breakfast. Windows overlooked the front or back lots. The sides of the hotel were blank and featureless. Featureless pretty much described the room, too: a bed, a toilet, a TV, and not much else. *But what do you expect for forty bucks? The Beverly Hills Hilton?*

Yeager cranked the air conditioning unit to Ice Age and fell onto the bed, fully clothed. Listening to the rattle and hum of air blowing from the vents, he closed his eyes for a minute and woke up four hours later. The room was cold enough to hang meat. The digital clock on the nightstand flickered the time in dim red LEDs: 10:15 p.m. Yeager stretched, rubbed his eyes, and headed for the bathroom.

Twenty minutes later, shaved, showered, and dressed in clean clothes, he took the elevator to the lobby. He interrupted a fresh-faced kid playing solitaire on a desktop computer, the screen reflected in his glasses.

"Is there a restaurant within walking distance?"

"Burger King." The kid pointed to the right of the main doors. "About a quarter mile that way. They stay open until midnight."

"Thanks."

"No problem, sir." The boy's eyes were already fixed on the computer monitor again. "Enjoy your stay."

The night had cooled considerably since dusk, perfect for a walk. In no hurry, Yeager strolled down the road, the night settling around him like a familiar blanket. That part of the Chicago suburb was almost rural. The two-lane road ran north and south. On Yeager's side, commercial and industrial buildings stood every few hundred feet, while the opposite side was lined with trees.

An overcast sky left long stretches of darkness between the few buildings that sported lone security lights. But for the glow of city lights in the distance, Yeager could have been the last man on earth. Nothing stirred but the roadside grit crunching under his work boots.

At Burger King, Yeager dug the last bill, a twenty, out of his wallet and got back a ten, three ones, and a dribble of change. Dinner for less than seven bucks. He could eat twice more on the way home without using a credit card. *Well, I needed to lose weight anyway.*

Yeager lingered over his meal, arranging the hamburger wrapper, making a place for the fries in one corner, then tearing open ketchup packets with his teeth and squeezing the contents into the opposite corner. He had the restaurant to himself. The employees behind the counter had retreated to the kitchen and were laughing and banging things around while they cleaned. "The Girl from Ipanema" crooned from tinny speakers.

He dipped in one or two fries at a time, chewing slowly. He stared into the distance, holding in his mind an image of Charlie Buchanan sitting across the picnic table from him at the rest stop. Fine, delicate features. Light skin and red hair, strands of it blowing across her face until she pushed them back with those long fingers. Her fresh, tomboy look was so completely different from Martina Ruiz Yeager, his ex-wife/aspiring actress, that they could have come from different planets. *Different galaxies.*

Martina was a bottle of nitroglycerin left too near an open flame, always ready to explode and rain shrapnel on anyone in the vicinity. Yeager got used to handling her with oven mitts and a flak jacket. She reminded him of a beautiful cat who showed her belly; he could rub it, but every once in a while, she'd bite him for no reason at all.

On the other hand, he sensed Charlie didn't have a mean bone in her body. She reminded him of apple pie and ice cream, rainy Sunday mornings, and Christmas dinner.

And she didn't wear a wedding ring.

Jesus, Abel. Quit being an idiot. You have a grand total of thirteen dollars and twenty-eight cents in your pocket. You gonna ask her to dinner at Burger King?

There were times Yeager missed being married. Missed having someone to share the highs and lows with. Sitting at a Formica table in a deserted fast food restaurant and eating bad food under the glare of neon, loneliness grabbed him around the heart and squeezed. Too many bad choices. Too many fuckups and bad decisions.

Black ice. Downshift, brake. No! Don't! Ah, goddamnit, she's spinning out. Pump the brakes, tap the trailer brakes, downshift. Control it.

Even talking to Martina, who always wanted more from him, was better than going back to an empty motel room and staring at the tube until his eyes glazed over enough to sleep.

Martina hadn't lasted through his first tour in Afghanistan before she packed her bags and headed to the West Coast. She broke up with him over the phone on a Tuesday morning. The crackly satellite connection at the fire base meant they had to yell to be heard, and she had to repeat it twice before he got it.

"I can't live like this," she said. "I owe it to myself to follow my dream."

"Follow your dream? You're a goddamn hairstylist, Martina. What dream are you following? Cutting Kim Kardashian's hair?"

"You'll never unnerstan'! I'm not gonna be a stylist forever. I'm gonna make somethin' of myself. I'm not gonna hang around McAllen, havin' babies, while you go play your stupid war stuff, you *pendejo* asshole!"

She hung up on him, and that was the last time he'd spoken to her. The papers arrived three days later. She'd obviously printed them off a website and sent them long before that last call. He signed them in under a minute.

Then he got drunk, puked, and passed out. Six hours and one helicopter ride later, he had hiked six miles into the Shah-i-Kot Valley in support of Operation Anaconda, which was a place his thoughts really didn't want to go.

Cowboy up, Abel. Time to get back to that swanky hotel room. He refilled his soda at the dispenser, tossed out the debris from his meal, and headed back into the night. The buzzing of the neon sign gave way to singing crickets as the Burger King lights faded away behind him.

He headed for the side entrance of the hotel. The lot, lit with regularly spaced overheads on metal poles, contained a collection of cars scattered along the perimeter. Bugs whirled over the side door's single overhead light.

Yeager paused at the edge of the lot, not knowing why. Nothing moved. On his left, at the back of the lot, his rig waited, which made him breathe easier. The smattering of cars created an obstacle course between him and the hotel door, the gaps between them cloaked in darkness.

He narrowed his eyes and studied those black pools, looking

for whatever had tickled his sixth sense. In Afghanistan, Yeager had lived for weeks in the bush, often on his own, cat-napping during the day and slinking around at night. He trusted his instincts.

Maybe I'm spooky from the fight in Arkansas. Yeager slipped across the concrete lot, senses open to input and eyes tracking.

Something skittered behind him, tinkling like a coin skipping across the concrete. He spun to look an instant before realizing he'd been suckered. Motion flickered next to a parked car. Yeager registered the image of a man, charging hard, swinging a baseball bat.

With no time to move, Yeager hunched and took the hit under his short ribs. Pain detonated in his torso, and he grunted explosively, doubling over, vision going dark. He grabbed the bat, but it was jerked out of his hands. A rush of feet sounded behind him, and he knew there were two.

Yeager dropped and rolled, fighting for breath as well as room to maneuver. He rose to one knee as two of the guys from the hijacking crew, both with bats, came right at him, murder in their eyes. Yeager sucked wind, trying to expand his lungs with enough oxygen so he could move. He had to get in the fight before the two refugees from the bush leagues got some batting practice on his skull.

His attackers stalked him, spreading out to divide his attention. The kid on the right was Hairflip, the hijacker who played traffic cop at the rest stop. He had a massive purple bruise on his left cheek. Eyes narrowed, Hairflip crabbed farther right, bat cocked. He spun the bat in little circles in the air as if he was waiting for a pitch.

On the left, Tire Iron, the one with close-cropped hair and deep-set eyes, showed white teeth in a nasty grin. He had the look of a bully used to winning. He swung his bat in little arcs as though he was on deck, taking some practice swings.

Yeager drew in enough air to loosen his diaphragm and get his lungs working again. The blackness around the edge of his vision cleared, and he levered himself up onto his feet. *Engage one at a time. Get in close, inside the swing. Disable and clear before the other one closes.*

Woozy and lightheaded, Yeager backed away, gaining time. He

wanted to puke from the dull ache throbbing in his gut with every breath. "Well, muchacho," he wheezed, thinking maybe he could goad the older one into a mistake. "That the hardest you can hit? Your momma hit me harder than that after I promised I wouldn't come in her mouth."

Tire Iron's eyes flared, but then he showed a thin-lipped smile. "You think you are funny?" He circled further left, and Yeager had to swivel his head back and forth to keep them both in sight. "I think it will be funny when I break your arm like you broke my brother's. Then I will think it is even more funny when I break every other bone the same way."

Yeager feinted left, toward Tire Iron, then bolted right, straight for Hairflip. *Too slow.* The kid saw him coming and swung. Yeager dodged the bat then closed in, getting in tight before being caught by the backswing. *Palm strike to the nose, followed by a neck-twist takedown.*

The palm strike and the takedown were both potentially fatal if not done correctly, but Yeager didn't much care. He slapped his palm into Hairflip's nose, and something crunched. Grabbing the short hair at the back of the kid's head in his left hand, he cupped Hairflip's chin with his right. *Twist and pull.* The boy had no choice but to go with the momentum, and he was on the ground before he knew what hit him. At least he went down fast.

Tire Iron came from behind before Yeager could disengage and reset. Yeager spun and ducked, out of balance and out of position. He avoided most of the strike, but still got clipped on the side of the head.

Light flashed behind his eyes. Without realizing how he made it there, Yeager was on the ground again, staring at the night sky. Warm, gritty concrete scratched his back. Tire Iron raised the wooden bat as if he wanted to split a log with one hit.

Yeager rolled left, and the bat cracked the pavement next to his head. He came off the ground and skipped away from the backhand swipe as the bat zipped past his midsection. Tire Iron came in hard, swinging for the fences.

Fuck, this is gonna hurt... Yeager dove in ahead of the swing, close enough that he mitigated the full force of the blow, and took the shot in his left side. He grunted with the impact but held on and clamped his arm over the weapon to immobilize it. He drove a right fist into Tire Iron's nose twice—*bap-bap*—hard enough to rock a fence post.

The hijacker's legs jellied, and he lost his grip on the bat. He stumbled back, clutching his face in both hands as blood washed through his fingers. He glared through wet, teary eyes. Yeager had to give the guy some credit; he could take a punch and still have some fight left in the tank. Yeager tossed the bat aside and made a come-on gesture with his sore right hand. A handgun popped, and the guy startled.

"Hey, *esé*," Victor Ruiz said. "You are fucking with the wrong gringo, homes. Nobody beats that white boy but me."

Tire Iron looked over his shoulder. Victor came across the parking lot, a gym bag over his shoulder and a stainless steel semi-auto pistol held down by his leg.

Yeager blinked. "Hey, Por Que. Nice of you to drop by."

"I had to walk from the airport, you know. It has made me cranky," Victor said. He was still about twenty-five yards away but closing. "Why don't you badasses put your hands up?"

Tire Iron backed away, and Hairflip scrambled to his feet to join his friend. Each cupped a hand under a bleeding nose. *Two broken noses in one night. May be a record.* Both assailants started sliding farther away from Victor and his gun.

"We don' wan' no trouble," Tire Iron made a *slow down* gesture with both hands. Moments before, he had been the king of the world, but now he was slinking away like a kicked dog.

"Oh, yeah?" Victor said. "You shoulda thought of that before you done pissed me off. Now you got loads a' trouble."

With unseen communication, both turned and ran at the same time, disappearing into the black field behind the motel. Victor raised his pistol.

Yeager held up a hand. "Not worth it, amigo. You kill one running away, they throw your ass in jail. They might anyway if anyone heard the shot and called the cops."

"*Sí.*" Victor walked over and patted him on the shoulder. "I wasn't gonna shoot 'em. Well, maybe jus' a little bit. On the edges, like. Let's get inside. Then we can talk about how I saved your sorry butt. Again."

"Saved me?" Yeager said. "From those candy-asses?"

"You gettin' old, man. Once upon a time, they'd have been pretzels by now."

"Well, join the club, Por Que. I need a beer."

"Cool, a party!" Victor grinned. "Do I get to wear a funny hat?"

<hr />

The motel room ice bucket came with a plastic bag liner, which Yeager filled with ice. He settled into the room's one chair, alternating the bag between his head and stomach.

Victor peered into his eyes for a second, declared him concussion free, then plopped onto the bed. He found the TV remote and started flipping channels. Victor stood only five-six, but he packed all of it with muscle. His Body Mass Index would put him in the obese category because he had twice the muscle mass of an average person his height. He looked like a short, Hispanic Arnold Schwarzenegger. "So, what the fuck, dude? You piss on these guys, or what?"

"Only stopped 'em from takin' my truck." Yeager winced as he applied the ice bag to the side of his head. "Where's Cujo?"

"He said he wanted to stay with the plane. He's funny that way. I don' worry 'bout him. That guy, he would survive a WMD attack."

"Or maybe start one."

Victor tossed the remote down after finding a soccer game broadcast in Spanish. He dug in his gym bag and produced a six pack of Negra Modelo. "I know you're too cheap to buy beer. Here."

"Thanks." Yeager popped the top and took a pull. Even warm, the beer tasted good going down. "You staying here or gettin' your own room?"

"Only one bed in here. I stay, I get it. I don' sleep in no beds with guys, tha's for sure," Victor said. "I don't roll that way, *esé.*"

"*Por que no?*"

Victor shot him a dirty look. "No need for cheap shots to a man who jus' saved your life."

"Did you get my stuff?"

"Yeah, I got your stuff." Victor set his beer on the nightstand and stuck his nose back into his gym bag. "My papa finished your gun. Nice sights, by the way. I went by your house, man, and I have to tell you... you ever hear about a thing called paint, dude? I mean, shit, your house, it wouldn't even qualify for a crack house."

"Paint costs money."

"Sure it does, but come on..." Victor placed a leather pistol case on the bed then scrabbled in his bag again.

Yeager retrieved the pistol case, zipped it open, and slipped out his Springfield Arms 1911-A1 Custom .45 Auto. There were two empty magazines in the case, and when he looked up, Victor tossed him a box of Winchester hollow-points. Victor's dad was a first-class gunsmith and had been installing tritium night sights on the .45, which was why Yeager hadn't had it on him when he was attacked at the rest stop.

"You can't afford paint," Victor said, "but you own a two-thousand-dollar gun there? Somethin' don' seem right, bro."

"Priorities. You bring the—"

"Yeah, I got everything you asked for." Victor took a long pull from his beer bottle. "Be quiet. Chivas is playing."

"Hate to miss that."

Yeager loaded the magazines and popped one into the base of the Springfield. He snapped back the slide, chambered a round, then set the thumb safety. *Nothing like an old friend to make you feel safe.* He breathed easier than he had in the last thirty-something hours. The checkered grip felt solid and deadly in his hand.

"What's wrong with your face?" Victor asked.

"Huh?"

"You're smilin, man."

"I am? That's tragic."

"You ain't done it much lately is all. Not since the, uh, you know. The wreck and whatnot."

"Something happened today."

"Duh."

"No," Yeager said. "I met this woman."

"A woman? Really? With, like, boobs and stuff? Wow, I'm impressed."

"Shut up, dickhead. I'm tryin' to tell you something." Yeager tipped more beer down his throat and set the bottle on the side table. "She was… *man*."

Victor cocked an eyebrow. "Tha's poetry, dude."

Yeager grimaced. "It's like, like I've been sleepwalking, you know? And today, I woke up. The fight with the hijackers woke me up, and Charlie woke me up, too, but in a different way."

"So… you're awake now. Tha's what you saying? Good to know, bro. You drivin' a truck and whatnot."

"There was this guy in the Stan with me, an 0358—"

"Remind me?"

"Force recon. A staff sergeant, same as me. Millnimow was his name. Anyway, Millnimow had been blown up twice by IEDs. Both times, every man around him was killed. He led one patrol into the bush, and they dropped into some deep shit that killed everybody but him. You get the picture? It's like he was a bad luck charm or something. After about six months of that, Millnimow looked like a dog wanting to lay down somewhere and die. He lost about forty pounds, never slept, just went through the motions until he finally walked into a bullet one night in the Helmand Province."

Victor pursed his lips in a brooding way and tipped his beer. "So you, you're like this Millnimow guy?"

Yeager nodded. "It's what I feel like, yeah."

"And these guys, they woke your ass up?"

Yeager gave a grim smile. "Not completely, but at least I can hear the alarm going off."

"Well, don' hit the snooze button, bro. You know what I'm sayin'?"

Yeager smiled, leaned back in the chair, and closed his eyes.

CHAPTER 7

Book Finders
Austin, Texas

WEDNESDAY EVENING, CHARLIE BUCHANAN PULLED into her reserved space in the parking lot next to Book Finders and switched off the engine. She stepped out of her bug- and dirt-splattered car and stretched her aching back and neck. Things cracked and popped that never did before. Long drives took more out of her than they did only a few years ago. Hell, everything took more out of her than it used to.

Her cell rang, and she missed a step when she saw her ex-husband's name on the caller ID. "Hello."

"Hey, kiddo," Steven said. "Wanted to see that you made it back from St. Louis okay."

"Yeah, sure." She held the phone away and looked at the caller ID again. Sure enough, it said *Steven*. "I got back last night."

"Good. Good. Everything go okay? The place I suggested work out?"

"Uh… yeah, I guess. The books were pretty good. Cheap, too, except for the shipping."

"The shipping?"

"Yeah, the guy was charging out the wazoo."

"So… what'd you do?"

"I used my own shipper."

"Oh," Steven said. "Well. That's good then. So you bought some books there?"

"Yeah, six pallet loads." She popped the trunk with her remote. "Anything else?"

"No, no. Nothing. Mainly wanted to check on you. Make sure everything worked out. Okay, then. See you."

Charlie said goodbye and touched End. *Strange.* Steven had never been very interested in her book business, but he'd suddenly gotten all excited about the place in St. Louis, telling her what great bargains they had and convincing her to check them out. Now calling to see how she did? What the hell was up with him?

Extending the pull handle on her suitcase, she slung her bag over her shoulder. She wheeled the case behind her into the store, chirping the car's alarm on the way.

For a Wednesday night in the summer, with no school in session, traffic in the store seemed heavier than normal. During the fall and winter, when the University of Texas filled up with college kids, the store could become packed in a hurry. Charlie didn't do textbooks—there were dozens of stores for that—but she sold the hell out of Cliff's Notes and reading list material.

She waved at Nita Lutz, the store manager, who was busy at the cash register. Nita smiled and gave her a look that said, "If you want to come help, I wouldn't mind." Charlie chose not to take the hint. If she became involved, she'd be working until well after closing, and she was so tired her bones ached. She loved Nita like a sister but not enough to work a late shift.

She used her passkey on the freight elevator and punched three for the top floor. The door opened onto a bare foyer with a tiled floor and unadorned walls. A heavy but plain wooden door across from the elevator led to her apartment. On the right side of the foyer, a steel fire door with a push bar led to a staircase and the alley behind the shop. Charlie unlocked her apartment door and maneuvered her bags into the living room, calling out, "I'm home!"

"*Hola, Señora* Buchanan!" Maria sang from the kitchen. A second later, she bustled into the room, drying her hands on her apron, a wide smile of greeting lighting her face.

Maria Mendoza had been with Charlie for years. More of a second mother than a housekeeper, she was in that indefinable age between fifty and seventy. In all the time Charlie had known her, she had never seen Maria frown.

After a quick hug, Maria said, "Good to have you back safe, Señora. Dinner will be ready in a few minutes, hokay? You get cleaned up and come eat."

"How's David?"

"*Bien*. He is in his room, working on a wooden car."

"*Gracias*, Maria." Charlie dumped her shoulder bag on the couch and crossed the room to David's bedroom. After a quick tap on the door, she opened it to find her ten-year-old son sitting on his bed and studying a set of instructions, bits and pieces of a Pinewood Derby car scattered around him. "How's it going, buddy?"

"Hey, Mom." David glanced up. "How was your trip?"

"Same old, same old. Nothing exciting." No way was Charlie going to bring up her part in the confrontation at the rest stop. David could be a worrier, and he'd fret if he heard she'd nearly been in a gunfight with a bunch of bandits. "How's the car coming?"

"It's not." David held up a rectangular block of wood slightly bigger than his palm. "This is what we're supposed to cut the car shape out of, but I don't know how."

Charlie frowned. Since she split with Steven, there had been times where she didn't have the skills to do the "boy things" that David needed. She hated fishing, couldn't throw a ball, and her skills with power tools were rusty. About all her daddy had ever taught her was how to handle a gun and manage money.

Goddamn you, Steven, if you could've kept it in your pants... This is your job! Charlie played that thought back and reconsidered. *Who am I kidding? Steven would be as clueless as I am and have less interest in learning.*

"And you're supposed to mount these wheels," David continued, "on these nails, sticking 'em in these slots, and the whole thing can't weigh more than five ounces." He tossed the block on the mattress and flopped back on his bed with a sigh. A thin boy with a serious expression, David wore wire-framed glasses that made him look old and wise beyond his years. He insisted on being called David, never Dave or Davey.

"Don't worry, baby." Charlie sat next to him and stroked his sandy-red hair. "Maybe we can get Tomas to help."

Tomas, Maria's brother, did the occasional odd job for her, everything from electrical to plumbing to drywall, and all with the same cheerful outlook as his sister.

David never showed it, but Charlie often wondered if he wasn't secretly disappointed in her, as if maybe he blamed her for his father's philandering and lack of attention. The one time she'd gotten him to open up about his bi-weekly visits with Steven, she got the impression that his father spent most of their time together on the phone, working on deals.

The confrontation at the rest stop kept bubbling up in her mind. Maybe if she left out her part of the incident... Brightening her tone, she said, "I saw this guy take on three outlaws and deck 'em all."

"Really?"

"Yeah, it was like Chuck Norris or Jason Statham or something. The three guys were down when I showed up, but I heard later that one had a knife and the other a tire iron. And then, this other guy..."

"Dinner!" Maria called from the other room.

"Come on, kiddo." Charlie pulled David to his feet. "Let's go eat, and I'll tell you the rest of the story."

<hr />

Comfort Inn
Wheeling, Illinois

Early Thursday morning, Yeager's cell phone rang as he tightened the last nut on the Peterbilt's battery cell bridge.

Victor was sitting in the open door of the cab, reading a magazine, one of those with pictures of freakishly muscled men on the cover. Without looking up, he announced, "Phone's ringing."

"Thanks so much." Yeager pushed the answer button with a greasy finger. "Yeager here."

"Mr. Abe... Abelard Yeager?" Male voice, deep Southern accent.

"Abel is fine."

"I heard that," the man chuckled. "This is Sergeant Jurdan of the

Arkansas State Police. We're investigating the attempted armed robbery of your truck, Mr. Yeager."

"Uh huh." *About time.*

"Coupla questions."

"Sure." Yeager tucked the phone under his ear and rooted a red shop towel out of his box. "Shoot."

Jurdan took him through the hijacking then asked, "Where'd you learn them moves?"

"Courtesy of the United States Marine Corps."

"Semper Fi, buddy," Jurdan said. "Anyway, you ought to know, our intel guys IDed the leader of the merry band of outlaws you tangled with. They had some new facial-recognition software that they got to play with. Made 'em very happy, you know. Geeks with their toys."

"Okay, I'll bite. Who is it?"

"Humberto Cruz." Jurdan paused for a moment, as if waiting for Yeager to add something. When Yeager didn't respond, he continued, "He operates a hijacking ring south of Monterrey, Mexico. He used to work for Los Zetas, the drug cartel enforcement bunch, before branching out into hijacking, human trafficking, and whatnot. He's a bad hombre, Mr. Yeager. You're lucky you met him and lived."

"Lucky Miz Buchanan showed up with a gun. You think she's in any danger?"

"Naw, prob'ly not," Jurdan said. "It's a business for these guys, right? All they want is the truck. It's not like it was personal or anything."

"Any luck finding Mr. Cruz?"

"We're following up on some leads. Have you seen these fellers since the attempted hijacking?"

Yeager was tempted to say he'd seen at least two of the gang last night, but that would lead to a lot of questions he didn't want to answer—like how his friend from Texas had flown up with an illegal pilot, carrying guns in his gym bag, and capped off a round in the Comfort Inn parking lot. Next thing he knew, somebody would be questioning both of them about carrying weapons. Eventually, they might even get around to Cujo. Yeager shuddered just thinking about it. Cujo talking to the police would not be a pretty sight. "No."

"Well, that's all the questions I have for now." Jurdan sounded a little surprised that Yeager didn't have more to add. "If you see them ol' boys again, give me a call at this number."

"Sure," Yeager said. "Appreciate you keeping me in the loop."

"You bet."

Jurdan signed off, and Yeager wiped the phone with the rag from his pocket. He gave Victor a rundown of the conversation.

"Humberto Cruz, huh?" Victor chewed his lip and stared off across the parking lot. "I've heard that name, I think. Somewhere."

"Another cousin, maybe?"

"Ver' funny, gringo."

"Well, one thing's for damn certain," Yeager said. "Cruz is pissed about something. This is about more than a truckload of copper."

Victor nodded solemnly. "My people carry grudges a long time."

"Oh yeah? And who're your people? Short, muscle-bound assholes?"

"Handsome Mexicans, esé, what you think?"

"Shit, Por Que. Your people been in Texas longer than mine. How's that make you a Mexican?"

"See, it's like this." Victor tossed the magazine onto the seat. "It was Mexico before it was Texas. You people stole it when you sneak attacked Santa Ana, dude. Is why I'm still carrying a grudge, you know?"

"Ah. Clears it up."

"You through dickin' around with that engine, homes? Give me a ride to the airport. I gotta check on Cujo, get to him before he gets too far into his stash. When he flies stoned, altitude becomes an arbitrary concept, you know?"

Yeager nodded, but his mind was filled with questions. What did Cruz want? If what Jurdan said was accurate, why did the gang leader's boys show up again last night and try and take him out? And some of the things Cruz had said during the hijacking had sounded more personal than *just business*. If Cruz was taking it personally, was Charlie really safe?

CHAPTER 8

Big River Wholesale
St. Louis, Missouri

NAUSEATED AND DIZZY, DAREAS THOMPSON tried to sleep Wednesday night, but he couldn't seem to get any rest. He finally gave up and threw the sheets back at four o'clock in the morning. He sat on the side of his bed and rubbed his aching shoulder. *Must have pulled a muscle. Lifted something wrong, I guess. Maybe comin' down with a cold, too.*

He yawned and scratched his fuzzy chest. It was pick-up day. *Better stage the money pallets. Get that done before anyone clocks in.*

He ate a Jack-in-the-Box breakfast in the car on the way to Big River Wholesale. To keep the peace with his queasy stomach, he only had two breakfast sandwiches and hash browns instead of his usual morning meal. The headlights of his Escalade washed the front of the building when he pulled in at oh-dark-thirty. He opened the SUV's door. Sweat beaded on his forehead the instant he left the comfort of the Cadillac's air conditioning and was rolling down his face by the time he finished climbing the stairs to the main entrance.

After switching on the warehouse lights, he fired up a forklift and unlocked the secure cage containing the money pallets, six skids, each with a square core of small bills carefully banded, weighed, and shrink-wrapped. Stacks of books surrounded the core, which were in turn surrounded by cardboard and shrink-wrapped again. Dareas assembled the pallets, scrawling seemingly random numbers on the side that indicated the dollar amount in each. He did the math in his head and came up with sixty million dollars for that shipment alone.

Getting cash from the United States to Mexico was a problem for the cartel. In the years Dareas had worked for the Sinaloa in the U.S., he had run every money-laundering scam the big boys could think of. The idea of smuggling cash inside pallets of books was the latest in a number of techniques to get cash back in the hands of the drug sellers.

Every ten, twenty, fifty, and one-hundred-dollar bill dropped into the hand of a street dealer was stacked into piles of cash in the dealers' home bases. With hundreds of dealers in each city, selling thousands of dollars per day in crack cocaine, powdered cocaine, heroin, pot, X, meth, and a pharmacy's worth of other street drugs, those piles of cash added up quickly.

Each of those piles—suitcases full—was moved upstream to the dealer's supplier, who aggregated their take into pallet-sized piles. The suppliers delivered those loads of cash to one or more collection points in the city. In St. Louis, for example, the main collection point was Big River Wholesale. And Dareas moved several pallet loads of cash back to Mexico inside loads of cheap, easy-to-get books.

The cartel knew within a few thousand bucks how much each shipment contained, so Dareas kept his fingers clean. He had seen firsthand what happened when people got greedy and the cartel found out.

Dareas's predecessor had skimmed and skimmed, then his skimming had turned to scooping. By the time the cartel hitters were done, the man looked like something eaten by a lion and vomited back out. The bosses had shown Dareas the remains as a lesson in appetite control, and it had worked. He'd lost his breakfast and all the meals he'd eaten for the past week, right there on the warehouse floor.

He lined up the six money pallets behind door number one. In a rare burst of industry, Dareas also pulled the six skids of books purchased by the pretty redhead. Too bad she'd gotten away. He had her phone number on the PO; maybe he should give her a call, set up a date for the next time she came back. Her pallets, he put at the second door. The two lines of staged pallets looked identical. *Hidden in plain sight.* Nobody would know the difference.

Grateful to get inside the air-conditioned office, Dareas braced himself for a moment, overcome with a bout of dizziness. He tottered around his desk, vision going dark around the edges, and all but fell into his chair. The leather protested with a woof and a groan.

Dmitri came in with two cups of coffee. "Here, boss. Half-and-half, six sugars."

"You ain't good for much, Dmitri, but you're damn regular about bringing good coffee."

"Is Russian blend. Make you strong, like me."

Dareas mustered a weak laugh then sipped from the cup. It really was nice coffee, with a spicy, cinnamon scent and a slightly bitter aftertaste. He wiped the sweat off his brow and massaged his arm, where the dull ache had flared to a sharp pain. *Shit, this ain't good. Better get myself to a doctor. This feels like some kick-ass flu.*

He drank some more coffee. Printing the shipping labels was his next task. He had to print the labels or the shipment wouldn't go. *A little flu virus will be the least of my worries if the shipment doesn't go out.*

Dareas gathered both sets of labels and got to his feet. A knife of pain—*no, a big fucking sword of pain*—stabbed through his chest, driving him to his knees. He must have yelled or something because Dmitri ran back down the hall. For some reason, the little Russian was smiling. His mouth moved, but Dareas couldn't hear any sound. Another railroad spike of pain hammered his chest, and dirty linoleum filled his vision. As he fell, the shipping labels spiraled out of his hands and fluttered across the floor in a blizzard of white.

His last thought was *Well, that's a fuckin' mess.*

Round Rock, Texas

Harlan stopped the Challenger at the gatehouse for the Sandy Creek private community in Round Rock, a suburb of Austin. A rent-a-cop came out, and Harlan handed off his identification.

After consulting a clipboard, the guard returned his license. "Go right on through, Mr. King. You need directions?"

"Nah, I been here before." Harlan gunned the car through the retreating gate.

Skeeter flicked his cigarette butt out the open window and yawned. "Wonder what this place looks like at Christmas."

The streets lamps glowed orange, and every house had bright porch lights and wall-mounted security floods under the eaves. Landscape lighting added accents while ensuring shadows were kept to a minimum. Fit-looking people in summer clothes from Neiman Marcus or L.L.Bean strolled the twisty residential sidewalks. Joggers in spandex and flashy red warning lights weaved between the walkers, their running shoes as clean and spiffy as if they had sprung out of the box that morning.

He pulled the rumbling Challenger into the driveway of a two-story house as big as an aircraft hangar. A lighted, arched entry dominated the front; tall windows on either side revealed a grand staircase in the foyer. White stone construction, rough-hewn wood balconies, and a red-slate roof gave a vague impression of Spanish, Texan, and modern architectural styles splashed together with more ambition than taste.

John Stone answered the door. Pudgy, with a round face and bulldog eyes, he wore his black hair long, pulled into a ponytail. Bone-white ostrich cowboy boots added another inch to his five and a half feet. A personal injury attorney, John did TV commercials, calling himself the Rock of Texas. He came on harder than a Southern revival preacher, claiming he'd get clients big settlements if they were injured at work or in a car crash. "Insurance company messing with you? Crush 'em against the Rock!" Harlan laughed out loud whenever he saw it.

They must do wonders with makeup on his TV commercials. He doesn't look like the Rock of Texas now.

Stone held the door with one hand and motioned with a Corona in the other. A piece of lime floated in the beer. "C'mon in, boys. Been expectin' ya."

The attorney led them to a sunken living room decorated in what Harlan thought of as Nouveau Southwest. Indian-style print blankets and branding irons adorned the walls, alongside cattle skulls and a Henry repeating rifle over the fireplace. Circled in the middle were a couple of cattle-hide sofas and leather chairs. *Bonanza* in the suburbs of Austin.

"Where's Hoss and Little Joe?" Harlan asked, as he always did.

Stone laughed. "Ass-fuckin' Miss Kitty! Y'all want a drink?"

"Yeah, sure. Rum and coke."

"Bourbon, straight up," Skeeter said.

They settled around a coffee table cut from the heart of a sequoia, sanded and polished to a glow. Harlan yawned and stretched. They'd spent the better part of three days in the car, from Dallas to Texarkana to St. Louis and back to Austin. His eyes were gritty and tired.

"Your money's there." Stone handed Harlan a buff envelope. "How'd it go in St. Louis?"

"Like a charm." Harlan tossed the packet to Skeeter, who opened it and riffled through the bills.

Stone leaned forward and put his elbows on his knees, giving Harlan his most sincere, convince-the-jury look. "Dmitri do it?"

"Yep. The warehouse manager, Thompson, is sick as a dog from that stuff Doc Buchanan gave us. Should be ready to drop any second."

Stone grinned. "Okay, then. I talked to Buchanan, and he came through on the wife, too. Call Dmitri and tell him to switch the load to Book Finders in Austin. His ex bought a nice-sized load yesterday. Double the dose if Thompson's not dead yet."

"This is all pretty complicated, Stoney. Why not just knock off the truck when it leaves the warehouse? Stick a gun in the driver's belly and have him drive it where we want it."

"Two reasons, Mr. King." Stone tipped the last of his beer into his mouth, sucking the dregs around the lime wedged in the neck of the bottle. "The cartel may be running security on the rig. We wouldn't see 'em 'til they dropped in and butt-fucked us. And two"—Stone touched a finger to his nose and winked—"when they do figure out where the truck went, I want the trail to lead right to the good doctor. Once you boys take care of him so's he disappears forever, the Sinaloa bastards will be chasing a ghost. *Hah!* Get it? Chasin' *his* ghost, right?"

"So we're double-crossing Buchanan?"

"Anything wrong with that?"

Harlan shrugged. "Ain't no skin off my pecker."

⟫∗⟪

Big River Wholesale
St. Louis, Missouri

When Yeager pulled in, an ambulance was blocking the loading dock of the warehouse. He parked his rig on the other side of the lot and took the key but left the engine idling. Yeager hopped out, locked the cab, and went to the warehouse office.

High, thin clouds traced the skyline, and the heat of the morning sun turned the muggy air into a steam bath. A ship's horn sent up a mournful wail. The Mississippi sliced the edge of St. Louis a couple of blocks to the east.

Big River looked like any of a thousand mid-sized warehouse-based businesses where Yeager had either dropped or picked up loads. Painted white at some point in the Napoleonic era, the single-story brick building squatted between an auto repair shop and a place called A1 Imports. A set of narrow steps led to a glassed-in office to the right of two open, dock-height freight doors.

Paramedics and firefighters bustled around the near dock, struggling with a huge, sheet-covered form on a gurney. Three guys at the base of the door grunted and swore as three on the dock cussed back, lowering the overloaded gurney.

This don't look good. Yeager climbed the steps and pushed through the office door, making an electric chime *ding* somewhere in the back. He didn't have to wait long before a thin guy in gray coveralls entered from the warehouse. He had mouse-brown hair, flattened and sticking up on one side, and a long nose protruding from a narrow face.

The guy said, "Good-bye," into a cellphone then put it away in his coverall pocket before addressing Yeager. "I am to be helping you?" He spoke in a Slavic accent with all the cheer of having a prostate exam. The man picked up a paper cup from the desk and gently placed it in the wastebasket.

"Are you the boss?" Yeager asked.

The guy seemed to be working over the question in his mind. "Yes... yes, I am the boss. Dmitri Kazulin is the boss here now. The old boss, he is dead."

"Sorry to hear that."

"I am not."

"Oh." Yeager nodded. "Okay, then. I'm here to pick up some skids for Austin. Books."

"What kind books?"

"I don't know. Books. For Charlie Buchanan, Austin, Texas."

"Ah, yes, I know this one. Book Finders." Dmitri held up his index finger then sifted through a loose pile of papers on the desk. "Manifest here somewhere. Back up, door one. You wait for leave the ambulance."

"Door one," Yeager repeated. "Wait for the ambulance to leave."

"Is what I say." Dmitri smiled for the first time, showing top and bottom gray teeth. "Dmitri take care of everything."

Book Finders
Austin, Texas

Charlie spent Thursday morning in her office on the bookstore's ground floor, matching invoices to shipments from her two biggest book suppliers, Ingram and Baker & Taylor. Her single-cup coffee maker gurgled and dribbled her third cup of the day, filling the room with the aroma of cinnamon.

Lined with walnut bookshelves and decorated with earth-tone furniture, her office resembled a comfy den more than a place of business. Books were stacked on every available surface. The only anomalies were the sleek twenty-three-inch monitor, keyboard, and mouse on the polished oak of her desktop. She looked up at a tap on her office door.

Nita Lutz stood in the doorway. "Hey, welcome back."

"Hey, yourself. What's been going on?"

Nita's voluptuous figure, broad shoulders, and wide hips exuded the sultry sensuality of a young Kirstie Alley. Charlie figured that in another ten years her friend's infatuation with fried food, coupled with her tendency toward heaviness, would have her shopping in the Plus sizes.

Nita briefly brought her up to speed on store business then asked, "So how was your trip? You find anything good?"

"We have six skids of remainders due to arrive tomorrow."

"Awesome!" Nita selected a dark roast K-cup and started it brewing. "Online stock's been getting pretty thin."

"Oh, and you're never going to believe what happened..." Charlie filled Nita in on the confrontation at the rest stop.

"So this truck driver, was he cute?" Nita asked.

"Cute?" Charlie bit her lip. "No, I don't think *cute's* the word I would use. More like... uh, think Russell Crowe in *Gladiator,* and you have a better picture."

"Oh, so melt-your-bones hot then."

"Hah! Yeah, I guess, now that you mention it. But I wasn't thinking about his heat factor right then. More about getting out of there without getting shot."

"Charlie"—Nita pulled her cup from the dispenser and added creamer and Sweet'N Low—"how long have we been friends now? Seven years? Eight?"

"Yeah," Charlie said, drawing it out. "About that."

"You're telling me you saw a superhot guy take out three baddies like Jason Statham, you save his ass from getting shot, and you *didn't notice* his super hotness?"

"Well, I noticed, but I, uh, had other things—"

"Yeah, I'm calling bullshit on that." Nita sipped her coffee, leaving a red lipstick stain on the cup. "Was he married?"

"I..." Charlie looked at her monitor and hoped her neck wasn't turning red. "I don't really know."

"Fail! Jeez, woman, how do you ever expect to hook up again?"

"I guess I'm out of practice." Charlie leaned back in her chair and rubbed her scalp with both hands, mussing her hair. The heat from a flush was definitely working its way up her neck. "Well, you'll get a chance to meet him. He's bringing the skids from St. Louis."

"Oops, skids." Nita straightened and snapped her fingers. "That reminds me. I guess I better get the forklift fixed."

"It's broken? *Again*? How am I supposed to get the pallets off the truck?"

"The guy's supposed to come Saturday morning. If you can get the trucker to bring them on Saturday, I'll come in and unload."

Charlie sighed. "You don't have to do that. I live upstairs, you know? Easier for me to do it."

"No, no, I don't mind at all. And don't you have that thing?"

Charlie winced. "The Chamber luncheon. I forgot."

Nita smirked. "Hey, look on the bright side. Ask Superman to spend the night. You might get lucky."

"Fat chance."

Nita laughed and closed the door on her way out.

As if conjured by magic, Charlie's cell phone rang, and Abel Yeager's name showed on the display. She thumbed it on. "Well, hey, stranger. How'd you know we were talking about you?"

"You were?" A roar in the background muffled his rich baritone. He sounded as though he was calling from the space shuttle.

"Just telling my manager you were bringing me some books. Everything okay?"

"Yeah, I got your order, but listen. I need to tell you something." He cleared his throat. "That guy at the rest stop, the one with the white hair. You know? With the gun? His name is Humberto Cruz, and he's a pretty bad guy."

"Really?" Charlie's insides chilled, and she sat up straight. "How bad?"

"Not sure, but I think he's got some kind of bone to pick with us. His guys showed up in Chicago and made another run at me. Not the truck, but at me, you know?" He gave her a rundown of his second altercation. "I don't think you're in any danger, but I thought you ought to know."

Not in any danger? "How can you be sure? I mean, do you think he knows who I am?"

"No, I been thinkin' about that, and I can't see any way. Unless he shows up at the Arkansas State Police headquarters and requests a copy of the police report. I called the detective, and he promised to let me know if that happens."

"Oh." She listened to the background roar for a few seconds then remembered what Nita had said. Charlie told him about the dead forklift and the estimated repair time. Something compelled her to add, "Hey, look, do you have any place to stay in town?"

"No," he drawled. She could almost picture his frown. "I generally sleep in the cab if I have to overnight somewhere. Last night was an exception."

"I'd hate for you to be put out on my account." Charlie had no idea where the words were coming from; her mouth seemingly had a mind of its own. "Stay here with me and David. There's plenty of room."

"But Cruz—"

"Better yet, if this guy Cruz shows up, there'll be two of us to deal with him. We made a good team last time, right?"

"Uh, yeah, I guess you're right."

Charlie counted the seconds while she waited for him to continue.

At the count of eleven, he said, "Let's talk about it when I get there, okay? Maybe you'll have your lift fixed by then, and the point will be mute, right?"

Moot, she almost said but bit her tongue in time. "Works for me. See you when you get here."

Abel said goodbye, and she keyed off the phone. The Cruz thing was a concern, but deep down she wondered how the guy could be a threat to her. He didn't know who she was or where she lived. Besides, Abel had beat up the hijackers not once, but twice. Cruz surely knew he should cut his losses and move on.

Now, how do I tell Nita I invited a strange man to spend the night? She'll have kittens.

Charlie realized she was wearing a silly grin.

CHAPTER 9

NewGen Biotech
Austin, Texas

A T TIMES, DR. STEVE BUCHANAN found the emptiness of the NewGen Biotech building depressing. A two-story cube of red granite and tinted glass, NewGen hid behind a screen of trees, about as far out on Mopac Expressway as one could go and still be in Austin.

The rare visitors entered via an access control door operated by the receptionist, Loren Gaffney, stationed in a lobby of chrome, leather, and glass. If the visitor was somebody Steven wanted to see, Loren would call him on the intercom. She would then escort the person through another access control door, down a short hall, past framed prints of scientists from Madame Curie to Jonas Salk, to his corner office.

Every other door in the facility not only had access control readers, they also featured neon-red warning signs. The signs informed people of terrible biohazards beyond the portal, and unauthorized entry could result in criminal action.

For the last three years, the only thing behind those doors had been an empty shell, nothing but metal studs and sheetrock walls. Steve had sold all the equipment, fixtures, and furniture, from the electron microscope and autoclaves to the restroom faucets and towel racks. The only working toilet left was the one between Loren's desk and Steve's office. Everything else in the building was a sham.

With Loren at lunch, Steven had the place to himself, a small pea in a very large pod. He clunked a bottle of Laphroaig 18 on his desk, took a tumbler from the same drawer the bottle had come from, and filled the glass with a four-finger measure. Both feet on his desk, hands resting on his stomach, cradling a glass of single malt, Steve reflected on his bad luck.

The walls surrounding him were a testament to his past. At first, the world had rocked along for Steven Buchanan exactly the right way. Medical degree from Texas Tech University. Residency at Johns Hopkins. Next to the fancy-looking medical sheepskins hung the press release for Aminoxicil, his company's first biotech NOX inhibitor released nine years ago. The one that worked. Photos of him playing golf with a former President and pictures of him sailing a single-mast schooner off the Gulf coast hung on his office wall. He kept one photo of him and Charlie, taken right after their wedding, and a baby picture of David on his desk.

Two years had passed since the divorce. *A great time. The best. Too bad I got caught.*

Steve considered himself a man of passionate tastes, and he'd found the more he sampled, the more he wanted, until the urge to try new and different things became insatiable. He searched for the finest-tasting food, the best whiskey, the fastest car... and the hottest women.

A conservative man—a less driven person who was content with the status quo—would have cashed out when Aminoxicil hit it big and his personal bank account hit ten million. On top of the money, he was married to a hot-looking woman and had a beautiful son, along with their three-thousand-square-foot apartment over a bookstore in downtown Austin.

The first affair—one of three that Charlie didn't know about— happened six months after they were married. She was a college intern from the University of Texas, working in the research lab, nineteen years old, tits like cantaloupes, and tanned, muscular legs. *Tawny.* Steve snorted and topped off his scotch. *No shit, for a fact, Tawny Lyons.*

After Tawny, there were four or five more, two of which Charlie *did* find out about. And that was that for marriage and fatherhood.

Which I was never cut out for anyway. After that, things always seemed to go wrong. The stock market crash. Stupid lab assistants. Bad temperature control. Idiots for partners.

Upshot of it all, he couldn't duplicate the success of Aminoxicil. He just couldn't make another damn drug that worked. He lost half his cash in the divorce and poured the rest down a stinking money pit, chasing another NOX inhibitor. Then, instead of cashing out, he conned people into investing in biotech research he knew wouldn't work. He even tried to con his old buddy John Stone, which turned into the most dangerous game he'd ever played.

So he was sitting in his mostly empty building, sipping scotch, and waiting for the Feds to come knocking at the door with warrants and guns and handcuffs. Somehow, he didn't think they would wait for Loren to buzz them through.

Steven sat up and pulled a thumb drive from his shirt pocket. He plugged it into his laptop and logged on. Clicking and keying his way through his bank accounts, one after the other, he updated the spreadsheet on his thumb drive with the latest balances and stared at the total.

$12,235,382.96

Was it time to fold? Was twelve mil enough? Gas up the boat, run up the sail, and head for Costa Rica or Argentina? With the last deal, he should at least double his money, giving him about twenty-five million.

If he left, he'd miss... not much at all. He had never warmed up to David, and Charlie was a lost cause. So he didn't know why he was sticking around. It was time to pack up and head out of Dodge.

"Why the fuck not?" Steve keyed some transactions, moving money here and there, cleaning up a few loose ends.

He closed all his windows and ran his disk-shredding program, killing all traces of his activity. Moving quickly, he printed out a letter to Loren, giving her a month's severance and a brief thanks, and left the single page on his desk.

It took him ten minutes to destroy all his paper documents and another ten to gather the few bits and pieces he wanted to take with him, which did not include his picture of David. Nor the one of

Charlie. With one last look around, Steve switched off the lights and closed his office door.

Three minutes later, he was in the Infiniti, burning a path out of the parking lot. He didn't look back.

———————◆———————

Interstate 35
Sixty miles north of Austin, Texas

Yeager found himself humming along with a song on the radio. What in the hell had gotten into him? A little dust-up with a couple of punks, a smile from a pretty woman, and all of a sudden a few rays of sunshine had pierced his gloomy cloud.

That, and maybe his luck had finally turned around.

On the way out of Chicago, he stopped by a freight terminal and fell into a full truckload headed to Dallas. And after he dropped that load, he picked up another partial load bound for Austin. All of which meant that he actually stood to make a profit for the trip.

"Now if I can only find something in Austin headed for McAllen, I might could pay a bill or two." Speaking his thoughts aloud was a habit he'd fallen into when he first started driving long distance. When he got sleepy, he'd not only talk but sing as well, which was why he never picked up a dog to ride along with him. *Why subject an animal to such cruelty?*

"After I drop this load, I can stop off at Charlie Buchanan's bookstore. She'll be so happy to see me, she'll leap into my arms and pledge her undying love. Yep, I can see it now. Why else would she ask me to spend the night?" He chuckled. "Get real. She lives with a guy named David. Probably a stockbroker or a lawyer. Definitely not a screw-up like me."

By the time he reached Charlie's store, the sun had dropped below the rooftops, and darkness was bleeding into the alley. A single sodium light on a wooden pole near the street hummed and flickered to life.

Charlie opened the small delivery door moments after he pushed the buzzer.

"Oh, Abel," she said, twisting her hands together. "I didn't think you were going to make it."

Somehow he had forgotten how damned good-looking she was. Her thick red hair fell around her shoulders, framing her fashion-model face. She wore a simple pair of jeans and a cotton button-down blouse in lemon yellow. His heart did a double-thump in reaction.

"Flying monkeys couldn't keep me away."

She bit her lip. "The forklift's still broken. My store manager tried to get it fixed, but the guy hasn't come yet."

She looked so worried, Yeager felt an overpowering urge to make everything better, like maybe heave the pallets off by brute force if necessary.

"I am so sorry," she added. "The guy is supposed to be here by tomorrow to fix it, but I couldn't get him out tonight, no matter how much I begged him."

"No problem," he said. "It's late anyway. I can come back in the morning, if that's okay. Is there a fast-food place close by?"

"Oh no, absolutely not!"

"Huh?"

"No way you're eating in a fast-food joint because of my faulty forklift." Charlie transformed from hand-wringing to decisive in a heartbeat. She had that look of determination women got when they felt guilty but wanted to cover it up by doing something positive.

"Say that three times real fast," Yeager said. "Faulty forklift, faulty forkift, flaltly florkfiftht."

She laughed.

"But really," Yeager said, "it's not a problem. I do it all the time."

"No, Mr. Yeager, I insist. You're staying to supper. David and I can never finish all of Maria's cooking. Have you eaten yet?"

He shook his head.

"No? Good, then it's all settled. Lock your truck and come on. I'd love for you to meet David."

Oh goody, Yeager thought. *Let's go meet the boyfriend.*

Interstate 35
Eleven miles north of Austin

Humberto Cruz answered his phone as he sat, stalled in traffic on Interstate 35, entering the outskirts of Austin. "Where is he?"

The sun was an orange ball touching the horizon, shooting laser beams into his eyes. He pushed the passenger-side visor over, but it didn't help.

"Stopped at the back of a bookstore. At the dock," Hector reported, his voice blurred by wind and traffic noises. He gave Humberto the address. "And you won't believe this, boss. That woman, you know, the one at the rest stop with the gun?"

"*Sí.*"

"He is with her," Hector said. "She opened the warehouse door, and he went inside. They have not come out, and the truck is still there. I think there's an apartment over the store."

Humberto strangled the steering wheel with one hand and his phone with the other. His jaw tightened. Maybe Yeager had known the woman, or maybe they became friends after she pulled a gun at the rest stop. No matter. They were both in it together, and both would suffer the same fate.

"How many men have you gathered?" Humberto asked.

"Four, plus me."

"Guns?"

"*Sí.* Rudy brought them."

"*Bueno.*" Humberto smiled for the first time in days. "We will hit them tonight. We will take the truck and anything in it, then we will pay a visit to the driver and his lady friend with the *pistola grande*, hey?"

"I would like that very much, boss," Hector said.

"Just watch them. Nothing else. This is my time. Do you understand?"

"*Sí, jefe.*"

Humberto thumbed off his phone. Finally, after waiting so long, he would end it. *Tonight.*

CHAPTER 10

Book Finders
Austin, Texas

"THERE'S BEEN A STORE OF some kind on the main floor for over fifty years." Charlie heard herself babbling but was unable to stop, on a verbal canoe without a paddle. Why was she getting so rattled? "The upper two floors were offices, but when I bought the building, I converted them to a living space. The top floor is where David and I live, and the second floor has guest rooms, where Maria lives. Also, we have some storage space and a game room down there."

The freight elevator clunked to a stop at the top floor, and Charlie punched the button to raise the two sets of doors. They split horizontally and retracted, half into the ceiling and half into the floor. Charlie had managed to chatter nonstop the entire time. *Get a hold on yourself, woman! It's not like you've never had a man in your house.*

But as she thought about it, she realized there hadn't been a man in the house—aside from Tomas—for a very, very long time. *And there won't be now if I don't get a grip on my tongue. I sound like a pompous twit, talking about buying the building. Sheesh.*

Charlie opened the apartment door and waved Abel ahead of her. The living room was decorated in what she called JCPenney chic: comfortable, traditional, and livable. She had chosen a tan sofa with matching chairs, along with mahogany veneer end tables and a coffee table. All of the furniture was arranged around a faux fireplace because trying to retrofit an old office building with a real fireplace had proven to be the mother of all architectural battles. Lamps and track lighting provided the illumination. In the corner, to the left of the fireplace, a tall cabinet concealed the entertainment center.

"Maria! David!" Charlie called. "We have company!" She turned to Abel. "Wait 'til you meet Maria. She's such a gem. I think she believes David's really hers, and I'm only around to pay the bills and bring home the groceries."

When the short, plump housekeeper bustled into the room, she was wiping her hands on an apron and looking flushed from working in the kitchen. She beamed at Charlie then did a double-take when she saw Abel.

Charlie smiled at the look of comic surprise on Maria's face, then her jaw dropped when Abel launched into a greeting, and the two began trading bursts of Spanish so fast that Charlie couldn't keep up. In a few moments, he had Maria laughing and chatting as if they were old friends. Charlie examined him while they talked, wondering at the new facet of his character. At the rest stop, while engaged with the hijackers, he'd moved with an unhurried speed that fooled the eye, a liquid blur of motion. After that, what she'd noticed was how still and quiet he became, not fidgeting, scratching, or even seeming to breathe, utterly focused. Then downstairs, he'd gotten downright silly, trying to say "faulty forklift" three times. A smile lit up his eyes, which, Charlie decided, were puppy-dog brown.

When the two new best friends paused, Charlie said, "Abel will be staying the night in the guest room, Maria. Would you see that everything's fixed up down there? And set another place for dinner."

"Of course, Señora." Maria winked at Abel. "I hope you like pollo con mole, Señor Abel."

"Ah, Maria," Abel said, "you know how to get to me, don't you? Can I ask if by any chance you're single?"

The portly housekeeper giggled and slapped his arm. She trundled back to the kitchen, passing David, who had slipped into the room almost unnoticed.

"And this is my son, David," Charlie said, holding out a hand to draw her son closer. "Say hello to Mr. Yeager, David."

David held out a hand and greeted Abel the way he did most strangers, with the minimum acknowledgement he could get away with. She thought she saw a look of surprise cross Abel's face, but it was gone before she could be sure.

Abel shook the boy's hand solemnly. "So David is your son?"

"Mom," David said, dismissing the stranger without further comment. "When will Tomas be here to help? The derby runs in a couple of days, and I'm not ready."

"I don't know. I called him, but he has a job to do in San Antonio and might not be back in time. You might have to skip this year."

David sighed, looking crestfallen. Head down, he turned and shuffled toward his room. Charlie's heart squeezed, and she twisted her fingers together.

"What derby?" Yeager asked.

"The Pinewood Derby race for David's Boy Scout troop," Charlie said. "They have one every year, usually in March. This year, it was postponed because a water leak shut down the school on race day. They recently rescheduled for Monday, and we still haven't built his car."

"You know..." Abel rubbed his chin. "I used to be pretty good at building Pinewood Derby cars. Maybe I could lend a hand."

David stopped at the door to his room and looked back. "Really?"

"Sure." Abel nodded. "You got any tools?"

"We have all kinds of stuff downstairs," Charlie said. "In the storage room."

"Then why don't we take a shot at it?"

David scrunched his eyes, clearly skeptical. "Mom?"

"But you're a guest," Charlie told Abel. "It's not fair to make you work for your supper."

"Work? Building Pinewood cars ain't work. It's fun."

Twenty minutes later, Abel and David were in the storage room, which doubled as Tomas's workshop, digging through boxes and speaking in the arcane language of power tools, files, friction, and other manly stuff. Charlie grew bored quickly and left them to it.

In the kitchen, Maria looked up when Charlie came in. "Oh,

Señora Charlie," she said with a roll of her eyes, "what have you done brought home?"

"He's only a guest, Maria." Charlie felt the heat flush on her throat and knew she was getting that red, blotchy thing that traveled up from her collarbone when she was embarrassed. "He brought my books down from St. Louis, and the forklift died, and he didn't have anywhere to go, so I thought that it was only good manners that he stay here..." She trailed off, realizing she was babbling again.

"Ai-eee!" Maria blew on her fingers and shook her hand. "Did you see his arms? Like these." She held her hands apart as if holding an invisible watermelon. "I think he could pick me up with one hand."

"I think he could pick you up with one wink."

Maria shouted a laugh and returned to stirring a simmering pot on the stove. "I think I'm not the only one, no?"

Charlie opened the fridge and leaned in so the cool air wafted across her face, hoping it would chill the bright red flush she knew was there.

When Charlie ventured downstairs to tell Abel and David to wash up for dinner, whirring sounds of a drill motor drowned out her voice. In an attempt to be heard, she yelled, "Time for dinner!" which was when the drill stopped, leaving her shouting into the silence.

They glanced up from the workbench, gave her grunts of acknowledgement, and went back to work. She watched for a moment, noting David's intense expression as he soaked up everything Abel did, studying the man as carefully as a math exam.

A warmth she hadn't felt in a very long time spread through her. Steven had always treated David as more of a possession than a child, a trophy to add to his wall of fame. *See, everyone? I'm a normal American guy with a beautiful wife and a child.* Her dreams of watching David grow up with a father, someone who would teach him to fish and ride bikes and play ball, had been relegated to a tiny corner of her soul where it had shriveled up and disappeared. The strength of that feeling rising again nearly made her gasp with its power.

Charlie went back up to finish setting the table. After several minutes, she marched downstairs again but met with the same result. She finally sent Maria down with a wooden spatula to fetch the boys away from their toys.

At the table, Charlie said a short grace. As soon as the "Amen" left her lips, Abel and David dug into their food like wolves.

"I guess working on Pinewood cars gives you an appetite," she told Maria, who beamed. Nothing made Maria happier than feeding people. She had long since despaired of fattening up Charlie. Abel looked to be her next target.

"It's not any ol' car," Abel said after swallowing some iced tea. "First off, we named her, which you gotta do with cars, or else they fail you."

"Yeah, Mom," David piped up between bites. "She's called the Buchanan Burner. We're gonna make her wedge shaped for aerodynamics and add weights to bring her in at five ounces."

Charlie raised an eyebrow. "Why is it suddenly a 'she'?"

"Abel says that cars and boats are always called 'she.'"

Charlie looked at the trucker, who shrugged and said, "I don't know why. It's a Rule. Capital R."

She smirked. "Sounds like a Man-Law to me."

"Don't forget"—Abel pointed a fork at David—"we have to leave a space to add or remove weight, in case the scale is off."

"Yes sir, I'll remember."

David continued jabbering about filing nail heads and sanding wheels and balancing the weight. Biting back a smile, Charlie paid little attention to the specifics as she let David's enthusiasm wash over her. Normally, David never gushed about anything.

After dinner, David reluctantly went to bed. Maria returned to the kitchen.

Charlie motioned for Abel to sit on the couch. "I've got some Scotch my ex left behind. I don't drink Scotch, but I think it's supposed to be the good stuff." She found the bottle and showed it to him.

He raised his eyebrows. "Macallan, twenty-five years old. Yeah, I think I can manage that without choking."

After serving him a drink, she poured herself a small glass of

Baileys and settled onto the other end of the couch, tucking her feet up under her. Maria puttered around the kitchen, cleaning up. They could hear her singing from time to time as she worked, a Spanish love song that she strangled on the high notes and drowned on the low ones.

Charlie cleared her throat. "So, um, have you always been a trucker, Abel?"

"It feels like only the last thousand years." He tasted a small sip of his drink. "I drifted into it really. When I came back from Afghanistan, a friend of mine, a real whack-job named Victor, knew somebody in the business and hooked me up. The company sent me to truck driving school, and I hit the road."

"Do you like it?"

"Not so much, anymore." Abel sipped his Scotch, seeming to savor the whiskey, holding it in his mouth a moment before swallowing. "At first, it was great. After getting back, I needed the time alone to clear my head of all the blood and death, get back to being a civilian again." He quirked a rueful smile, making his sad eyes even more doleful. "Back then, every time a balloon popped or a door slammed, I'd drop to the ground and roll for cover. Driving gave me a lot of quiet time, let me relax."

"So what happened?" Charlie leaned over to the table and set her glass down. Her blouse gaped at the front, and she noticed that his eyes flicked to the opening of her shirt and snapped away. Deliberately, she held the pose for a second to see what he'd do.

He took a strong pull from his highball glass and studied the upholstery, the coffee table, and the wall art, looking everywhere but at her. Charlie reclined and brushed her hair back, very pleased at having knocked him off balance. *Jesus, Charlie, your hormones are completely out of control.*

"What happened was that the guy I worked for retired and sold me the business. Nowadays, there ain't no such thing as a peaceful drive. I do math in my head all day, over and over. And worry, like, will I get a load? How much will it be? How much fuel will I need, and how much will it cost? Things like that."

"So why don't you quit?"

"Can't. I owe the bank too much for the truck. Things were going pretty good at first, then a woman in a four-wheeler spun out on black ice right in front of me. I couldn't stop. Busted up the rig, busted up my ankle." Abel finished his drink and set the empty glass on the coffee table. "Worse'n that, she... the woman in the car... died. I hit her when I jackknifed." He stared at his hands for a bit, picking at a thumb. "She was pregnant."

Charlie gasped. "Oh, Abel."

"Yeah." He sighed. "It took eight weeks before I could get on the road again. The woman's husband sued me, and my insurance company took a bath. They dumped me, and I lost a lot of customers that I haven't ever gotten back. Higher insurance rates, higher fuel, and less income." He flashed a weak smile. "Some days, I'm happy to make fuel money."

"Now I feel bad. I knew I should've paid you more."

"Hah! No way. You saved my butt. I would've done it for free." He chuffed a short laugh. "Look, I don't know what got into me. Spillin' out all my troubles like some kinda whiny brat. I apologize for bein' such an ass. Must be better whiskey than I thought."

"No, not at all," Charlie said, reaching over to touch his forearm where it rested on the back of the couch. "I'm enjoying your company. Also, you could be a serial killer, and as long as you build that damned Pinewood car, you'd be welcome to stay and tell me all your troubles." *And stare at my boobs with those puppy-dog eyes.*

Watching him from the corner of her eye, Charlie took her time leaning toward the table to fetch her Baileys. Yep, he did a full check of her cleavage, discreetly done, but there nevertheless. Abel cleared his throat and pushed to his feet, picking up his empty glass.

"Do you want another?" Charlie asked. "There's plenty more, and I'm sure not going to drink it."

"No." He headed for the kitchen. "Thanks anyway. It's best not to get too used to the good stuff."

He disappeared through the archway and spoke to Maria in Spanish. The housekeeper laughed and said something back that made him chuckle. Charlie finished off her drink and stood. She waffled, unsure what to do or, more accurately, what she *wanted* to do. *Should she make a move? Let him make a move?* She flopped back down on the sofa and huffed. *What a mess.*

Although she didn't consider herself a class snob, there were some obvious differences in their backgrounds. She came from a blue-blood Dallas family, had a college degree, drank Starbucks lattes, and owned a shoe collection that probably surpassed his entire wardrobe budget. *Oh, God. I can just imagine taking Abel home. "Look, Mom, I hooked up with a truck-drivin' man!"* Her mother would fall dead in her Pradas. *So why am I so... attracted to him?*

When Abel came back into the room, moving with that liquid grace she found so intriguing, she said, "You speak Spanish very well. You're so fast and natural, I can't even keep up."

He stopped behind the sofa and put his hands on his hips. "Ex-wife." He didn't look inclined to sit down again.

"Ex?" she asked, toying with her glass and not looking at him.

"Yeah, I got married out of high school to my best friend's sister. Latina woman. Ever she got mad at me, she'd start yellin' in Spanish. Seems I had a lot of practice learnin' a foreign language." His rueful smile flashed. "Last I heard, she was in LA, trainin' to be an actress by waitin' tables or some such." He shrugged. "It's for the best."

Abel wandered around the room, looking at the paintings on the wall and the knickknacks on the shelves. He stopped at the bookcase and tilted his head to read the titles. "You know, you can learn a lot about a person by seein' what they read."

"What do my books say about me?"

"I have no idea. I tried to read a book once, but my reading aloud annoyed the other inmates."

"The other *what?*"

He glanced over his shoulder and grinned. "Gotcha."

"Abel Yeager!" She threw a sofa pillow that hit him in the back.

"So where's Mr. Charlie Buchanan?"

Aha! Finally, he's curious about my marital status. Maybe there's hope yet.

"Steven and I divorced," she said. "Six years ago. He had a taste for other women. Many other women."

"Aw, damn." He grimaced. "I'm sorry."

"Not to worry." She smiled. "It was a long time ago. He's a doctor. Owns a biotech company. He made a potful of money on some kind of thing that's supposed to keep enzymes—bad enzymes—from forming in your system and causing tumors." She shook her head. "David barely knows his father. Steven doesn't visit much."

Abel covered his mouth to stifle a yawn. "Well, Charlie, it's gettin' late. Time to grab some shut-eye, so I can get up early and work on a champion Pinewood car."

"Oh!" Charlie jumped up. "Let me show you the spare room. The room's plenty big; it has its own shower and a queen-sized bed. It has to be better than your truck's sleeper. So what do you say, Mr. Yeager?"

Abel blinked and raised an eyebrow. "You drive a hard bargain, Ms. Buchanan. It's a deal."

CHAPTER 11

Book Finders
Austin, Texas

YEAGER FOLLOWED CHARLIE ON A quick tour of the apartment. He memorized the layout through force of habit—*Law Number Three: Know the Territory.* He found it difficult to relax without knowing the ways in and out of any building where he was staying overnight. The second- and third-floor entrances had identical vestibules. Both apartment doors had simple latch bolt locks, the kind where the spring-loaded tongue of the lock slipped over a small plate and snapped into a hole. They were cheap and ineffective from a security standpoint.

To the left of the elevator, a set of fire stairs opened off the vestibule. Yeager gave the steel emergency exit door a tug to verify it was locked. Inside the stairwell, the upper floors could be accessed with a key. After Charlie wished him a good night and went back upstairs, Yeager propped open the second-floor door and slipped down the emergency stairwell.

On the first floor, another steel fire door, latched on the inside with a push bar, led into the warehouse. Yeager assumed it was alarmed as part of the store's security system. On the way in, he'd noted a cipher lock on the other side. Anybody wanting to go up the stairs would need a numeric code to open the push-button lock. That provided a better measure of security than the other doors, but it could still be defeated with a pry bar and determination.

Yeager climbed back to his room. He sat on the bed, playing

back the evening on slow motion in his head. He wanted to relive every minute and experience every sensation in greater detail.

Working with David had washed away the feeling of gloom that had followed him for months. A simple meal with Charlie and her son, the warmth of Maria, and the joy of sharing their home had jolted his heart like a defibrillator. And a couple of times, he could've sworn Charlie had been throwing him some come-on looks. He laughed. *You're delusional.*

For six months or more, even before the accident, he'd been sleepwalking through his days. Maybe it was the difficulty of making the transition back to civilian life, or the stress of running his own business. Or maybe Martina's leaving hit him harder than he wanted to admit.

Then came the wreck, and with it, the realization of what he'd done to an innocent woman and her child. She wasn't some wartime collateral damage. She had been an expectant mother, anticipating the birth of her firstborn.

The accident investigators had cleared him in their report, stating he reacted appropriately, given the circumstances, but questions and doubts ate at his gut. What if he'd been more alert? What if he'd been in a little less of a hurry and kept his speed down? He knew the possibility of icy patches existed. He should have paid more attention.

He once heard a captain say something that had stuck with him. "Guilt is an acid that corrodes a man's self-image, etching it with scars that never heal."

Charlie Buchanan didn't have an interest in him. She'd treated him to a room and a meal out of a sense of kindness and decency, nothing more.

The buzzing of his cell phone pulled him back to the present. "Yeager here."

"Yo, *esé.*"

"Por Que. What's up?" Yeager pinched the phone with his shoulder and worked at the laces on his boot.

"I finally remembered where I heard the name Cruz, bro." He paused for a couple of heartbeats. "You ain't gonna like it."

"Hit me." The left boot thumped to the floor, and he crossed his right leg to reach the next.

"I did some checking to be sure, and I nearly peed my pants when I found out." Victor took a deep breath. "Rosaria Santiago. Humberto Cruz is her daddy."

A bucket of ice water washed Yeager from head to toe. His boot remained suspended by one hand, forgotten. "You're sure?"

"I wish I was joking, dude. I really do."

"So all this is about..."

"The wreck, yeah."

Somehow, Yeager wasn't surprised. Oddly, he felt a strong sense of relief. The bill for the worst day of his life was coming due. "So this is about revenge."

"He laid low during the trial, y'know? When that *puta* lawyer was butt-fucking your insurance company? But I remember hearing somewhere Rosaria's maiden name was Cruz, so I checked it with a guy I know in the *Federales,* and sure enough, she's Humberto's only child."

"One or a dozen, it doesn't matter, not when it comes to kids. I understand why he's pissed."

"So, yeah," Victor said. "Anyway, he must've decided to come north and finish the job. Y'know? Ruin you then shoot your ass, *cabrone.*"

Yeager ran his hand through his hair. He needed a shower. *Rosaria Santiago.* Yeager squeezed his eyes shut.

A small car—a Camry—slams on its brakes when it hits the ice. Downshifting, tapping the trailer brakes, Yeager curses and yells at her not to do it, even though he knows she can't hear him. The truck floats across the ice. Steering goes loose, brakes useless. The view pinwheels. Shuddering, the trailer breaks free, moving the entire rig sideways across the road. A pair of headlights shines through the side window.

"You still there?" Victor asked.

"Yeah. Just thinking."

"Don' hurt yourself, *hermano.*"

"This guy Cruz probably ain't gonna give up. I'm in the middle of downtown Austin, so I can't see him trying anything here. I'll be in McAllen by Sunday. Let's hook up then and maybe come up with a plan on how to deal with this guy."

"Sounds good."

"Thanks, Vic. Good to know what I'm up against."

"What *we're* up against, *hombre*. One for all and like that, y'know?"

Yeager snorted a tiny laugh, said goodbye, and tossed the phone on the bed. The very thing that had been slowly suffocating him for the past few months was the—*what was the word? catalyst?*—of his renewed spirit.

Crushing Rosaria Santiago and her unborn child in the tinfoil tomb of their Camry had poisoned Yeager's life with a guilt that ate away at him. Then Cruz's attack had brought Charlie into his life and energized him in a way he hadn't felt since… well, since Afghanistan.

Dealing with Cruz is a problem for tomorrow. Mission priority is to take a shower and get some sleep.

CHAPTER 12

Book Finders
Austin, Texas

Hector Castillo sat in a car on Fifth Street, across from the bookstore where he had last seen the trucker and the red-haired woman from the rest stop. After they had gone inside, Hector and Julio had maintained surveillance. No one had left all evening, nor did anyone take the truck away.

At well after midnight, all the lights were out in the building, and traffic had dwindled to a trickle. One block over, on Sixth Street, the traffic would be heavier, even with the college kids from the University of Texas out for the summer. Sixth Street—a lineup of music clubs, bars, and shops—remained open all night.

Hector lit a cigarette, blowing the smoke out his open window. It would be much more fun to be club-hopping, dancing with long-legged, blond college girls, than sitting in a car all night, aching to take a piss. Humberto Cruz, the prick, had saddled Hector with watching the front doors and the emergency exit in case they flushed the quarry too early.

Something wasn't right about the new job. Cruz had said they were going to steal the guy's truck. He promised them all a lot of money. Instead, all they'd gotten was bruises, and Cruz was still following the guy around, looking for more trouble. Targeting the trucker for death didn't make sense. Cruz claimed it was because the guy had made them lose face, but if that was it, they should just steal his truck and be done with it. It was sitting there behind the store, waiting to be taken.

Twice, patrol cars passed his position, though none of the cops gave him a second glance. But how long would that last? Soon, some prick of a cop would notice him sitting in a car, doing nothing, and would have to harass him for being Mexican. He needed to find a new spot, so they didn't keep seeing him in the same place. Fifth was a one-way street, so he could pull forward and use the mirrors to watch, or he could make the block and find a place farther back. Cruz was taking a long time. He should have been there by now.

His walkie-talkie squawked on the seat beside him. Hector picked it up and keyed the button. *"Si?"*

"Humberto said to tell you to stay put. They are going in." Julio was watching the alley behind the store.

"Humberto's there?"

"Sí. They just drove past me in the van."

"Bueno." Hector tossed the radio on the seat.

It wouldn't be long. After the bookstore had closed and all the workers had filtered out, Julio had gone down the alley and cut the phone lines. Then he and Hector had set up cell jammers around the building, cutting communication. Cruz and the rest of the guys would go in, find the people, and kill them all. Then they would take the truck and whatever else they could find and get the hell out of Texas for a while.

Goddamned state. Texas recently executed a Mexican citizen, ignoring protests from the Mexican government. The *Tejano pendejos* were insane, and Hector wanted to be long gone when the bodies in the bookstore were found.

He shifted in his seat. Soon he would need to use the empty coffee cup. But if the shooting started and the trucker and his bitch ran out the front door, he didn't want to have his dick in his hand, half-standing in his seat trying to piss in a cup.

No, he could wait a few more minutes. It should be over soon, and then he could take a leak in peace. He lit another cigarette and grimaced, adjusting again.

Soon. It'd better be soon.

After the call from Victor, Yeager had gone to bed restless and edgy. When the door opened, he snapped awake. For a fuzzy moment, he thought it was a continuation of his erotic dream of Charlie crawling into bed with him.

She stood, framed by the dim light of the hall. A big nickel-plated handgun gleamed in her hand. "Abel, wake up," Charlie hissed. "Trouble."

"Talk to me." He swung his legs out and grabbed his jeans off the chair back. In one motion, hopefully before she got an eyeful, he whipped the jeans up and fastened the button.

Next, he shoved his hand under the pillow for his Springfield .45. He kept it cocked and locked, so there was no need to cycle the action or check the chamber. He knew the condition of every weapon he owned, and those he carried, he kept ready for action.

"A van came up the alley," Charlie whispered. "No headlights. Five guys got out, carrying guns, and headed for the warehouse door. I tried to call 9-1-1, but there's no dial tone."

"Cruz. How did he find us so fast?" He shook his head. The how didn't matter right then. "Okay, what about your cell?"

"No signal." She frowned. "And that's weird because I always get signal here."

Yeager checked his cell—no signal. "Jammer."

"What? Are these guys spies?" Charlie took a step into the room. Her nightshirt wasn't sheer, and the meager hallway light cast her in a shapely silhouette.

He blinked and rubbed his eyes. "You can get cell jammers on the Internet these days." He brushed past her and moved into the hallway. "Where's David?"

"I sent Maria to his room. She took a frying pan and locked the door. She's armed and dangerous." Charlie tried for gallows humor, but the tremor in her voice gave her true fear away.

Yeager used the internal staircase to the top floor, taking the steps two at time. Charlie followed on his heels.

"There any way out of here I don't know about?" Yeager asked. "Fire escapes? Stairs? Elevators?"

"There's another set of fire stairs"—she pointed down the hall toward the bedrooms—"that comes out at the street in front."

"Okay," he said, pausing at the apartment door. "They probably have somebody watchin' that door, but I don't think they'll come up that way. You see who it was?"

Charlie shook her head. "I couldn't tell."

She was trembling, but so slightly Yeager almost couldn't tell. She held the big revolver down by her leg. Her bare leg, Yeager noted. The nightshirt barely covered her upper thighs. *A half-naked woman holding a gun. Victor will never believe me.*

"The dead phones are enemy action. They've cut us off. No alarms, no police unless we get lucky and somebody calls in the ruckus." He thumbed his .45's safety off. "Here's the deal. They'll come up the fire stairs either to the second floor and up these stairs, or all the way to three and in your front door here. Get down behind that sofa, where you can keep everything in sight. Point that cannon downrange and shoot anything that ain't me."

"Or a cop."

"Yeah, or a cop. Any get past me, you're the last line of defense between David and the bad guys, so don't hesitate. Shoot 'em until they don't move anymore."

"I know," she flung back over her shoulder, already headed for her post. "Be careful."

Yeager smiled, watching her backside. Damned if she wasn't one hell of a woman. Smart, brave, and her legs... "Holy shit," he muttered. *Time to get to work.*

He slammed through the apartment door fast and hard, sweeping the .45 from left to right. The vestibule was empty, the freight elevator silent. The neon fixture seemed as bright as a summer afternoon after the dark apartment.

He headed for the fire stairs. With a little luck, maybe he could get down to the warehouse while the enemy was still trying to get in. It would be one on five in an enclosed space, but he'd put his experience up against a gangster's any day.

Big River Wholesale
St. Louis, Missouri

The specialist wiped his hands on a shop towel and looked at his boss. "That is all he will say. We can get nothing more from him." The specialist spoke Spanish with a heavy Nahuatl accent.

"Is he telling the truth?" Enrique DaSilva asked.

The specialist, thick and strong through the middle, was dressed in working man's clothes and looked more like a janitor than a torturer. He pursed his heavy lips in thought. "Yes, I believe it to be so. Some men paid him to give the manager a drug that would cause a heart attack. That day, he diverted the shipment."

"But he has not said who these men are?"

"No. Either he is very tough, or he doesn't know."

DaSilva, touches of gray at his temples, wore a suit that cost more than some cars, so he stayed well back from the man slumped in the chair. The object of the specialist's attention had long since voided his bowels, and that stench, combined with the rank odor of blood and the reek of fear-sweat, assaulted DaSilva's nostrils. He found such things distasteful since he had achieved high rank within his organization. However, the loss of sixty million dollars required the personal attention of someone with his authority.

DaSilva turned to the other specialist in the room, a chubby and soft computer-forensics technician young enough to be still in school. "Well?"

The computer tech pushed his glasses up on this nose. "Th-th-there's a record of a shipment of six pallets to an address in Austin, on the same day as our shipment."

DaSilva brightened for the first time since he'd learned of the empty shipping truck with its dead driver. "The address?"

"Austin," the computer nerd said. "It's in Texas."

"Yes, thank you. I know. Print the address for me." He turned to the heavier man, who had indeed become a janitor. "When you are done, come to Austin and meet me there. I may have need of your services again. Soon."

CHAPTER 13

Book Finders
Austin, Texas

"Q UIETLY," HUMBERTO CRUZ ORDERED AS Fidel inserted the straight end of a pry bar into the doorframe of the bookstore warehouse.

His men huddled in the darkness, confronting the metal door to the right of the roll-up door, blocked by the trucker's rig. The only illumination came from Gallo's flashlight. All five were armed with either assault rifles or tactical shotguns and a variety of handguns.

Fidel nodded and put his weight on the pry bar. The door squealed, and the metal buckled slightly. He took another grip, adjusted the tool, and shoved. An inch at a time, the door crunched away from the frame, revealing a frame brace across the jamb. The crosspiece functioned like the bar on a fortress, securing the door to the frame.

Fidel huffed. "This will take a few minutes, boss. The door has a—"

"I see it," Cruz growled. "Continue."

With a grunt from Fidel and another screech of metal, the door jerked partway out of the frame. Chupa tapped him on the shoulder, and Fidel traded off the pry bar. The door would give up the fight any minute. *And about time.*

Cruz glanced around, a mouse of anxiety nibbling at him as he stood by the back door of this warehouse, in the dark with guns, in a race to get in and get the job done before the cops noticed them. "Julio, check in," he muttered into the radio.

"Sí."

"Status? Police?"

"Nothing, *jefe.*" The radio crackled with static. "All clear."

The night remained quiet but for the screech and scrape of Chupa gnawing on the door. Time dribbled through their fingers. The cross-frame lock bar had been an unpleasant surprise and had already caused too much delay. Cruz's stomach acid flared up, and he swallowed to make the heartburn go down. Using his shirt sleeve, he wiped sweat from his forehead.

Chupa heaved on the pry bar one final time. The door sprang open. From inside, the whine of the security panel signaled the start of its countdown. But the alarm would go nowhere if Hector and Julio had done their job properly.

"Go, Chupa," Cruz ordered, patting the man on his broad back.

Chupa grabbed his shotgun from beside the door and shoved in first, followed closely by Fidel, Juan, and Gallo.

Cruz entered last, pulling the door shut as far as it would go, given that it was mangled out of shape. "Fan out. Not you, Juan. Stay here, watch for the *policia.*"

Juan frowned but complied in silence. Their flashlights pierced the gloom inside the warehouse, slicing and dancing through the darkness and reflecting off floor-to-ceiling racks and workstations with postage meters and shipping supplies. A forklift hulked in the gloom. To the left, a twenty-four-foot-square open area for unloading trucks had been swept clean and bare. Beyond that were the shelving units, three rows aligned so workers could look down their length. To the right, a set of swinging double doors with small Plexiglas windows led to the store's sales floor.

Cruz checked on the double doors, which joined imperfectly in the middle, and found them locked from the store side. The clerks must have secured the warehouse first then exited via the front of the store. Without more pry-bar work or maybe a shotgun blast, the sales floor remained inaccessible. Cruz decided to leave that as a last resort, in case they found—

"Here!" one of his men called from a dark aisle between two

bookshelves. The man waved a flashlight, and Cruz saw Gallo on the far right aisle against the interior wall.

Cruz hurried down that aisle and, in the unsteady beam of his flashlight, found a door secured with a keypunch lock. "Chupa! Get the pry bar."

Chupa came at a jog, shotgun in one hand, bar in the other. He slammed the metal tip into the doorframe and heaved. With no locking bar across the frame, Chupa made short work of the door. It sprang open with a metallic crunch and revealed a staircase dimly lit by emergency lighting. The stairs were contained in a concrete-walled space that went all the way to the ceiling. They doubled back, turning at a small landing at the halfway point between the first and second floors.

Cruz edged in and looked up. He twisted and turned every way he could, trying to see if anyone had noticed their arrival, but the stairs were built so the landing on each floor blocked his view beyond the halfway point.

Nothing moved, and the only sound was the insistent scream of the alarm panel begging for attention back in the warehouse. Nevertheless, as he moved closer to the first step, the hairs on the back of his neck stood. Without looking back, he motioned for the men behind him to go first. Gallo surged ahead, forcing his way to the front.

The young think they will live forever. Well, let's see if that's true. "Gallo," he whispered to the wiry little hombre. "Check it out. Find if they have rooms upstairs, or what." Turning to the next in line, he said, "Chupa, go right behind him. Fidel, stay here and guard our backs."

Gallo moved up the stairs, an HK assault rifle held in front of him like a TV cop. "Come on, Chupa. Follow me."

Cruz held back a pace, allowing the two men to go ahead. Chupa stopped on the first landing while Gallo advanced. When the smaller man made it to the second floor landing, Chupa started up. The scuff of the men's shoes and their panting sounded loud even over the distant squeal of the alarm panel.

Cruz jumped at the loud bang of a pistol shot. Chupa yelled and hopped back to the landing, blind-firing two quick rounds from his shotgun. Gallo tumbled down the stairs like a marionette with its strings cut. He was dead before he landed at Chupa's feet.

Chupa, standing on the first landing, fired upward again and again, cranking the pump action in a blur. Cruz's ears rang from the repeated blasts, and he hugged the wall.

"What are you shooting at?" Cruz screamed.

Chupa stopped shooting and looked at him, confused. "I don't know! The bullet came from up there!" He blasted another round upstairs, emptying the shotgun.

Chupa stared at the weapon, seeming at a loss as to why it failed to fire. Cruz had seen that look before, men in combat so jacked up on fear and adrenaline that they turned stupid and forgot simple things, like taking off the safety.

Or retreating to a safe position to reload.

Chips of gore-covered concrete exploded behind Chupa's head. The big man stumbled into the wall, his face twice its normal size from the pressure wave of the bullet that had passed through his forehead. He fell in a heap, wearing a wide-eyed look of surprise.

Cruz screamed and pointed his CAR-15 around the corner of the stairs, keeping his body out of harm's way. He let off a full magazine up the staircase, fire-hosing thirty rounds in a matter of seconds.

When the magazine ran dry, he popped in another one and retreated back into the shadow by the door. He fixed the CAR's sights on the corner where the trucker would have to appear if he wanted to come down. Fidel crouched beside the open door, eyes wide and a white-knuckled death grip on his shotgun. Juan shouted from farther away, wanting to know what was happening.

Frustration and anger clawed at Cruz's throat. "You motherfucker!" he bellowed up into the stairwell, which stank of blood and gun smoke. He could barely hear his own voice over the ringing in his ears. "I will fucking kill you and piss on your dead face, you fucking piece of shit!"

After a heartbeat of silence, a quiet chuckle drifted down, followed by an ice-cold voice. "Bring it."

CHAPTER 14

A TRICKLE OF MOISTURE RAN DOWN his face, and Yeager swiped at it. The back of his hand came away streaked red. A bullet fragment or concrete chip had cut a groove from the side of his nose to his cheekbone. He hadn't noticed when it happened, but once he knew about it, the wound began to sting. He counted himself lucky that was the only damage he'd taken.

The loudmouth who had promised to piss in his dead face—and it had to be Cruz—continued to scream curses up the stairwell, but he had switched to Spanish after Yeager's taunt. Yeager sat on the bottom stair directly above the second-floor landing and listened to the rant. Nice technique, he decided. He would give it a seven or eight for style and enthusiasm, but Cruz couldn't hold a candle to Martina, who could jumpstart a nuclear reactor with the volume, language, and venom of her cussing.

Yeager switched out magazines. Slipping the partially spent one into his hip pocket, he took stock. He didn't feel too bad about his position, and time was on his side. The longer he held off the invaders, the better. Cruz would want to end this little adventure quickly, but he wouldn't have counted on or planned for a siege situation. He had to be shitting bricks down there, expecting either cops or witnesses to show up at any moment. Since he'd whiffed on the quick kill, he might cut his losses and go away.

Yeah, and pigs might fly to the moon in cherry-colored rocket ships. I just hope these guys didn't bring grenades.

Humberto Cruz. Revenge for his daughter had brought him here. Charlie, David, and Maria were in danger because of Yeager. More debt to add to his ledger. *Charlie. David. Maria. These guys won't touch a hair on any of the Buchanan family. Not. A. Hair.*

Several seconds ticked away in silence. Dust blown loose in the flood of lead twisted and curled in the weak yellow light, tickling Yeager's nose. He pinched back a sneeze. The stairs were covered in grit, new and old, and it crunched under his butt when he shifted position.

Cruz started issuing orders in Spanish, and Yeager strained to listen. The man spoke in the kind of overloud voice that old people used when they couldn't hear. *His ears must be ringing worse than mine.*

Something, something... "Sprinkler valve off..." *Something...* Then a word came through loud and clear: "*Fuego.*"

Fire.

"Shit," Yeager muttered. "I wish he hadn't thought of that."

All that Cruz and his gang had to do was shut off the water to the sprinkler system and light a fire in the warehouse. They could then sit back munching popcorn while they watched the place, including the inhabitants, go up in flames. Or they could pick Yeager and his friends off when they rushed outside in a panic.

Think, Abel. His instincts screamed for him to take the offensive, but charging downstairs into a crew of gunmen, from the lighted stairwell to the dark warehouse, would get him killed quickly and messily. Had he made it down earlier and played hide-and-seek in the dark, it would have been a different story, but the crooks had the advantage there. *No, direct assault won't do at all.*

Yeager rose onto the balls of his bare feet and crept across the landing to the apartment's second-floor door. Cruz shouted something, but Yeager couldn't make out the words.

Yeager inched through the apartment door like a teenager sneaking home after curfew. The stairs to the third floor were on his left, and directly in front of him, a hall led to the front of the building. *Two doors on each side, bedrooms on the left, workshop and storage room on the right.* Silver light gleamed from the casement window at the end of the hall. *Get a look at the street? Or go upstairs first?* Yeager debated. *Window or warning?*

He started up the stairs. "Charlie!" he stage-whispered. "It's me—Abel."

"Okay. Come on up."

He poked his head up far enough to see Charlie standing behind the sofa, revolver dangling.

"What happened?" she asked. "I heard shots."

"Two down." He bounded up the remaining stairs and crossed the room. "But listen, they're planning on lighting a fire and burning us out."

Her eyes widened. "A fire!"

"Yeah. I heard 'em talkin'. So I'm going out front to try to get around back before they figure out how to turn off the sprinklers." He touched her arm and slipped past her, heading across the living room for the hall. "I don't know how many are out front, so I need you to cover me from the window while I flush 'em out. When they go for me, lay down some cover fire so I can... eliminate the problem. Then you grab David and Maria and follow me out. Get to safety. Where's that other fire stair?"

"Here," she said, opening the last door on the left.

A business office lay beyond: desk, chairs, a computer monitor glowing with a spiraling screen saver. The office window overlooked the street. An exit sign glowed over a plain utilitarian door in the room's far corner.

"Good. Cover me from here," Yeager said. "Keep back from the window. Shoot through the glass if anybody makes a move on me."

"But—"

"Oh, and watch your back. If they figure out I'm gone, they could come up the stairs."

"Wait." She grabbed his arm.

"What?" Yeager could feel time bleeding away, and he was itching to move.

"Don't go around back. There's nothing in this building worth you getting killed over. I'll cover you from the window like you said. Then we'll go down and all get away. We can call the police—"

"No." Yeager shook his head, pulling away. "This guy's after me, not you. I brought this problem to your door, so I'm not going to let them hurt you or burn your house down. Besides, they've tried to kill me twice now. They don't get to try anymore."

Yeager stopped at the exit, one hand braced on the push bar. His adrenaline spiked. The world dialed into focus like a camera lens being twisted. His hearing turned up, and time slowed to a carnivore's rhythm. He knew the feeling well. What he hadn't realized was how much he missed it.

He pushed open the door and slipped out, not looking back.

⸻ ❖ ⸻

The door swung closed, and Charlie shivered. She had never been tested by violence. Physical confrontations were so far out of her comfort zone, she struggled to think clearly. Hyperventilation threatened to take over her breathing. Her pulse hammered, and her skin felt cold and clammy. Ants seemed to be crawling on the back of her tongue.

She crept up to the window, stood to the side of it, and scanned the street below. She saw a few parked cars but no passing traffic or loitering pedestrians. Hunched down, she crossed to the other side of the window. Looking west on Fifth, she found the scene pretty much the same. Puddles of amber light reflected off car windshields, concealing any potential occupants.

Yeager would hit the door any second. An alarm bar on the street-level door would scream holy hell when pressed, something she'd found out by accident when she forgot to unlock it before going out. *Wish I'd thought of popping the alarm on the door to attract attention. Too late now, though, and it might not have helped anyway.*

She cocked her revolver and steadied her grip with both hands, holding the piece low, muzzle down. She took several deep breaths, trying to calm her nerves, but the pounding in her chest threatened to reach overload. She had to wipe her hands, one at a time, on her shirt to dry them off.

Even though she was waiting for it, she jumped when the door alarm squealed. Sucking in a shuddering breath, she tried to focus on the street. She moved in front of the window. In her desperation not to miss anyone coming for Abel, she forgot about showing herself as a target. For tonight at least, she'd negotiate from behind a Smith & Wesson .41 Magnum.

There! A car door opened across the street, and a dark-haired man jumped out. Focused on something below her, possibly Abel, he started to raise the radio or cell phone he had in his left hand, while pointing a pistol with his right. In an instant, all the jittery nervousness flushed away, and she brought the Magnum up in a shooter's stance, nerves calm, hands rock steady. The red tab on the front sight snapped into perfect block with the rear, and she placed the target on top of the sight-picture, as if she stood at the firing line on the range, facing nothing more dangerous than a paper target.

Letting out a half breath, she squeezed the trigger with a gentle caress.

CHAPTER 15

Book Finders
Austin, Texas

HECTOR CASTILLO SQUIRMED AND GLANCED at the clock on the dashboard. Cruz entered the building across the street twelve minutes ago, and since then, Hector hadn't heard a word. The leather creaked as he shifted again, trying to find a comfortable position for his aching bladder. How long did it take to break in and kill two people in their beds? They should have been finished, everyone long gone before the cops showed up.

He checked the clock again. *Thirteen minutes.* Hector liked the little dial-type clock, along with all the other amenities in the big Chrysler. It was a real gangster car, black and shiny and tough on the outside, creamy leather on the inside. If the cops ran the plates, the car would come up clean. But the stainless steel Smith & Wesson .40 caliber semi-automatic pistol on the seat *would* be a problem, as would Hector, a Mexican with an arrest record in two countries.

Hector had the motor running, blowing the air conditioning to keep out the muggy air and mosquitoes. The AC fan and the engine made so little noise that he had no problem hearing the shriek of the emergency exit when it sounded. The trucker burst out of the building and curled into a crouch, his handgun tracking like a turret from left to right.

Hector's bladder clenched in pain. *What? Why is he out here? What happened to Humberto?*

The trucker apparently didn't spot Hector behind the tinted

glass, since he jogged for the corner across the street to Hector's left. The man wore jeans but no shirt and no shoes.

He's going around back! Hector jerked the handle and butted his shoulder into the door. He grabbed his gun and radio on the way out. Each hand filled, Hector's heart thumped. His tongue buzzed with fear. Aiming one-handed, he swung the weapon to bear on the trucker. His thumb stabbed for the push-to-talk button on his radio.

Boom! The concrete at his feet exploded. The trucker skidded to a stop and spun to face Hector. The passenger window next to Hector crunched and shattered. He never even heard that shot.

"Fuck this." Hector dived back into the car.

Another round from the cannon slapped into the roof, blowing a hole through it and thudding into the upholstery. He tossed the gun and radio on the floorboard and slapped the shift lever into Drive. Huddled behind the dash, Hector stomped the gas pedal before the transmission engaged, causing the car to leap ahead. The rear window starred from another impact. Hector didn't know which gun had caused it, and he didn't care.

He floored the accelerator, and the big car flew, engine winding up with a powerful hum. He peered over the dash enough to keep the car in a straight line but didn't sit all the way up until he was six blocks away from the bookstore.

Twelve blocks away, blowing through another stoplight, he realized his pants were soaked.

Yeager paused, making sure Hector wasn't coming back and none of his friends were coming out to play. The taillights of the big Chrysler bobbed up and down as it bounded over a dip in the road, sparks scattering from the undercarriage. He jogged halfway into the street and looked up at the shattered third floor window and waved an "all clear." Charlie appeared, waved back, then disappeared.

Not every day that you ran across a woman who'd back you up in a gunfight, he mused as he trotted for the street corner, and with a gun big enough to launch a space shuttle.

On his first tour in the sandbox, a grizzled sergeant from Alabama with service medals dating back to the Spanish-American War had taught Yeager about tactics in a firefight. Once, seeing a squad pinned down in a box canyon, Yeager had scrambled up, ready up to charge headfirst into the firefight.

Sergeant Masterson had grabbed Yeager's arm and pulled him back down. "Hold up, boy."

"Fuck 'hold up,' Sar'nt," Yeager, then a Private First Class, screamed back. "We gotta bust those guys out."

"And we will, son. But one thing you gotta learn is how to hurry carefully."

That lesson became *Law Number Five: Hurry carefully.*

It came back to him from time to time, especially when he forgot something important, like reconnaissance. He rounded the corner and sprinted for the alley. He was already past the second watcher before he realized there was one. Stepping out of a dark gap between two buildings on the other side of the four-lane street, the slender, dark-haired man wasn't much more than a flash of motion in Yeager's peripheral vision.

Sergeant Masterson had once addressed the platoon. "In most firefights, civilian and military, the number of rounds expended exceeded those few that make contact with their intended target by an order of magnitude. In the grip of adrenaline, even trained marksmen can blow through entire magazines at astoundingly close ranges and hit nothing more than dirt." Then he spat a stream of tobacco juice onto the dusty Afghanistan road. "If I see any of you pussies wasting ammo, shooting without looking, going full rock 'n' roll, or trying any Wyatt Earp trick shots, or using your weapons in any manner except aimed, disciplined fire, you better hope the Tally-ban gets you before I do."

Yeager was glad his old sergeant couldn't see him being a total jackass. Yeager registered the movement to his left and classified it as a threat, processing the information through his combat-trained mind at overclock speed. Before the thought had fully transformed from recognition to conscious reaction, he was sliding to a stop and pivoting left, weapon locked in both hands, torso rotating. The target picture coalesced over his sights, and Yeager instantly confirmed "threat" and "weapon," at the same moment his finger took up slack on the trigger. It was the most heinous violation of Masterson's rules that Yeager ever committed: a snap shot in the dark, at a moving target more than thirty yards distant.

But it hit the would-be ambusher—dead, solid, perfect—center mass. The guy spun backward and landed in a pile.

I wish Por Que had seen that shot. He'll never believe it, not for a minute.

Yeager shook off his own shock and continued his run for the alley. He paused at the corner—better late than never—to check for more watchers.

Book Finders occupied the entire corner of Fifth and San Jacinto. The alley behind the building extended a short way before the cut-out for the dock indented to the right. Yeager's rig took up most of the free space. He had left it backed up to the overhead door, parked parallel to the alley. A van, presumably the assailants', blocked the lane.

Yeager skirted the van, checking the interior for the enemy before moving past it. He winced as sharp bits of gravel and other debris jabbed at his bare feet. A can tinkled down the alley when an unexpected gust of wind rattled through the night. A bite of cooler air followed, blowing off some of the muggy heat and chilling the sweat on his bare chest.

Moths battered the single, murky sodium vapor light mounted over the dock. A car horn blared, followed by a squeal of brakes, the sound muted by the intervening distance of several streets. Close by, nothing moved, and no traffic passed. Fifth and San Jacinto were unaccountably empty.

Where the hell is everybody? Downtown Austin on Friday night, even at three o'clock in the morning, there ought to be people. Kids partying, delivery drivers, cops, something. It was a mystery he didn't have time to solve.

He checked around the front of his rig and found the warehouse door mangled, hanging open at the top of a short stairway.

Fidel and Juan couldn't find the sprinkler riser anywhere inside the warehouse perimeter. When they looked outside, they finally found a door on the exterior wall labeled Authorized Personnel Only.

"In here," Fidel said and popped the door with his pry bar.

Pay dirt. The room was a simple square of concrete, reeking of dust and cobwebs, containing two standing pipes with a huge valve in the middle of each. The valves, mounted about waist high, were controlled by large wheels, like those on a submarine hatch. Each wheel had a padlocked chain running through it, locking the valve open to prevent the kind of damage they intended to inflict.

"It's locked," Juan said and raised his Mossberg pump shotgun, holding the muzzle an inch from the dangling padlock on the right-hand riser.

"No!" Fidel screamed.

Juan frowned at him. "What?"

"You will kill us both, stupid."

"Don't call me stupid."

"I will call you stupid if you shoot that gun in here."

Juan looked around and apparently reconsidered the idea of firing a shotgun inside a closet-sized room full of concrete and steel. "Okay, genius, how do we get the lock off?"

"With this." Fidel slung his assault rifle and inserted the tip of his pry bar inside the one of the chain's links and started to twist.

The door swung shut behind them, and Fidel cursed until Juan dug out his flashlight and pointed it at the chain. Inside the enclosed space, they were sweating and panting within seconds.

"Did you hear that?" Juan asked.

"What?"

"It sounded like gunfire."

Fidel shrugged. "Probably Humberto, bravely killing more stairs."

After a few minutes of grunting effort, Fidel snapped the links on both chains. Seconds later, the sprinkler riser valves were closed.

"Come on." Fidel mopped his face with the tail of his snap-buttoned shirt. "Let's tell Humberto so we can get this over with. This job has been a fucking nightmare."

"No shit." Juan twisted the handle and shouldered open the door.

CHAPTER 16

Book Finders
Austin, Texas

YEAGER GLIDED AROUND THE FRONT of his truck and headed toward the warehouse steps. A door to the left, less than twenty feet away, swung open, and a Hispanic male emerged, wearing tight jeans, boots, and a Western shirt. The man held a pry bar in his right hand and carried an assault rifle slung over one shoulder. The guy froze, a Looney Tunes expression of surprise on his face. Yeager followed the man's thoughts as though reading from a book: *Rifle slung, pry bar in one hand, man with pistol. What do I do? Go for it or run like hell?*

The guy tried to do both at once, and Yeager shot him, a double tap to the chest. The pry bar clattered to the floor. The man in the Western shirt slammed back into the wall, bounced off, and slumped to the floor. Yeager tracked him with the muzzle of the .45.

The steel door banged open a second time. A bulky man in black jeans and a Tecate T-shirt rushed out, fire blooming from the muzzle of a pump shotgun. Driven by instinct, Yeager leaped to the side. Pellets zipped past his face, slashing the air.

Yeager fell hard, scraping a bare shoulder on the greasy asphalt and jarring his gun hand to numbness. His head bounced off the concrete. Stunned, all he could do was roll, trying to stay out of the spread of pellets as Mr. Tecate fired again, and then again, shotgun muzzle tracking left, following Yeager's tumble.

Yeager rose on one knee, snapped a shot at a blurry target and missed. He blinked, acquired the target, and fired again, slide locking back. The last round zipped downrange and hit high and to the right of the Tecate emblem.

The shotgun discharged into the air. Mr. Tecate spun away, grunting. Yeager leaped up and slammed the empty pistol into the side of Tecate's head. The skull cracked with a dull dropped-melon sound.

The Latino man collapsed, eyes rolled back into his head. Dead or not, Yeager couldn't tell.

Sucking wind as if he'd run a marathon, Yeager retrieved his partially spent clip from his hip pocket and hot swapped with the empty one in his .45. Dropping the slide release, he chambered a round and checked his perimeter. Still clear.

Sergeant Masterson's voice echoed in his head. "Too much time sitting on your fat ass behind the wheel and not enough PT, Private Yeager."

"No shit, Sergeant," Yeager gasped, flicking sweat off his forehead with the back of one hand. "I'll get right on that."

The dock area became quiet in the aftermath of the shooting. No more bad guys spilled from the sprinkler riser room. Yeager checked and made sure it was empty. The moths carried on, whirling and dancing around the overhead light, but the cicadas had stopped. Or at least he thought they had. It was hard to tell over the ringing in his ears. The warehouse door creaked a tiny bit in the puff of wind that stirred through the dust and trash of the alley. The invitation was implicit. Come on in and finish the party, said the open door.

"Where the fuck are the cops?" he muttered. "What do you have to do around here to get some attention, set off a bomb? The second invasion of Texas by Mexico is going on here, and nobody gives a shit."

The road rash on his right shoulder woke up and started to sting, the blood getting tacky in the cool breeze playing through the alley. A crumpled paper bag, lifted on magical currents, spun in circles then skittered away.

Thunder rumbled, and the damp chill of the wind raised goose bumps on his bare skin. He realized he'd been staring at the warehouse door for several seconds, putting off the inevitable.

"Well, Humberto, you got any guys left, or is it down to you and me?" He started forward in a crouch. "Let's find out."

Charlie stayed at the window long enough to see Yeager head for the corner. The concussion of the big Magnum rang in her head as if someone had clapped cymbals over her ears, and the flash had left a ghost image on her vision. Wind gusted through the shattered window, stirring the curtains and breaking her loose from her trance.

She ran for her bedroom. One thought kept popping up from the back of her mind as she shucked into yesterday's jeans: *I just shot at someone. A real, live person, not a paper target.*

She slipped on a pair of flats, ran to David's room, and pounded on the door. "Maria, it's me. Open up."

The lock clicked, and Maria eyes appeared in the gap, followed by the rest of her as she flung the door open. Maria swept her into a bear hug, the cast iron skillet in her hand thumping Charlie in the back. "Ai, *mi hermosa*, what happened?" Maria cried, holding Charlie at arm's length to inspect for damages. "We heard *chooting*!"

David stood by his bed, a baseball bat held at the ready, his eyes serious and concerned but not frightened.

Pride in her son blossomed in her chest, and she smiled and held out a hand. "Come on, you two. We have to get out of here while the coast is clear."

What is taking those jackasses so long? Humberto Cruz held a Molotov cocktail he'd retrieved from the van, prepared originally to eliminate the evidence once they shot the trucker and his whore in their bed. He snapped the lid of a Zippo lighter open and shut, pacing from the door to a mountain of books piled on the floor and back again.

He heard something that sounded like shots. Two, no, three shots. Then nothing. Cruz cocked his head, trying to determine the source. Pocketing the Zippo, he unclipped the radio on his belt and keyed the mike. "Hector. Check in."

Nothing.

"Julio?"

Again nothing, but another shot sounded—closer, he thought. The trucker must have flanked them somehow. He paced in a small circle, tapping his head with the hand holding the radio, trying to jar loose a thought, a decision, a plan. He was getting old and soft. First, he had backed down at the rest stop, then he let others take the lead up the stairs, and he was just standing there, not knowing which way to jump when guns were being fired.

Cruz sighed. *It is time to retire, hey?* "But not until I kill this *pendejo* truck driver," he muttered.

Cruz retrieved his Zippo and snapped open the top. He flicked the wheel, and a healthy tongue of flame ignited, glowing in the dark warehouse. He dangled the gas-soaked rag over the yellow flame.

He jerked, surprised, when gunfire boomed outside the door. A scattering of shots sounded and then silence. Cruz closed the lighter and returned it to his pocket. He strode to the warehouse door.

Charlie paused at the fire door, which still screamed in alarm, and pushed it open enough to reconnoiter the street. Seeing nothing but a passing car, quickly gone, she shoved the door open the rest of the way and dragged Maria and David outside.

A scattering of shots from around back made her heart clench, but she resisted the impulse to go see what had happened. Instead, she concentrated on getting her son and friend to safety. The Downtown Austin Marriott Courtyard was the closest place she could think of that would be open at such a late hour, and it was only a block and a half away on Fourth Street.

As she walked, she kept her head on a swivel, ignoring David's questions and Maria's prayers. Hustling as fast as Maria could go, they crossed the street and slid to the left, rounding the corner of Trinity and Fifth, headed south. As they made the corner, she thought she heard another gunshot.

Muttering a prayer of her own, Charlie jostled David and Maria in front of her and kept them moving toward the Courtyard, all the while glancing back over her shoulder.

※

Yeager started for the warehouse door, holding the .45 in a two-handed grip, finger alongside the trigger guard. His foot had barely touched the bottom step leading to the back door when it banged open. Humberto Cruz filled the doorway. Yeager recognized the dapper little man from the first time he'd seen him at the rest stop in Judsonia, Arkansas.

Cruz looked much the same. He wore dark slacks, a white Guayabera shirt, polished loafers, and an aura of meanness. The only difference was that he looked... Yeager wasn't certain. Defeated? Resigned?

"Humberto," Yeager growled.

The Mexican crook stiffened, and his eyes widened. "You know my name?"

"Everybody knows who you are, Humberto. Cops in two states and the Feds are all looking for you. Best for you if you give up. The thing with your daughter... I'm sorry, but it was an accident. She hit her brakes too hard."

Cruz smiled almost sadly. "No, *Señor* Truck Driver, I don' think so." He stepped forward, and the mangled door closed behind him with a squeal. He was holding a bottle with a rag dangling from the neck. It took Yeager a few seconds to realize it was a Molotov cocktail.

Cruz fished his free hand in his pocket, and Yeager tensed.

Cruz paused, seeming lost in thought. "I remember my daughter. Full of life. I miss her every day." He shook his head. "All my men are dead, yes? *Sí, muerte.* And you have a gun in hand, and I do not. I have no chance to kill you. It would seem that you win." He hung his head and brought his hand out of his pocket. He was holding something shiny. *A lighter.*

"Stop!" Yeager yelled.

Cruz's hand kept moving. Yeager shot him once in the chest. Cruz stumbled but didn't go down or drop the lighter. Yeager shot

103

him again, center mass. Cruz bounced off the steel door but still didn't fall. Drunkenly, stumbling, he lit the Zippo with one flick and held it to the gas-soaked rag.

Yeager shot him again, but Cruz was driven by a will beyond mere flesh and blood. Sometimes Yeager had bad dreams where he fired again and again into an enemy with no effect, but that had never happened in real life. Cruz raised the Molotov cocktail, aiming it not at the building but directly at Yeager.

Yeager shifted aim and fired one shot at the whisky bottle full of gasoline. The bottle shattered, drenching Cruz in sheets of flaming gas.

Cruz shrieked and stumbled down the steps, and Yeager leaped backward. The flaming man staggered a couple of steps then collapsed onto the concrete parking apron, shrieking an inhuman cry of pain.

Yeager clenched his teeth and took a couple of breaths to settle his aim. He carefully put one bullet through Cruz's head. The scream cut off as if he'd hit the power button on a CD player. All that was left was the crackling of the fire and the smell of burning meat.

And, finally, the sound of sirens wailing in the distance.

CHAPTER 17

Austin, Texas

STEVEN BUCHANAN KNOCKED ON APARTMENT 404 of the Windswept complex after midnight. He kept one hand in his pocket, toying with the thumb drive containing his bank account information. In the other, he carried a bottle of wine.

The place was a few blocks from the UT campus. Rock music thrummed from a nearby unit, and a bunch of twenty-somethings sat on tailgates and lawn chairs in the parking lot, drinking Bud Light and laughing. They all wore knee-length shorts and baseball caps turned backward, with either flip-flops or running shoes and no socks.

The door opened, and Nita Lutz said, "Hey there."

"Sorry I'm late." He slid past her, catching a scent of some fiery perfume as he brushed against her tits, which poked out from her satin robe like warhead-tipped missiles. "Had more stuff to clean up than I expected."

"That's all right." She closed the door and swished into the kitchen behind him.

As he set the wine bottle down on the counter, she wrapped her arms around him and pressed against his back, molding her body to his. She laid her head against his back. "I just got home myself. There was a cash discrepancy in the till, and I had to stay late to fix it. You know how Charlie is when the books don't match."

"Hah! Do I ever."

He turned in her arms and tilted her chin for a kiss, which turned into a Nita Special: a warm, soft mouth and an acre of tongue, a kiss that involved her entire body. *One thing about Nita, she puts everything she has into it.*

When they broke apart, Steven took a moment to admire her gray eyes, thick black hair, and full, slightly puffy lips. Of all the women he'd screwed before, during, and after marriage, he kept coming back to her. The things Nita did with her tongue made sex with other women like screwing a rubber doll. She had the libido of a succubus, and if she had a limit, he had yet to find it.

"I did what you asked." Her eyes sparkled with mischief. "Now are you going to tell me why?"

He raised one eyebrow. "You did?"

"Yeah, even better than you wanted. Instead of keeping Charlie out of the book skids, I got the truck to stay there overnight. Charlie has the hots for the driver."

"A truck driver?" A momentary stab of jealousy caught him by surprise. Charlie was the only woman who could run a close second to Nita in bed. Plus, Charlie could have a conversation about more than celebrity weddings and divorces, too. He pushed past her and sifted through her utensil drawer for the wine opener. "That doesn't seem likely."

Her hands slid into his pockets from behind and cupped his equipment. He tensed when her fingers brushed the flash drive. "Ooh, look who's jumpy," she cooed. "Don't worry, baby. She doesn't know about us, so if you want to go back and save her from her blue-collar slumming, you still can."

"Amazing she never found out." Steven located the opener and extricated himself from her grip. He brushed the outline of the thumb drive in his pants with a casual swipe of his free hand. "About us, I mean. That time you gave me a blow job in the office..."

She giggled. "I know, right? She walked in, what, two minutes after you zipped up?" Her eyes sparkled. "And she never suspected a thing. What a loser, that girl."

"Hey, I was married to her," he said, only half teasing. "Have some respect."

He poured two glasses of red wine, and they carried them to

the living room sofa. She laid her head in his lap and stroked his leg while he sipped the wine and flipped channels on the remote.

"You seem a little distracted tonight, baby," Nita murmured against his thigh. "And you never answered my question. What's in the pallets that you want so bad?"

"Mmmm." He set the wine glass down on the end table so he could fondle her ample bottom.

She moaned appreciatively. Maybe he should take a piece of tail with him when he ran for it. If he took anybody, it would be Nita, but he knew himself too well. Six months—a year, tops—of nonstop Nita on a small boat and he'd want to chuck her overboard in shark-infested waters.

"Ooh, baby doll." Her cheek rubbed his stiffening cock through his slacks. "I love how you're playing with my ass. I've got some new lube, so why don't we head to the bedroom and see what else you can do with it?"

On the other hand, how bad could it be?

Nita Lutz's jaw dropped when Charlie called Saturday morning and told her what had happened. She sat up in bed and checked the clock: 9:34 a.m. "A shootout? At the store?"

"Yes, at our store. The entire place is a crime scene."

Incredible. Did this have something to do with Steven's pallets?

"I'm dropping David off at Maria's brother's now," Charlie continued. "Then I'm going to the courthouse to see about getting Abel out of jail."

"Abel?"

"The truck driver. He's the one who shot it out with the gang. We think he's the one they were after, too."

Steven made a noise in his sleep and rolled over. Nita carefully rolled out of bed, took the cordless phone into the living room, and closed the door behind her. Nude, she curled up on the sofa and crossed an arm under her breasts. Gooseflesh pimpled her skin, and she shivered.

"So I think it's best," Charlie was saying, "if we close the store today and give everybody a paid day off."

"So how many people were killed?"

"Five or six. I'm not sure."

Nita realized her nipples were hard and her crotch slightly damp. "Is there much blood?"

"Nita, I don't know. It's not like I went down to look. Listen, speaking of that, when the cops release the crime scene, I'm going to need someone to do cleanup. I've called Tomas, and he's ready to come in, but I don't know how long this thing at the jail's going to take. I hate to ask this, but can you—"

"I'll take care of it. Don't worry. I'll get the online orders ready to ship, too."

"You don't have to—"

"No, don't worry. It's fine."

They talked for a few more minutes, but Nita barely paid attention. When she hung up, she tossed the phone on the sofa and padded back to the bedroom. Steven's clothes were crumpled on the floor, and a metallic glint caught her eye. A small thumb drive had fallen from his pocket. She picked it up and set it on the bedside table.

She studied the man in her bed. Blond hair, square chin and the body of a Ken doll. *Except with a real dick.* She chuckled silently. Her little cutie was up to no good. First, he'd asked her to keep Charlie away from the book shipment. To the best of her recollection, Steven had never given the book business more than ten seconds of attention. Then, he'd made a big deal out of Charlie buying some books in St. Louis. He told Nita to stay away from the shipment when it came in. And early that morning, somebody had shot up the bookstore. It all fit together somehow.

Steven mumbled something and cracked his eyes open.

"Hey, sleepyhead." Nita traced the outline of his semi-hard erection under the sheet. The tingle between her legs grew from a tiny buzz to a harmonic vibration. "Wakey-wakey."

She needed to find out what her lover boy was up to. It sure wasn't a sudden passion for literature. Whenever Steven became that interested in something, it always involved money, usually in bonus-sized amounts, which meant she needed to know what it was. So she could get a piece of the action. Fortunately, Steven had a lever that, when handled properly, unlocked all his secrets.

Nita pulled the sheet back and took him in her mouth.

Austin City Jail
Austin, Texas

Yeager spent the rest of the night, and a good part of Saturday, in jail.

When the Austin cops had arrived on scene and learned the body count, they couldn't get the cuffs on him fast enough. After in-processing, Yeager used his phone privilege to wake Victor, who called a cousin, David Garcia, an Austin lawyer.

Yeager met Garcia for the first time in a sterile interview room—white walls, scratched-up table, two folding chairs—at ten o'clock on Saturday morning, six hours after his arrest. His first impression of the young Mr. Garcia: razor sharp. The attorney had a laser-guided haircut and a tailor-made suit cut from a cloth so rich that lint ran away in terror. His shoes were polished to a shine that the Queen's guard would envy.

"So, Mr. Yeager." Garcia spoke in clear Midwestern-American English, at some point having eliminated all traces of his Hispanic roots. "You have caused quite the uproar."

The lawyer clicked the latches on his briefcase and drew out a thick sheaf of papers. He closed the briefcase, set it aside, and took a pen from inside his suit jacket. Yeager lost a mental bet when, instead of the expected shiny gold Montblanc, Garcia brought out a generic plastic roller ball.

"Let's get started," Garcia said. He uncapped the pen and adjusted his rimless glasses. A lock of black hair escaped when he glanced through the documents in front of him. "The Austin PD is still processing the scene... five bodies, one burnt to a crisp, the rest shot to pieces. It may take them the rest of the day to sort through all that."

"How's Ms. Buchanan? David? Maria?"

"They're fine. In fact, Ms. Buchanan told me that she would be posting your bail, once we get a hearing on that."

"Bail?" Yeager sat back and scratched under his ribs. He'd been issued an orange jumpsuit stiff from heavy detergent, and it itched. "I'm eligible for bail? I figured as many as I killed, they'd lock me up for a while outta spite."

Garcia's smile, though genuine, could be measured in millimeters. "Here's how this is going to play out, Mr. Yeager."

The young attorney recapped his pen without having used it, tamped the papers into a square stack, and lined everything up neatly on the table. "First, let me illustrate how I will be addressing the media, who are already baying at the doors for a statement. You, Mr. Yeager—an honest, hard-working veteran of the United States Marine Corps—protected a beautiful daughter of the State of Texas and her young son from the depredations of a gang of ruthless Mexican banditos. Outgunned, outnumbered, and with no thought of the risk to your own life, you engaged a superior force of armed intruders and defeated them all, protecting the lives and property of innocent civilians."

Garcia gave another tiny smile. "Mr. Yeager, attorneys have wet dreams about clients like you."

Yeager held up a finger. "One correction. Those guys were after me. Oh, and two"—he flipped up a second finger—"I absolutely had a thought to the risking of my own neck."

Garcia nodded. "No doubt. You are a skilled warrior, trained by the best in the world. However, by the time I'm through with the press conference, your name will be mentioned in the same breath as Travis, Crockett, and Jim Bowie."

Yeager tried to reach an itch between his shoulder blades.

"Now," Garcia said, "the DA is not an idiot. He knows the circumstances here as well as I do. The reality is, even without any grandstanding on my part, it is unlikely that he would seek to try this case."

"So what happens next?"

"We will first go to an arraignment, where you will be formally charged and a bond will be established. That charge will last only until the DA presents the case to the grand jury, whereupon he will undoubtedly ask for a No Bill, which the grand jury will approve. At that point, you will be cleared of all wrongdoing in this case."

Yeager frowned. "What's a No Bill?"

"It basically means that there's not enough evidence to prosecute."

"How long will all this take?"

"I expect a few months."

"Months? I have to stay in jail for months?"

"Not at all. I expect the judge will set a reasonable bail, for which Ms. Buchanan will post a bond, and you'll walk out of here this afternoon. The rest will be legal tomfoolery."

"Can't happen soon enough," Yeager said, scratching his thigh.

CHAPTER 18

THE ARRAIGNMENT PLAYED OUT PRETTY much the way David Garcia had predicted. The courtroom drama was spoken in a language other than standard English, some of which Yeager followed, specifically the part where Garcia entered the plea of "Not guilty."

Bail set, bond posted, Yeager walked out of the Austin jail with David Garcia at four o'clock in the last of his clean shirts and jeans. Charlie had not only posted his bond, she had also brought him his bag. She hugged him fiercely in the waiting area when they buzzed him out.

"Wow. That made a stay in jail worthwhile," Yeager teased as they walked to the exit. "How's David?"

"He thinks it was all one big adventure. He's staying with Maria's brother, Tomas. Maria's staying there, too. Tomas and Sonia have about twelve kids in the house at any one time, four of their own and the rest either neighbors or relatives. David loves it over there." The bright light of the glass exit door spilled across the floor. "David can tell Tomas's two boys all about the gunfight at the bookstore. He'll be a hero for days. Or at least until they fire up the Xbox."

Garcia walked a few steps ahead, prepared to meet the reporters outside. They hit the main doors, and a small crowd of news people lit up the scene with camera strobes. Deflecting the "how do you feel" questions with a "No comment," Yeager let Garcia do all the talking. As promised, the attorney promoted the gunfight at Book Finders as if it had been a reenactment of the Battle of the Alamo.

A reporter asked about the relationship between Yeager and Charlie, which was when Yeager got fed up with the whole lot and excused himself. Tugging Charlie with him, he plowed through the middle of the crowd and headed to the parking lot. Charlie beeped the remote on the BMW, and they dove in, the clutch of reporters trailing behind. They accelerated away from the lot and were soon lost in traffic.

Charlie told him she had rented a two-bedroom suite at the downtown Marriott, adding that she couldn't sleep in her own place until all traces of the attack had been cleaned up. "Besides, it's too soon."

Yeager scrubbed a hand over his face. *How am I supposed to read this? A night in a hotel room but separate bedrooms. To hell with it. I'm too tired to read clues.*

The warmth of the afternoon sun shining through the car windows acted like a drug. Only able to catnap in jail, Yeager had a bad case of the yawns, and his eyes drooped. If he put his head back, he'd be asleep in minutes.

Charlie wore shorts and a sleeveless button-down top. The blouse gaped at the neck, revealing a white bra strap and an expanse of pale neck and collarbone. The muscles in her thigh danced when she shifted gears. Yeager felt a tingle in his groin and had to look out the window. *Maybe I'm not too tired after all.*

Charlie gave him a rundown on how she, David, and Maria had bolted out of the apartment the night before and run to the Marriott, the same one they were headed to—and called the cops from there. The night staff had nearly had heart attacks when she ran in with a gun tucked in her waistband.

"I'll bet," Yeager said. "And Maria with her rolling pin probably finished them off."

Charlie laughed. "Frying pan."

Yeager cracked his neck and leaned his head back for a second.

He jolted awake when Charlie pulled into the valet parking area in front of the hotel. They rode the elevator in silence, eyes playing the glance-and-shoot-away game. Yeager's mind refused to engage. Not a talkative man anyway, he floundered in a sea of helplessness, acutely aware of the situation. *Hotel room. Beautiful woman. Holy shit.*

The suite door opened onto a central living area with a sofa, chair, and big screen TV. To the left was a mini-kitchen and a small table with two place settings. Bedroom doors stood ajar on each side of the living area.

"I checked in this morning after the police came," Charlie said. "But I had to go back with one of the cops and pack bags for me and David. The place was insane, gawkers standing around everywhere. I closed the store and gave everybody the weekend off."

She pulled a cell phone from the back pocket of her shorts and flopped onto the sofa. *Except I don't think this woman knows how to flop. She moves like a dancer.*

"Chinese or pizza?" she asked. "Your choice."

Yeager stood in the center of the room, hyper-aware of Charlie on the sofa, bare legs and narrow waist, and the bedroom doors only a few feet away. "Whatever you're having is fine. I'm going to clean up, wash the stink of jail cell off me." He gestured with his bag. "Which one's mine?"

Charlie pointed with one hand, the other already dialing her cell. "I feel like a Chinese feast. Lo Mein, egg rolls, broccoli beef, Szechuan chicken. Sound good?"

"Absolutely."

Yeager spent a long time in the shower. While playing in the sandbox overseas, he'd developed a particular skill set. More so than the average soldier, he became adept at killing people. In a firefight, or one-on-one, in daylight or darkness, it didn't matter; Yeager owned a pale horse, and he rode it hard.

One of the things that gave him an edge was his ability to compartmentalize the act of killing, box it up and put it away in a corner of his mind. No hesitation, no remorse. *Bang. You're dead, I'm not.* He'd developed rules to regulate the art of war.

Lost in thought, he let the water sluice over his head until the bathroom fogged with clouds of steam. He didn't feel bad about killing men who wanted him dead. Near as he could figure, it had to be done, like cleaning up trash from a tipped-over can. *Hold your nose, and get it over with.*

Cutting off the water, he dried and dressed again in his jeans and work shirt, which were still relatively clean. He stepped into the living area, toweling his hair, and missed a step when he found Charlie laying out the Chinese food on the low table in front of the sofa. He was surprised he had been in the shower *that* long.

"Hey, stranger," she said. "I thought you got lost in there."

"Nearly drowned."

"Dig in."

He didn't hesitate, filling his plate and digging in. "So what's the plan?"

"Plan?"

"What are we going to do about your books?"

"Oh. The books."

"I know you probably want to get the place cleaned up some before you get the forklift guy in to fix the machine. You have somebody who can clean up for you?"

"Tomas and Maria are on that already." She took a bite of an egg roll. "Tomas came back from San Antonio to help. They'll have the place spotless in no time. I'm thinking I can get the forklift guy in by Monday and get you unloaded that afternoon. Sound good?"

Yeager nodded. "Okay. I wasn't really going anywhere on Sunday anyway. Monday, I'll have a chance to head down to the freight terminal, maybe find a load. Gotta keep moving in this business."

"Will they allow you to leave town? I thought the cops always said not to leave town."

He chuckled. "I'll stay in touch with Garcia. Come back when they want me."

"Ah."

The light outside the curtains of the hotel room had faded. The room had grown darker while they talked, and neither had bothered to switch on the lights. The air conditioner clunked on and started to hum. Yeager looked at Charlie, meeting her sky-blue eyes and reading something he hadn't seen in a long time.

Without a word spoken they moved together in the center of the sofa. Her lips were as soft as he'd imagined. Light as a dream, her scent filled his lungs with heat and dimmed his vision. He cupped her face, conscious of his work-hardened hands on her delicate skin as they kissed. He pulled her close and traced the outline of her back through her thin cotton blouse.

They groped and kissed like teenagers on their parent's sofa, all fire and passion and fumbling, trying to touch everywhere at once. Charlie broke away, panting a little, and Yeager studied her face, soaking up the heat from her eyes.

"Let's go to bed," she breathed.

"I thought you'd never ask."

Days Inn
South of Austin, Texas

Hector watched the replay of the press conference on the six o'clock news. The truck driver was with his *puta,* and his lawyer stood there like a brick, acting all the big shot.

So. Humberto was dead. So were Chupa, Juan, Gallo, Fidel, and Julio. The whole gang had been taken down by one truck driver. Incredible.

"And you ran away," he whispered in the darkened motel room. He'd gotten a room in a no-tell motel on the south side of town. All the doors opened onto a central parking area, and the bed smelled of industrial-strength chemicals. "Like a coward, you ran away. And pissed yourself."

He had failed to act in the way a man should act. Somehow, he would have to make amends. He would need to strike back at the trucker, if for no other reason than he would be killed on sight if he slunk home, the only survivor, with nothing to show for it.

He was alone. Nobody could tell about how he ran. Hector could write the story and change the ending to make himself the hero. All he needed to do was pull himself together and go back for another visit.

**Denny's Restaurant
Austin, Texas**

Harlan and Skeeter met John Stone for dinner at a Denny's off
Interstate 35. They got a table in the back. The waitress was a perky
little college student, blond hair with dark roots, cute nose, and a
slight overbite.

After she'd taken their order, Stone watched the waitress swish
away in her mid-thigh skirt. "My, oh my. It's been a long time since
I had me one-a them."

"One of what?" Harlan asked.

"A long-legged split-tail like that, Harlan my friend." Stone leaned
back in the booth. "Mm-mmm. Ass sweet as vanilla ice cream."

"No shit," Skeeter said. "I may come back here at closin' time and
take her for a ride in the country."

"No playtime for you," Stone warned. "Not until Buchanan calls
and we go for the money."

Harlan sipped his ice water and kept his eyes on Skeeter. There
was no telling which way the crazy peckerwood would break. Stone
talking to Skeeter as if he were a child might be enough to set
him off.

"Well, one thing's for sure," Harlan said, keeping his voice low.
The other customers averaged about a hundred years old and were
likely hard of hearing, but there was no reason to take chances.
"The cops are all over that place today. It'll be a miracle if they don't
look in the truck and find the money."

"We would've heard it on the news if they found it," Stone said.
"What I want to know is, what the fuck happened there?"

"Damn good question," Harlan said. "A big freaking shootout,
right when our truck full of money shows up. Can't be coincidence."

"You sure the money's there?"

Harlan shrugged. "Dmitri did his job. He called right after the
truck pulled out. Said the switch was made."

"I think that slimy fucker is up to something."

"Who? Buchanan?"

"Yeah, Stevie Buchanan. Never trust a con man."

"Why do we need him, anyway?" Harlan asked.

"His ex-wife owns the bookstore. What better place to get a load of books delivered? He did his job and got the woman to buy from Big River, like we wanted. Everything was going along fine—"

Stone shut up as the waitress bounced back to their table and said, "Y'all from out of town?" She filled their cups from a full pot of coffee.

"We're desperados on the loose," Stone drawled. He pointed at the name tag on her left breast. "That one's named Aubrey? What's the other one called?"

Aubrey's face froze in that polite waitress smile. "Gee, sir. I've never heard that one before. Your order will be right out." She hustled away from their table.

Skeeter grinned, showing tobacco-stained teeth. "Oh, yeah. She wants you, Stoney. Anybody can tell."

"I flash the python at her, she'll be all over me like a Baptist on free beer."

"Python?" Harlan asked. "You got a snake in your pocket?"

Stone leered and grabbed his crotch. "Anyway. Everything was happening like it was supposed to. Somehow, that dipshit even got the truck to stay there overnight. Today he was supposed to keep wifey out of the way while we grabbed the pallets off the dock. But, well, shit..."

Harlan nodded and stirred creamer in his coffee. "Somebody else starts a fight, and they's cops all over the place."

"I tell you, it's gotta be Buchanan."

"Let's go find him," Skeeter drawled. "Squeeze his nuts with a pair of channel-locks."

Harlan nodded. "I think you're right. The boy ain't returning my calls. That right there's a bad sign."

"Any idea where we ought to look?"

The lawyer scratched his thin growth of beard and stared into the distance. Stone didn't even notice when Aubrey brought the dishes, set them out, and left. Harlan scooped a forkful of fried potatoes and had it halfway to his mouth when Stone said, "I'll give you his home address. Go there first. Then try that NewGen place."

"NewGen?"

"Yeah, it's out on MoPac. His office where he's running his scam. Stupid fuck tried it on me, which is how I come to hook up with him in the first place. He has a cute little sex-a-tarry. Lori or some such. Ask her where the boss man went."

Harlan shrugged. "Shouldn't be too hard. She doesn't want to talk, I'll give her to Skeeter here."

CHAPTER 19

Austin, Texas

THE CARTEL TROUBLESHOOTER CALLED HIMSELF Enrique DaSilva. To protect his family, he had adopted a different persona when he started muling drugs for the cartel forty years ago. Reprisals against a person's loved ones were commonplace even then, and taking another name insulated his mother and sisters from all but the most determined enemy. He had almost forgotten his birth name, Pablo Martinez.

His mother was gone, and both sisters were married to high-ranking cartel managers. They were safe and protected behind walled compounds near Mexico City. Even so, the habit of carrying the name DaSilva had stuck so long, he couldn't change it.

Plus, it scared the living shit out of people when they heard that DaSilva was coming to see them. No one would care about Pablo Martinez, the goatherd.

The driver's door of the Escalade thunked open, and Pedro, back from a scouting trip, dropped into the seat. They were parked on Fifth Street, several blocks from the bookstore where the shipping labels showed the money had been delivered. Police swarmed around the place. There were enough flashing lights and gawkers and commotion for a circus.

"So what is happening, Pedro?"

The two men in the back seat leaned forward.

"Some kind of shooting." Small and quick, Pedro reminded DaSilva of a crow or a grackle. Dark-skinned, intelligent in his own way, with bright, darting eyes, he remained one of DaSilva's steadiest men. "It's all over the news, they said." Pedro fiddled with the radio, settling on a Spanish language station that featured news and traffic. The station was playing a Miller Lite commercial. "Ten or twelve men tried to break into the bookstore, and all were killed by somebody inside."

"Ten or twelve?"

Pedro shrugged. "It's what they said."

"And who killed them?"

Pedro shrugged again. "One guy, they said. Must have been a badass, no?"

"Did they say anything about the money?"

"Nothing. Just the shooting. People are pointing at grease spots in the street, thinking they are blood stains. One window on the third floor is broken out. That's all I could see."

"Somebody else after our money?" *Who could it be?*

Pedro shook his head and shrugged yet again. It seemed to be his default response.

The commercial ended, but they had to wait through traffic and weather before the announcer started on the news. The male news anchor had one of those perpetually excited voices that made a broken water main sound like a biblical flood. Talking about the shooting at the bookstore, he was nearly hysterical.

"Only six, he said," DaSilva commented after the segment. When the anchor cut over to a story about the city council, he turned down the radio. "Not ten or twelve. And no mention of the money."

"Maybe they are keeping it quiet."

DaSilva rubbed his chin, staring at the sluggish traffic on Fifth. Everything was backed up from the cars having to detour around the circus at the bookstore. "Maybe. But have you ever heard of cops keeping quiet about that much money, hey?"

"Not likely, no."

"We need to find out who shot up the bookstore," DaSilva said. "They had to be after our money, which means the people in the bookstore must know what they have. Why else would they fight so hard for it?"

"If the cops find it, we will lose it all."

DaSilva nodded. "Nothing for it. Unless we walk up to the police and say, let's have our money back, hey?"

Pedro smiled. "Say we are needy and poor. Americans always give to the needy and poor."

DaSilva grunted. "All right. Use the GPS-thing in the dashboard. Find us a place to stay. We'll have to wait for the cops to clear out then see what we can see later."

Pedro tapped at the GPS unit for a few minutes. "There's a Marriott a block away."

"Good. Let's go. I need a shower and then to call some people I know. Maybe find out who was massacred last night, hey?"

⸺⸺✦⸺⸺

The cops finally let Nita go in the store at a quarter after five that evening. Tomas brought in his cleaning equipment, and Nita locked the front door behind them. She ignored the small gathering of gawkers outside, who were shading their eyes and pointing.

She found nothing nasty in the warehouse, except for the broken doors and a strong stench kind of like a barbeque grill left out in the rain. In the emergency stairwell, the overpowering, coppery stink of blood hung like an invisible mist. Dried burgundy splotches of human tissue were splattered on the walls and steps.

She decided it was like looking at pictures in a true crime book, one of those gruesome stories about serial killers or axe murderers. She studied the patterns of blood sprayed on the walls, and a chill ran down her spine when she realized some of the chunks of goo were human brains.

"Please, come away," Tomas said, taking her arm. "Let me clean that up. Please, *señorita.*"

"Uh… sure." She forced a smile and walked stiff-legged to the overhead door. She unlocked the padlock, kicked the bolt holding the door closed, and used the rattling chain to roll it up.

Good. The truck was still there.

⸺⸺✦⸺⸺

Downtown Marriott
Austin, Texas

There's something about a woman's hip, Yeager thought, *that can move a man like no other sight on earth.* That line from under the ribs to the top of the thigh. One of his lieutenants, a ring knocker, had called it sublime. Yeager wasn't completely sure what that meant, but he knew for a certain fact that it was one of the most exciting places on a woman's body. *Forget all that stuff about breasts and so on, nothing beat the lust that holding a woman's hips could generate in a man.*

He traced that line on Charlie's body under the covers with one finger, earning a satisfied hum in return. The red LEDs on the bedside clock read 1:33 a.m. He wasn't sleepy at all, which was amazing, considering all the night's activity.

Charlie drowsed on her side, bare bottom turned toward him, which pleased him fine. His work-roughened hand contrasted sharply with the creamy-soft expanse of her hip. He roamed that hand over those interesting places, tracing the outline of hills and valleys.

Charlie purred and rolled to face him. "You're not going to sleep at all if you keep that up."

"Sleep's overrated." He ran his hand over a whole new set of hills and valleys, exploring the mountain ranges and the wild places.

Charlie arched her back and gasped. "Ooooh. I think you found the right spot."

Yeager leaned over and took one pink nipple into his mouth, tonguing it with gentle swirls.

"Jesus, Abel," she moaned. "You can stop that in five or six hours." Her hand found him already stiff and ready. "Oh, my. Whatever shall we do with this?"

"I'm hoping for the same thing we've done a couple of times now."

"You've already set a personal record for me."

"Me, too. Let's go for the gold medal." He covered her mouth with his.

"Steven?" Nita asked.

Steven Buchanan pressed the cell to his ear with a suddenly sweaty palm. "Yeah, baby. Is it still there?"

"Oh, yeah. I've never seen that much money in one place in my whole life."

"Not many people have. Okay, hide it again and lock up. Come back home, and let's figure out what to do."

After a beat of silence, Nita whispered, "Are you sure? Just leave it?"

"Nobody knows it's there but you and me. We need to think of a way to take it without anyone knowing."

"Uh… okay."

After he hung up, Steven paced Nita's small apartment. A bass beat played from a car stereo in the parking lot, fuzzy and distant through the walls of the apartment. He hadn't meant to let Nita know about the money hidden inside the stacks of books, but the more he thought about it, the more he realized how inevitable telling her had been. With her in the know, he had a ready-made ally inside the bookstore. Already he could see some possibilities unfolding.

Like a way he could maybe take it all and cut Stone and his crew out of the deal completely.

CHAPTER 20

Downtown Marriott
Austin, Texas

I T WAS LATE ON SUNDAY morning by the time Yeager signed the tab for a room service breakfast for two. He gave the bell boy his last bill, a five, and frowned at the empty space in his wallet where money had once lived.

Charlie came out of the bedroom, wearing his work shirt and nothing else, two buttons done up. *How do women do that? Put on a man's shirt and look better than an underwear model? Maybe Victoria's Secret ought to take a hint.*

"Morning," she said and padded over to him for a hug.

Her tousled, apple-scented hair tickled his nose when he pulled her close. Her velvet skin felt vibrant and warm beneath his cotton shirt. She molded into him. He combed his fingers through her hair and cupped her cheeks in his hands. Her face looked so small, so delicate. He kissed her and pulled her close, cupped her bottom. Charlie hummed and squirmed against him.

He let her go and got another kiss to start the morning. "Breakfast?" he asked.

"Mm-hmmm."

At the table, Yeager dug into a Denver omelet with fried potatoes on the side. Charlie slathered a croissant with strawberry jam from a miniature jar.

"So what do you think happened?" she asked.

He paused, fork halfway to his mouth. "We're not going to talk about our feelings now, are we?"

She laughed. "No, caveman, you get a break on that for a day or two. I didn't mean last night. I mean why did they come after us again?"

Stabbed some potatoes with his fork, he thought a second. "I killed his daughter. It was an accident, but I'd say Mr. Cruz made it personal. Remember me saying how a woman was killed when I jackknifed the truck? Her husband hired this bastard of a lawyer, who sued my insurance company until they said uncle, but I guess that wasn't enough."

"So they tracked you all over the country? That's... insane."

Her shirt fit tight across the bust. His groin stirred. Yeager swallowed and dragged his eyes back to his plate. *What the hell's up with that? I haven't been this horny since I was sixteen and Martina took her bra off for the first time.*

Charlie didn't nibble at her food like most women he'd known. She took healthy, big-girl bites of her croissant, somehow without dribbling a single crumb. She smiled at him when she caught him watching and winked one blue eye. *Wow.*

He didn't realize he'd said that aloud until she said, "Wow is right."

"I have to say, I never expected this."

"So now we're going to talk about our feelings?"

"Hah! I guess I had that one coming."

Charlie finished her coffee. "I think you had more than one coming last night."

Yeager snorted coffee and had to hold his nose for a second.

"I know for a fact," she added, "that I saw Jesus at one point."

"Well, you asked for him enough."

She laughed. "Finish your breakfast, caveman."

"You ready to get back?"

"Oh, hell no." She got up and came around the tiny table to stand in front of him. Unbuttoning her shirt, she pulled it open, revealing two hardening nipples, an expanse of lean belly, and lower, a tiny patch of reddish hair.

"You need to eat up," she said, straddling his lap, "'cause you're gonna need your strength."

Wow.

NewGen Office
Austin, Texas

"You think she's tellin' the truth about her boss?" Harlan asked. He patted the top of Loren Gaffney's head.

The NewGen receptionist didn't look up.

"Sure." Skeeter made the word sound more like "shore." "Anything's possible. Hell of a coincidence, the guy runnin' off right when the money hits town."

"No duh. You think this gal knew about the money?"

Picking at a pair of gardening shears, Skeeter shook his head. He dug at something stuck on the blade then flicked away a bit of Loren's flesh. "Nah. She woulda told by now."

"Along about the third toe."

"Prolly right."

"So our Stevie Buchanan is in the wind?" Harlan asked. "Either spooked and ran, or he's making a play on his own."

"Scared of the bad-ass John Stone. The Rock of Texas."

"Hah. Scared of Stone? Only if he caused a car wreck. Let's bust." Skeeter jerked his head at Loren. "What about her?"

"What about you, tiger?" Harlan asked Loren. "You want to live?" She nodded.

"Well, you have to promise me something."

"Anything." Her voice came out dry and raspy. "Anything," she repeated a little louder.

"You have to be a good girl and promise to eat your peas and drink your milk." He held his serious expression for a beat, then he cracked a smile. "Sorry, darlin', I was fuckin' with ya."

Harlan pulled a gun from his waistband and shot Loren between the eyes.

At two o'clock on Sunday afternoon, Charlie parked in the side lot of the bookstore. She gathered her purse and things while Abel climbed out and grabbed their bags from the trunk. The sun burned holes through the heavy gray clouds, and all trace of a breeze had died. It looked to be another warm, humid day in Texas, already approaching ninety degrees.

Even before she made it to the door, sweat broke out and stuck her cotton T-shirt to her back. But it didn't matter. Nothing could kill the smile that kept trying to break out. Pleasantly sore, her whole body seemed to vibrate from the inside. Warmth climbed her neck when she thought about how much like a cat in heat she'd acted last night. And how much she still wanted to act that way. She'd said things, and done things, she never would have believed she could say or do. And wanted to do more.

Fumbling with her ring of keys, she noticed her hand trembled a little. A couple of college kids came up.

"Is the store open?" one asked.

"No." Charlie turned the key in the lock. "Not today. Sorry, we're closed for cleanup."

The kids looked puzzled but moved on.

Abel came up behind her. "Should've told them the truth. You're closed because the owner's been busy getting laid."

Charlie barked a laugh and pushed open the door. She shut off the alarm at the keypad. The inside of the store seemed oddly dead, lit only by sunshine from the windows, no music playing, no customers or staff moving around and talking. More like a funeral home than a bookstore.

Fitting, given the men who died here the other night. She still had a hard time wrapping her mind around that thought. *Five men dead. Five men attacking her, her family, and her friends. Her store. Her home.* No matter that the attackers were all dead, the sense of violation remained. Her territory had been invaded, and her safety and security rocked. It was going to take some time to get back the sense that all was right and well and good.

One thing is true, she thought as she locked the door behind Abel and led him through the store to the warehouse, *things have certainly changed around my house.* She remained very aware of

Abel's presence, feeling a flutter in her stomach whenever she remembered the sex.

Not just sex, but…comfort. Safety.

But the sex.

Oh, my God.

The surge of dampness between her legs surprised her. She hadn't felt this way ever, not even with her ex-husband. That last thought triggered a twinge of guilt. She pushed open the warehouse doors, forgetting for a second the recent carnage that had taken place there while she wrestled with thoughts of Steven.

Then the smell hit her. Heavy bleach, overlaid with something… *Charred meat?*

Nausea made her dizzy for a moment. *How would this place ever get to be home again?* Every time she walked into the warehouse, or up the fire stairs, the reminder of men dying would linger, imprinted in the walls.

She glanced at Abel. *How did this quiet man with the sad eyes defeat five armed attackers then turn into such a passionate lover? Almost in the blink of an eye. Her lover.* What kind of man had she taken into her bed? That question failed to generate the kind of fear she expected.

Is he safe to be around David after all? Would he react violently if she, say, burned the toast? Then she remembered last night, and a flush of warmth blossomed in her belly.

In the freight elevator, she leaned against his solid frame, soaking up the strength and power that rippled off him in waves. *So what was he? Beauty or a beast?* "How did you do it?" she asked.

"Do what?"

"Turn into such a ninja warrior and, uh, take care of all those guys with guns."

The elevator clunked to a stop, and she pushed the button for the doors. He didn't speak for so long that she thought he wouldn't answer.

It wasn't until they were in the apartment and he had dropped the bags by the door that he murmured, "You mean, how'd I kill so easy?" He crossed to the sofa and sat back with a sigh.

She snuggled next to him. "You don't have to talk about it if you don't want."

"No, it's best you know who you're tangled up with." But then, he turned silent, staring at the far wall. His eyes seemed to lose focus.

His voice, when it came, sounded as if rubbed across fine grit sandpaper. "In Afghanistan, there was a time the Tally-ban started using women and kids as suicide bombers. Didn't make the U.S. news all that much, but nothin' those people do to women in that country makes the news. My first tour. My first time in the field. Green as grass. We're manning a checkpoint on a road to nowhere, from somewhere else. Stopping traffic, checking for *insurgents*, you know. Insurgents, my ass. Terrorist, chickenshit, backstabbing bastards is what they were. I guess that don't make the papers much, either."

She made a sympathetic noise in her throat and rested her head on his chest. She trailed her fingers in gentle patterns on his thigh.

"Anyway," he continued, sounding annoyed at his own bitterness, "men, we were ready for. Women, we were ready for. Then this kid wearing a jacket comes out of nowhere. It's, like, a hundred and ninety degrees, and the kid's wearing a jacket. He's approaching on foot, out of the middle of nowhere. All of us could tell something was wrong with his eyes, with the way he walked. He sort of stumble-shuffled. It was wrong, you know? Just wrong."

"We tell him to halt, but he keeps coming, kind of stumblin' and draggin' his feet, like he's some kinda zombie. The sergeant on the checkpoint, a real badass and a tough sonofabitch, he starts yellin' that if he don't stop, we'll shoot, blah, blah, blah, all that, you know."

"Of course, he didn't stop. He gets closer, and I can see it's a skinny kid, not much older than David. Sweat's runnin' down his face, and his eyes are zoned out. About thirty feet away, he reaches for his chest. All the guys knew what the kid was about to do. Even the sarge knew. But none of them wanted to... to take the shot. It's not how we're raised, you know? To shoot a kid. But soon as he reached for his chest, I didn't hesitate. Three rounds, head shot."

He deflated with an extended sigh. "The kid was strapped with an explosive vest packed with ball bearings and nails. He'd gotten any closer and tripped that switch..."

She put her hand on his. "But you did what you had to do. You saved their lives. You shouldn't feel bad about that."

"He still haunts my dreams. Now. But at the time it happened... no hesitation. Boom! I dropped him like a can of toxic waste. I do the hard thing when I need to. Took me a while to figure out that other people don't... or can't. I've always done the hard thing without thinking about it. It's like a... which one is it that's the monster, Jekyll or Hyde?"

"Hyde."

"Right. Always get those confused. It's like there's a Hyde in me, waitin', ready to come out and tear ass. I invented these silly rules. I call 'em Yeager's Laws. The first law is: Come home at the end of the day." He looked at her with a grim smile. "Not original, I know, but it helps."

"Well, I'm glad we got to come home. Thank you."

He waved her off. "Have to think I brought the trouble, so you got nothing you need to thank me for."

"Aside from last night."

He laughed, breaking the seriousness from his face like a clay mask. "Yeah, there is that, of course. If you recall, I got something outta that deal, too. I've been pretty much a robot these past few months. I feel like I'm coming back to life after being in a coffin."

He put his arm around her, pulling her close. She breathed in his scent and soaked up his heat, which seemed to radiate off him like pavement on a hot day. For some reason, she felt safe with him, despite the story he'd just told. She would need time to think about that new information and decide how she felt about it.

But in the meantime... "Hungry?" she asked.

"Yeah, I could eat. Woman like you around, I'm likely to waste away."

"Can't have that," she said, getting up from the sofa. "Let me see if I can find some sandwich fixings."

She strolled to the kitchen and rooted around in the fridge.

Pulling out bread, sliced lunch meat, and mayonnaise, she called, "Is turkey and mayo okay?"

"Sounds like heaven."

Smiling, she pulled out the chopping board and started humming "Edge of Seventeen." Going to the sink and washing a tomato, a strong sense of déjà vu hit her. She'd been standing in that exact spot the night everything had started. She looked out the window again, remembering the scene of the five men coming down the alley, sneaking past Abel's truck.

A flash of orange outside drew her attention. A Dodge Challenger, one of the new ones, was creeping down the alley. Her heart gave a heavy thud, but the car kept on, moving down the narrow lane until it was out of sight. But something else looked wrong.

"Abel?"

"Yeah?"

"Did you move your truck?"

"No, why?" he asked, coming into the kitchen.

"Did the police take it?"

Frowning. "Nooo... not that they told me. Why?"

"Because it's gone."

CHAPTER 21

"**H**OLA!"

"Victor." Yeager hunched over his laptop, his cell phone clamped between his cheek and shoulder.

"Oh, man, don' tell me you're in jail again."

"Not this time, buddy. But I've got some trouble."

"No shit? What a surprise."

"Listen, man," Yeager said. "They took my truck."

"Who took your truck?"

"Hijackers, I guess."

"Didn't you kill all those guys?"

"I reckon not. Least not all of them."

"Well, shit, *ese*. What is it about your crappy old Peterbilt, huh? Ever'body wants to steal it?"

"I guess it's a good thing we installed that GPS thing, huh?"

"You got him? You know where it is?"

"Yep, I know where it is," Yeager said. "That's the good news. The bad news is that it's already in Mexico."

"Damn, dude, that's a long way from Austin. Where you been all this time? Taking a nap?"

"Something like that, yeah." Yeager tapped the mouse pad, zooming the map while trying to ignore the heat creeping up his neck. "They crossed the border down by Falcon. Going through Nueva Ciudad Guerrero now."

"How'd they get across the border? No, forget I said that. These are pros, no? What do you want to do?"

"I want you to go to the Locker and load up the Huey then give me a ride down to Mexico."

After a short silence, Victor asked, "The Locker, homes? You serious?"

"I'm done screwing around, Por Que. I need firepower. The cops took my .45. And I need a ride down there."

"So you want me to fly you across the border now?"

"Yep."

"Man, I have customers, you know. Contracts and shit. I'm supposed to say, Sorry man, but I got a *gringo compadre* needs to go steal back his piece-of-shit truck?"

"When did you turn into a citizen, Por Que?"

"Ah, man. That hurts."

"I'm offering you a chance to load up with all kinds of guns, fly a dangerous mission into enemy territory, assault an unknown number of hostiles, and you're whining about customers?"

Victor paused. "You mean I get to shoot things? Well, shit, man. You din't say that."

"I'll jump on the first thing smokin' into McAllen then call with an ETA. Gimme thirty mikes."

"Cool. What you want out of the Locker?"

"Bring it all, Por Que," Yeager said. "Bring it all."

Yeager thumbed off the cell and pulled up a travel site on the Internet to find the first flight from Austin to McAllen. He felt the weight of Charlie's stare and realized she'd been quiet since she gave him her WiFi password. He looked at her standing at the end of the sofa, but he couldn't read her expression. They hadn't been together long enough for him to learn her moods and gestures.

"What?" he asked.

"What's the locker?"

"Me'n Victor, we've been dabbling in the gun business—the *legal* gun business—since we were old enough to know which end to point downrange. We've put together a little collection we keep in a storage place. By now, we could pretty much take over a small country. At least for an hour or so."

She moved a vase on the table a half inch to the right. "What are you thinking about doing?" Her tone was neutral.

He sighed. "I'm going to get my truck back."

"Simple as that?"

He pursed his lips. "Yeah. Pretty much."

"You don't owe me an explanation, Abel." She sat on the chair across from him. She reached out and moved the vase back a quarter inch to the left. "It's not like we're married. I just..." She picked at the arm of the chair, plucking at imaginary lint.

Yeager concentrated on the computer screen, typing the information for a one-way trip from Austin to McAllen. Nothing direct. *Damn.*

"Why don't you file with the insurance company? Why risk everything sneaking into Mexico and tangling with another bunch of hijackers?" Charlie's questions came in a matter-of-fact tone, not judging and not whining. She looked more puzzled than anything else.

He opened his mouth to answer but found that he didn't have a good response. *Why was he in a lather to get into a fight? What did he have to gain?*

"Look at it this way, Abel," Charlie said briskly. "You're out on bail for multiple homicides. We know it was self-defense and you're not going to jail for it—knock on wood—but what if you get caught crossing the border into Mexico? How's that going to look? They'll bring you back and throw you in jail until your trial, which could take months." She shook her head, tossing her thick red hair back over one shoulder. "And I don't want to even think what would happen if the Mexicans caught you starting a war in their country. They'll lock you up, and you'll never be seen again."

Yeager scrolled down his list of flight results without really seeing it. Dammit, she made too much sense. He had no rational argument against anything she'd said. In the process of waking up from his long self-imposed sleep, his aggressive reactions had bubbled to the surface. His instincts clamored at him to hunt, to fight, to kill if need be, and to take back what was his. *How to explain that in words?* Everything that came to mind made him sound more like a dangerous animal than a rational human being.

He tried out a wry grin. "Um. I'm trying to save the deductible?"

She gave him an indulgent smile. "And so, if you get the truck back, where are you? Stuck in an occupation you don't want, fighting an uphill battle to make ends meet." She came around the coffee table and knelt in front of him, hands on his thighs. "Maybe this is a sign that it's time to move on. We don't really know each other at all, but that's something I want to change. If you go off and get arrested or... or maybe killed, then I lose that chance. I'm too selfish to want that to happen." She squeezed his thighs. "Maybe it's time to change direction."

"Damn. I hate a sensible woman."

"That's not what you said last night."

"Last night, you weren't sensible at all."

She stroked his legs, moving her hands higher and higher. "But I am now. Being sensible, I mean. I want you to stay here so we can get to know each other."

Yeager fought his anger, shoving it back toward its cage. The need to take action, to find the people who kept messing with him, boiled up from that spot in his hind-brain where his killer-self lived, a piece of himself he assumed long buried. "Charlie... " He paused, deciding what to say. "Charlie, I don't know if I can let it go."

She didn't reply, so he thought about it some more, watching her long, slim hands move on his thighs. *How good would it feel to sit here and let her work her magic?* Images kept popping into his head, derailing his train of thought: pale soft skin under his fingers; her legs, open and inviting; her head thrown back, eyes clenched, biting her lower lip.

He shook his head, forcing himself to think straight. "Let me call Victor back and tell him to stand down, at least for the night. I'll sleep on it, decide in the morning. Sound fair?"

"Hmm. More than fair. Help me with this zipper, would you, sweetie?"

**Hacienda Del Norte
Northern Mexico**

Enrique DaSilva stared at the handcuffed man in front of him. The prisoner was young, early twenties, with close-cropped hair. He sported a bloody nose and the beginning of a swollen right eye.

"Do you know who I am?" DaSilva asked.

The man twisted in slow circles, hanging by his cuffed wrists from a hook mounted to the ceiling's crossbeam. He gave a small head toss as if he didn't care, still acting tough.

"I am DaSilva."

The man's eyes widened, and he stared at DaSilva, his nostrils flexing. Sweat stained the collar of his T-shirt and dripped from the tip of his nose to join the pool of blood on the floor. Even late in the evening, the stables retained the heat of the day. A bare bulb, fly-specked and dingy, cast a yellow light, leaving most of the stall shadowed. The smell of dust and old hay mingled with the man's fear-sweat odor.

DaSilva stepped forward. "The name on your identification says Juan Gomez. But the hidden documents in your bag say Hector Castillo. Which is your real name? And how did you come to be driving a truck full of my money?"

"Money!" The word burst from the prisoner in an explosive gasp. His mouth gaped. A man who had the winning lottery ticket, but lost it, would look much the same. "But... there was no money."

"I have chased this truck all the way from St. Louis." DaSilva paced behind the hanging man, who craned his neck, trying to follow the movement with his eyes. "We were ready to take possession of our... misplaced goods in Austin when, like magic, there is no truck." DaSilva made a poof gesture. "We are forced to chase it again, this time following someone who has stolen it. All the way, I ask my men: Who would steal a truck if they didn't know what was in it? No, it must be someone aware of all the money in the back, hidden in the books. And when I call ahead and arrange to stop this truck, I find you at the driver's wheel."

DaSilva made his way around to stand in front of the captive. "So I ask again: Your name?"

The man didn't respond.

DaSilva nodded at Pedro, who uncoiled from his position by the stall door, took one step, and punched the captive in the crotch. The cuffed man woofed and tried to curl up, but hanging from the ceiling prevented it. All he could do was groan and twist in a slow circle, his knees half raised.

"Your name?" DeSilva prompted.

"Cas-Castillo," the man said through gritted teeth, his eyes clenched shut.

"And who do you work for?"

Silence.

DaSilva held out his hand, and Pedro dropped a heavy lock-back knife into it. With a flick of his thumb, DaSilva flipped out the blade. He snagged Castillo's right ear and cut it off.

Castillo screamed.

DaSilva tucked the hunk of flesh into the man's pants pocket. "Maybe you didn't hear me. Who do you work for?" he asked, enunciating each word as if speaking to an especially difficult child.

Castillo blubbered, snot running from his nose. Blood ran down the side of his face and stained his shirt collar.

The stall door swung open, and the specialist who had worked on Dmitri in St. Louis entered the cubicle. He wore a plain gray work shirt and gray chinos held up by a black belt. He carried a tool kit.

Finally, we'll get some answers. "I am glad you have come, old friend," DaSilva said.

The specialist nodded in respect and set his tool box down in the corner.

"I want to know everything," DaSilva told him. "Who this man works for. How they discovered our operation in St. Louis. How they knew which truck to go after. Most importantly, find out where the money is."

"*Sí*, Don DaSilva."

DaSilva glared at the prisoner. Castillo was more than halfway broken already. It would not take long for the specialist to finish the job. DaSilva spun on his heel, handing Pedro the knife as he passed. Pedro followed as he turned left down the central breezeway.

At the entrance, Emilio Santos, a burly man in a too-tight polo shirt, slacks, and cowboy boots, hustled across the paved yard to meet them. Santos ran La Hacienda del Norte, a waypoint in the cartel's pipeline of drugs headed north. La Hacienda housed a small number of workers and guards among the ranch's buildings and storage areas, along with a significant weapons cache. Located to the east of Monterrey, it had seemed the logical place to bring the truck once they'd intercepted it an hour south of the border.

The last of the day died with an orange glow to the west, and the first stars began to dot the cobalt sky. The breeze blew away the stuffy heat and smell of the horse barn.

"Well?" DaSilva demanded. He kept walking toward the ranch house, Santos falling into step beside him. Pedro followed at a discreet distance, close enough to hear but far enough back to maintain respect.

"Nothing," Santos reported. "We stripped every pallet. The money is gone."

"Damn it. What else?"

"The truck belongs to an owner-operator out of McAllen, a North American called Yeager. We also found a bag we think belongs to the man in there." Santos jerked his head in the direction of the horse barn. "It contained some forged papers, along with a laptop and a portable printer. The laptop has some blank templates for more Customs documents. Typical for hijackers."

"So the driver works for smugglers, hey?"

Santos made a seesaw gesture with one hand. "Could be. Professional thieves, hijackers, smugglers. Something like that."

"Anything else?"

"No, nothing."

They pushed through the waist-high gate in the white rail fence surrounding the ranch house and followed a stone path through a garden of native plants and decorative cacti mixed with rock. A traditional hacienda, the house was huge, with heavy adobe walls and a red-slate-tiled roof. Arches led to a perimeter walkway paved in red brick.

Santos opened the double French doors, and DaSilva stepped inside. Inside the cool interior, DaSilva crossed the library and sat in the leather chair behind the antique mahogany desk.

"Drink, Don DaSilva?" Santos crossed to a buffet that held an ice bucket, glasses, and a variety of decanters.

"Yes. Scotch, with ice."

Santos looked a question at Pedro, who shook his head and slipped into a chair by the doors. Pedro would remain alert but effectively invisible.

"I have not been here before. What assets do we have?" DaSilva asked. "How many men? Guns?"

"We have twelve guards," Santos replied, clinking ice cubes into a crystal glass with a pair of tongs. "Four on duty at a time, in rotating shifts. All armed with automatic weapons and sidearms. There are eighteen peons, mostly young girls and boys who work in the big barn. It has been converted into a workshop and warehouse where they break down the product into small packets for ease of transport." Santos brought DaSilva a drink then returned to the bar and poured a shot of tequila for himself. "The workers are housed in the barn next to the warehouse. The guards have the bunkhouse attached to the barn."

Santos downed the shot. "The security room is through there." He motioned with the hand holding the glass, pointing to a door on the opposite wall. "We have cameras positioned around the perimeter of the hacienda with IR capability. Analytic software will detect the approach of a human form and send an alert to the guard's screen. The guard will notify the security squad on duty, who will respond to the threat."

DaSilva nodded and pursed his lips in thought. The ice tinkled in his glass when he raised it for another sip.

"We have many sources on the local and federal police in this area." Santos chuckled. "So many, in fact, that I think we employ more than the government does."

"So we will have plenty of warning if anybody shows up unexpectedly?"

"Yes. Plenty of warning."

"Pedro," DaSilva said, "I want you to call our people in Monterrey. Get another ten or twelve men. Have them armed for war. When we find who has our money, we are going after it."

"Sí, Don DaSilva," Pedro said, standing. "It will be done." Pedro took out his cell phone and stepped outside to make the call. When the door opened, DaSilva heard the faint sound of screams coming from the stables.

Turning to Santos, DaSilva said, "Get me a bed-warmer. Something young."

CHAPTER 22

Book Finders
Austin, Texas

O N MONDAY MORNING, NITA LUTZ pulled her silver Corolla into the bookstore's side lot. The remains of seven years' worth of faded University of Texas parking permits curled on the windshield. Seven years into a four-year journalism degree, Nita had stopped wasting her parents' money, given up on school, and gone to work at Book Finders full time. *And now it's going to pay off, big time. Only not how I ever thought it would.*

The Corolla's door squealed when it closed, and she had to bump it with her hip to get it to shut all the way. At six o'clock in the morning, hers was the only vehicle, except for an orange muscle car on the far side of the lot, a hot-looking Dodge. *Just think. Soon, I can buy as many muscle cars as I want. And Ferraris and Jaguars and Aston Martins.* She giggled and gave the Corolla's door a solid kick, leaving a baseball-sized dent.

Nita scrabbled in her purse for the store keys. She had a thousand things to do in the next few hours to make everything come out the way she wanted. Her hands still shook, even an hour after leaving Steven. Last night had been so... exciting.

She didn't notice the blond man in the Hawaiian shirt with a toothy grin and whisker-stubbled cheeks.

Until he stuck a gun in her belly.

———✦———

Hacienda Del Norte
Northern Mexico

A knock at his bedroom door awoke DaSilva at eight twenty in the morning. After a long night on the phone and supervising the final details of the interrogation of the smuggler, Castillo, DaSilva had gone to bed late and slept poorly. The clumsy efforts of the peasant girl sent to please him had not improved his mood.

"Don DaSilva?" The knock repeated, a gentle tap as if the person hesitated to disturb him.

"Come," DaSilva ordered. He sat up in bed, ran his fingers through his hair, and rubbed the sleep from his eyes.

Santos opened the door and took one step into the room. From his expression, everything was not well.

"What is it?" DaSilva asked.

"Our captive died," Santos said. "Before he did, he said he worked for a small-time bunch of thieves. The Cruz brothers."

"*Excellente!* I know those little shits. I didn't make the connection before. I am an idiot!" DaSilva thumped a hand to his forehead. Santos's look of fear dashed cold water on his mood. "What?"

"The captive... the man, Hector. He died before he could tell us where he put the money."

"Shit! Can nothing go right?"

Santos handed DaSilva his shirt; the one from the previous day. The other clothes DaSilva had brought were being cleaned. He had packed lightly, expecting the recovery to take a day, maybe two, at most. The smell of stale sweat made him frown. As did the girl's bloodstains on the sheets.

"Have someone clean that up," he ordered, pointing at the bed. "It would appear the Cruz brothers are looking to take a step up, maybe take on the Sinaloas. Well, one is, anyway. Humberto is dead."

"Who is left?"

"Oscar," DaSilva said, shrugging into his suit jacket. "Oscar Cruz. We will need to find him and bring him here. Him and his family, hey?"

DaSilva ran his fingers through his hair again, pushing it into some kind of order. He glanced in the bedroom mirror and paused. *When did my hair go so white?*

"Come," he ordered Santos. "I need to make some phone calls."

<hr />

Book Finders
Austin, Texas

Charlie loaded the breakfast dishes in the dishwasher while Yeager worked on his second cup of coffee. It was some fancy dark roast stuff, strong as nuclear fusion, and Yeager decided he liked it pretty damn well. He carried his cup into the living room and settled on the sofa, at the end he was beginning to think of as his usual spot. For the first time in a long while, he had absolutely nothing that he needed to do. No load to haul, no maintenance, no paperwork. Nothing but sit there and sip the fine coffee. *Strange feeling.*

It dawned on him that he'd already made the decision in his subconscious, sometime while he slept maybe, not to mount a raid on the thieves who had stolen his truck. Not only was it needlessly dangerous, but he would have been pushing Victor against the wall, committing him to a criminal action that would risk his life and his livelihood. And all of that would have been for a diesel rig that was more albatross than anything else, or perhaps for his pride.

The apartment phone rang, and Charlie answered it in the kitchen. Hearing her voice made him smile. The throaty, silky sound reminded him of that actress who played in *An Officer and a Gentleman. What's her name? Debra Winger.*

"That was Nita, my manager from downstairs," Charlie said, coming into the living room. "She has a problem she needs my help on. She sounded kind of agitated, which isn't like her, so I better go see what it is. Want to come with me? I'll give you the nickel tour of the bookstore."

She wore a white short-sleeved knit top, denim shorts, and sandals. Her copper hair was pulled back in a ponytail. In contrast to Yeager, on his third day in the same pair of jeans and second day in the same tan cotton shirt, she looked fresh, clean, and astonishingly pretty. A hot sensation zipped through his chest every time he saw her.

"Sure." He drained his cup and set it down.

"You like books? What do you like to read?"

"You got anything with Dick and Jane in it?" he teased. "I can't get enough of them two, how they're always watching Spot run."

She laughed. "I'll show you the picture book section."

"Good."

In the freight elevator, Yeager wrapped his arms around her from behind. Charlie pressed her backside into him, leaning her head into his collar bone. They untangled when the elevator came to a halt. He followed her down the warehouse aisle, watching her butt more than anything else. Intent, enthralled, and plain goofy with infatuation, he realized too late his situational awareness had devolved to situational stupidity.

When Charlie halted abruptly in front of him, his brain took a minute to catch up. A flush of cold water ran through his veins, snapping him to full alert.

In the open area, a rake-thin scarecrow with a blade nose and heavy cheekbones stood next to a black-haired woman, holding a shotgun to her head. She was secured to a chair with clear packaging tape. Next to him, two younger men waited, both armed with pistols.

One of the two—a young Robert Redford clone in a brightly patterned Hawaiian shirt, snug jeans, and flip flops—stepped forward and grinned as though he was having the most fun ever. "Yo! Welcome to the party. Come on down."

"Who the fuck are you?" Yeager barked in his Staff Sergeant voice. "And what do you want?"

"Now, is that any way to treat a guest?" the blond guy said. His white teeth contrasted with his surfer tan. Faint laugh lines traced down each cheek. The guy could have been a fashion model, something out of the JCPenney Summer Gunmen catalog. "Come on and join us," Smiley continued. "Have a seat."

In front of the dead forklift, three wooden chairs were arranged in a rough triangle, with the woman taped the one on the left. She wore a maroon shirt with the words Book Finders embroidered over the left breast and a name tag with Nita in big letters and Manager in a smaller font below. Nita's mascara had run, giving her raccoon eyes. Both her hands and feet were secured to the chair. The clear packing tape crinkled when she moved.

"What are you doing with her?" Charlie demanded. "Let her go."

"I don't think you're in a position to bargain here, Mizz Buchanan," the third man said. Pudgy, with black hair tied in a ponytail, white shirt, and black slacks, the guy looked familiar.

"How do you know my name?" Charlie asked.

"Oh, Mizz Buchanan, I know lots of things about you." Ponytail held a short-barreled, nickel-plated revolver. He stood apart from the other two, off to Yeager's right, near the dock door. "Except for one very important thing."

"What do you want?" Yeager, assessing the tactical situation, hadn't moved.

It didn't look good. The scarecrow, the one with a sawn-off double-barrel shotgun, was a stone-cold killer. His flat dark eyes gave an impression of a soul stained black with blood. Yeager had seen the type. That guy would drop the hammer without a second thought.

"We want you to sit the fuck down and tell us a story. One that we'll enjoy," Smiley said.

Yeager's body reacted to the grinning lunatic at a cellular level. Blood rushed to his face, his nostrils flared, and an electric jolt of adrenaline jazzed through his chest. The guy held a blue-steel Taurus semi-auto, probably a 9-millimeter with a high capacity magazine, down by his side. In contrast to the cigar-store Indian with the shotgun, he looked like a man out for a picnic, totally at ease, without a care in the world.

"What my companion means," Ponytail said, "is sit down, or Spooky here blows the tits off the fat bitch."

Charlie looked over her shoulder at Yeager, his concern mirrored in her eyes. He read the clear message: *We can't win against three armed men, but if we give up we'll probably die.*

Yeager processed the scene, looking for an edge. He didn't

find one. *No choice but to play it out.* He nodded with an almost microscopic tilt of his head. Charlie stepped into the circle of chairs, taking the one on the left. Fists clenched, Yeager moved his feet with an act of will.

"See now? Lookit y'all," Smiley drawled in a buttery, put-on Southern accent. "We can all just get along here."

Keeping out of the line of fire, Smiley skirted behind the chairs and secured Yeager's arms with packing tape. The *scritch* of the tape as he peeled it from the roll was loud in the otherwise quiet room.

Turning to Ponytail, Smiley said, "All yours, boss."

"So here's the deal," Ponytail said. "A load of books showed up here in the last couple of days. I want it. Tell me where those pallets are, and we'll be, like, gone, y'know?"

"Books?" Charlie asked. "What could you possibly want with a load of *books*?"

Ponytail beamed at her as if she were a simple child asking a dumb question. "As I'm sure you know, it ain't the books. It's the prize inside that we want." He raised an eyebrow, looking from Charlie to Yeager and back. "No? You mean to say you haven't found the sixty million dollars yet?"

"What?" Charlie shouted.

"What are you talking about, nutjob?" Yeager growled.

Ponytail grinned wider. "Well, you sure put on a good act, I'll say that. Okay, I'll play along." He pursed his lips and paced in a circle around the three chairs, like a professor delivering a lecture... or a lawyer delivering a closing argument. "The Sinaloa cartel, from down in Mexico, has a cash flow problem: how do they flow all their cash from the U.S. back to Mexico? One way is to have their people here buy cashier's checks and mail 'em home. Another one is to buy a load of washers and ship them south, where the dopers sell 'em to Argentina at a loss. They call the difference in price the cost of doing business."

The pudgy man strolled behind Yeager, who followed his progress by watching the dark-haired woman's eyes. Nita breathed in gulps, and her face had turned a bright shade of red. Fresh wetness stained her cheeks.

"But one way," Ponytail continued, "is to smuggle big loads of raw cash in, say, a load of remainder books."

Yeager snapped his head around and fixed Ponytail with a glare.

"Aha!" the man crowed. "I see the light has begun to dawn. A former client and current employee of mine"—he gestured at Smiley—"learned of this money train through his... more dubious acquaintances, but he does nothing with the knowledge. Knowing the cartel as he does, my friend here doesn't want to take them on straight up. He's smarter than he looks."

Ponytail put a hand on Smiley's shoulder and gave him a pat. "But then a curious thing happened. Serendipity. You know what that means, Mizz Buchanan, don't you? Something fortuitous and completely random-like. I send my pals here to put the squeeze on a slimeball who's trying to scam me. While convincing Mr. Slimeball to return some money of mine, he tells us his wife owns a bookstore and maybe he can get the money from her. Can you guess where this might be headed? Yep, none other than Dr. Steve Buchanan, your handsome ex, threw you under the bus."

The guy tucked his nickel-plated revolver in his hip pocket and slid forward to loom over Charlie. "Now the word *bookstore* connects in my friend's brain here, and he comes to me with a suggestion. A damn good one, too, I might add. Why not, he says to me, he says why not have Dr. Steve buy some books from that special warehouse, and we'll have our pal on the inside, who told us about this scheme to begin with, switch up some shipping labels."

Ponytail straightened and waved his hands like a magician. "And *voil*à! Here we have a truckload of money sitting on your dock." He frowned theatrically. "But no... wait. We *don't* have a truckload of money. So where'd it go? Inquiring minds want to know."

"Steven took it," Nita blurted.

All eyes snapped to her.

"Stevie?" Ponytail's eyebrows looked like a McDonald's sign, twin arches climbing up his forehead. "Steve Buchanan drove off with a big truck? By himself? Or did he hire a trucker type, like this guy here..." He glanced at Yeager. "Well, not this guy. He's putting the moves on the missus here. But one *like* him, to drive the truck."

"I-I don't know." Nita licked her lips. "He asked me to stall the delivery because he wanted what was on the truck. He didn't say why."

The three gunmen exchanged glances. Charlie looked as if she'd had a brick slammed into her head.

"It's like we thought," Smiley said. "Buchanan ran off with the money."

Yeager shared another glance with Charlie, who still seemed dazed. The bookstore manager wore the same kind of lost expression, magnified by a big helping of pure terror. As far as Yeager could tell, neither looked as though she had an idea of how to get out of the mess they were in.

"I have a GPS unit on the cab," Yeager said. "It shows the truck's in Mexico."

"Mexico?" Ponytail barked.

"He's lying," Scarecrow said. "Let's kill 'em all and get outta here."

Nita made a noise in her throat, and fresh tears flooded her face. Charlie sent him a silent question with her eyes.

Ponytail scratched the stubble on his chin. "Mexico, huh?"

Yeager nodded and tried to project confidence. "East of Monterrey, last time I looked."

"And why ain't you called the poh-lice?" Scarecrow asked. His shotgun never wavered from Nita's head.

Yeager shrugged. "The cartel has it."

"He's lyin'," Scarecrow repeated.

"No, wait," Charlie said. "He's telling the truth. We were going to call the police this morning. Last night, we were..." She glanced at Yeager, and a flush brightened her neck. "We were occupied."

Smiley brayed laughter. "All right, my man!" He slid over and patted Yeager on the shoulder. "That's called customer satisfaction, for sure."

Yeager gritted his teeth and imagined killing the grinning bastard. Maybe twist the creep's head around first. After that, Yeager would get creative.

"Your money's gone," Yeager said. "Maybe by this Steven guy, maybe by the drug lords. You don't have a reason to kill anybody. Pack up and head out."

Ponytail resumed pacing, arms crossed, one hand worrying his bottom lip. Scarecrow kept watch on all of them. Yeager expected a snake's tongue to slither out and test the air for scent. By the forklift, Smiley tucked his gun in his pants and wiped his hands on his shirt. The scuffing of the leader's ostrich boots moving around behind them was the only sound.

"So you know where this truck is right now?" Ponytail asked. His voice echoed a little in the high-ceilinged space.

Yeager nodded. "I can find it, yeah. But maybe only the cab, not the trailer."

"But chances are they're not far apart."

Yeager shrugged again. The tape on his wrists crackled. "I'll be happy to tell you where it is. You're welcome to go after it."

"Well, I do appreciate the thought, my man, but hey, dude, come on. Why should we risk our ass when we've got you?"

The question fell into a flat silence, the same look of confusion on everyone's faces. Even Scarecrow stared at his partner, eyebrows raised.

"Think about it." Ponytail circled around to stand at Yeager's shoulder. "My man here's obviously some kind of ninja action hero, the way he took out all those baddies the other night, right?"

The stick figure with the shotgun said, "Stoney, what the fuck are you thinkin' now?"

Stoney? A lawyer named Stoney. What was it about that name…?

"Just this, Skeeter." Stoney squeezed Yeager's shoulder. "Mr. Ninja Dude here can go get us our money from those bad boys down in Mexico, while we relax here with the pretty *señoritas*. He don't come back with the money, we kill his favorite red-haired customer and her store manager. No risk to us. It's a win-win, dude."

"You're fucking crazy," Yeager said, craning his neck around so he could look at Stoney. "I'm one guy. Going up against a whole *cartel*?" The irony of using the same argument Charlie had given him last night didn't escape him.

"Whaddya think?" Stoney didn't even bother to look at Yeager, keeping his gaze fixed on Smiley. Apparently, Scarecrow didn't get a vote.

The blond gunman shrugged. "Nothin' to lose. We already took the money from the safe with this 'un." He jerked a thumb at Nita. "We take the women somewhere else and give him a couple days. He don't show, we kill 'em and leave with what we got. Cut our losses."

"Exactly." Stoney beamed. "That's what I'm talkin' 'bout. C'mon, honey," he said, motioning to Charlie. "Get up. You're comin' with us."

"Goddamnit, no!" Yeager strained at the tape on his wrists. "Leave her out of this. I'll get your money for you, but leave her alone!"

"Oh no, Mr. Ninja. I need a guarantee of good behavior. No cops, no FBI, no DEA, no Boy Scouts of America. The lady comes with us." He scuffed his way over to Charlie, took her by the upper arm, and pulled her up from the chair. "Get the bags," he ordered the punk by the forklift.

"Wait," Yeager said. "How'm I supposed to believe this? There's no way I'm trusting you to keep your word. We've seen your faces, John Stone. I know exactly who you are."

Stone raised an eyebrow. "Well, damn, I hope so. I paid enough for them TV ads; I should have some face recognition from 'em." He tapped his foot on the floor. "Well, here's how I'm going to put it to you. If you get our money back, you all go free. After that, you make all the noise you want. I'll say that you all was in on it. Stevie, the redhead, the gal with the boobs here, all of you. You too, Mr. Truck Driver. I'll drag all of us down if it comes to that."

Yeager swallowed the response on the tip of his tongue. Pushing the guy into a corner suddenly seemed like a bad idea. The plan of mutually assured destruction seemed possibly feasible. He needed time to think. "How do I get in touch with you?"

"Good point. Read off your cell number. Harlan, load it in your phone."

Yeager recited the number, and the blond guy, Harlan, loaded it into his cell phone. Then, he headed toward the main store, pulling Charlie along with him. She glanced back at Yeager and sent another silent message with her eyes. Either *get me out of this,* or *be careful,* he wasn't sure which.

Skeeter cut Nita loose and shoved her with the shotgun. "Get going."

She looked up, bleary eyed, and stood like an old woman rising from a wheelchair. Skeeter pushed her toward the door then used his lockback knife to cut a notch through the tape on Yeager's left wrist.

"You oughta be able to get loose in a few minutes. Don't foller us, or the bitches die."

Yeager locked gazes with the lean, dark-eyed killer. He tried to project enough venom with his stare to drop the man dead, but the guy just chuckled.

"Yeah, Mr. Ninja, you all that, aintcha?" he drawled. "I reckon you could maybe get our truck back after all." Still chuckling, he left.

The swinging doors thumped back and forth for a few seconds then stopped. Yeager was alone, taped to a chair.

And Charlie was gone.

CHAPTER 23

Book Finders
Austin, Texas

YEAGER TOOK EIGHT MINUTES TO get loose, every second spent cursing and sweating. Expanding the notch the skinny bastard had cut meant ripping the heavy packing tape with brute strength. He made good progress until the tape bunched up at his wrist into a thin band tougher than any rope. Sliding and twisting, tearing arm hair and abrading his hide, he jerked his hand free. From there, it was a matter of picking apart the wrapping on his other wrist.

He checked the store first, going to the front glass window and looking out. The door was locked, apparently by Stone and his gang. Traffic passed a dozen feet away, people going about their business.

Prioritize, you dummy. Yeager dithered for a moment, running through options. Get the authorities involved, or try to handle the problem on his own? If he called the cops, he risked being held in a jail cell while Charlie's time ran out. Fresh out of jail and there he would be, reporting the abduction of the woman who'd bailed him out.

Stone and his buddies weren't going to keep their end of the bargain. Pretending otherwise would be foolish. They would kill the women as soon as they put their hands on the money.

Calling the cops required convincing them John Stone, personal-injury lawyer, kidnapped two women at gunpoint and demanded Yeager recover a truckload of cash from the ex-husband of one of the women. Assuming the cops believed him, they would shove Yeager to the side. From the second the authorities became involved, Charlie's fate was out of his hands. He would be nothing but a bystander. *Unacceptable.*

Yeager jogged upstairs, snagged his duffel, and repacked it. Charlie's purse lay on the kitchen table. He hesitated then dug through it for her spare cash and credit cards. His over-strained credit wouldn't get him where he needed to go.

"Sorry, honey," he said. Hearing his voice in the empty apartment seemed strange.

He used his laptop to make a flight reservation, swearing at the slow browser window every time it struggled to load a page. After the final click, he jotted out a quick note to the cops about what happened on some stationery next to the phone in the kitchen, left it there, and took everything else back to the warehouse.

The broken warehouse door was held shut by a few twists of heavy-gauge wire. Yeager cursed some more at the delay as he unwrapped the wire. He pulled open the door and stepped into the Monday morning sun at thirty minutes after ten.

He headed for the Marriott, where he could get a cab to the airport. From there, McAllen.

After that: Mexico.

McAllen International Airport
McAllen, Texas

Yeager took another cab from the arrivals gate to a private hangar on the fringe of the McAllen airport. He paid the driver, who grumped about the short trip and scorched away from the curb. Yeager shifted his duffel from one shoulder to the other, already sweating in the morning heat.

Victor sat in a folding lawn chair, the metal kind with woven straps that cut your ass to shreds once it started to break down. He tossed back the last of his coffee, set the cup down, and stood, his head barely reaching Yeager's chin. They shook hands, an old friends' greeting that included one-handed back-slapping.

A ringing clatter and a curse erupted from inside the hanger. Yeager squinted into the shaded interior.

"Cujo," Victor said. "Working on his plane."

"Do I want to know?"

"No. You do not."

"I need some of that coffee. I'm about to lose my mind."

"Yeah. Let's get started."

Victor picked up his empty cup and led Yeager inside the building. Past the half-open sliding door, the interior smelled of oil and machinery. In the middle of the floor, a single-engine plane with the wings over the canopy took up two-thirds of the interior. Arrayed around the walls were tool boxes, workbenches, and odd bits of aircraft parts that Yeager couldn't identify.

Victor opened a small office on the right. Cujo stood on a stepladder, mounting some kind of gear under the left wing. Cables and wire dangled like the guts of a science fiction robot.

As Yeager approached, Cujo dropped a socket wrench, making another clatter on the floor. "Fuck!"

Yeager retrieved the tool. "Here."

"Hey, Abel," Cujo said as if they'd seen each other yesterday. "When'd you get here? Thanks, man."

"Just now. The fuck are you doing?"

Cujo grinned, showing crooked teeth through a shaggy beard. His hairy eyebrows danced up and down in glee. "You'll never guess."

Victor came over and handed Yeager a cup of coffee. "Cujo, uh, *found* a real live .50-cal, full auto. He's trying to figure out how to mount it under the wing. Arm his airplane for the coming apock-a-lips, you know?"

Yeager inspected the plane's wing. "Cujo, you fire a fifty mounted on an aircraft this size, you're gonna spin her in a circle. Assuming you don't rip the wing off."

Cujo stared at the wrench in his hand for a beat then said, "Oh."

Yeager looked from Cujo to Victor and back. Cujo, a red cotton bandana tied around his head, ducked his head and stared at his shoes.

"Is true." Victor shrugged. "But hey, the boy needs something to do. Like a hobby, you know?"

Yeager grunted and slurped coffee. Victor brewed some of the strongest, blackest coffee on the planet. He said the beans were roasted in a cave in Africa by the Zulus. It was even better than Charlie's.

"Talk to me, man," Victor said. "You look like shit."

Yeager jerked his head toward the office, and Victor followed him. Yeager dropped his duffel on the floor and slumped on the ratty visitor chair with white stuffing poking through where the leather had cracked open. Victor took the creaky swivel chair. Papers and engine parts threatened to spill over the sides of the desk. Everything from old calendars to faded and curled pictures had been tacked to the walls.

Another ringing clatter sounded from the hanger. "Fuck!"

Yeager shut the office door. "This is some crazy shit, my friend," Yeager said, trying to organize his thoughts. "First, the daddy of that woman from the wreck shows up in Arkansas, of all the damn places. The only thing stopping him from killing me was Charlie, who drops in like an avenging angel with a six-shooter. Then two of his crew pull that stunt in Chicago, at the motel—"

"Which is where I saved your ass like an avenging angel with a nine-mil."

"Yeah. Exactly like that. So I go to St. Louis, pick up a load for the woman who saved my butt, and take it to Austin. There, Humberto and his crew do a full-on invasion, armed out the ass. Charlie and I drop six of seven. One ran away; I think it was the same guy that you scared off in Chicago."

Yeager sipped more coffee. "I'm not out of jail long enough to take a leak, and somebody stole my truck and took it to Mexico. At this point, I'm thinking fuck it, I don't want the damn truck anymore. Soon as I reach that conclusion, these three hombres show up. One looks like a game show host, the other like a stick of jerky, and the third is none other than John Stone, famous ambulance chaser."

"Wait a second. The guy on TV? The Crock of Texas?"

"The Rock. Yeah, that's the guy."

"Dang, man, a lawyer and a crook. Who'd believe it?"

"He tells me the truck's full of money they stole from the Sinaloas and they want it back—the crooks, not the Sinaloas, though I imagine they're pretty pissed, too. They say Charlie's ex-husband was in on the deal and he must have stole it and run to Mexico. I'm not buying that. From what Charlie said, the guy was a doctor, a research doctor, at that. What's he know about drivin' a truck?"

"It's not rocket science, bro. Otherwise, you couldn't do it."

Yeager drained his coffee cup and set it on the desk. "But why Mexico? All he had to do was drive it across town, unload the money, and the run away. Going to Mexico with a truckload of cash? Nah. I don't see it."

"You think maybe this guy did it, the one from Humberto's crew?"

Yeager nodded. "He seems good. Or maybe the cartel people caught up with what's going on and grabbed their money back. Anyway, it doesn't matter. Stone and his buddies are holding Charlie and her female manager hostage and will trade 'em for the cash. No matter who has it, I gotta get it back."

"Damn, bro. You are having a seriously fucked-up week."

"Except for Charlie, I'd agree."

"That good, huh?"

Yeager shook his head, feeling a grapefruit-sized lump in his throat. "The best, man. The very best."

"Is okay, hoss. We'll get her back."

Yeager's phone buzzed, and he pulled it out of his pocket. A blocked number showed on the caller ID. "Yeager here."

"Hey, dude, wassup?" Harlan, the blond guy, asked.

"Listen, dickhead," Yeager said. "Those ladies get so much as a hangnail—"

"Yeah, yeah. Heard it, got the T-shirt. You'll hunt us till the ends of the earth, blah blah blah. Close?"

"Tattoo it on your forehead, cocksucker."

"Here's the deal. You have until Wednesday, ten a.m. We either make the exchange on or before that time or these sweet little *thangs* gets dropped on the side of the road with a bullet to the head. We clear on that, amigo?"

Yeager ground his teeth. "Where and when do we make the exchange?"

"You'll find that out later. Keep this phone on, dude, cause y'know, we want to keep in touch. And don't bother trying to trace this call. We're dropping this phone in the trash and movin' on."

Yeager tried to control his breathing, shifting the phone from one sweating palm to the other.

"Oh, and by the way, you'd better hurry," Harlan went on. "I think Skeeter's taken quite a shine to your honey, if you know what I mean. I don't know how long he's willing to wait."

Yeager started to reply, but the line died in his ear.

Rural road
East of Austin, Texas

Behind the driver, Charlie retreated as far as possible into the corner of the orange Challenger. In the driver's seat, the blond guy in the Hawaiian shirt turned off the cell phone and held it in his lap for a moment, out of her sight. He tossed a bit out of the window—the SIM card, she assumed—then started the engine.

"Well," he said, "I think that went well, don't you?"

Charlie, working on her invisibility spell, didn't reply. She wrapped both arms across her chest, fists clenched. *David. What will David think? He'll be so worried.* She kept trying to swallow with a dry throat.

Nita sat in the front seat, mascara painting her face into a tragic clown mask. The scarecrow sat behind her, holding a gun low so he could cover both of them with equal ease. A Ruger Blackhawk, probably in .44 caliber, a part of Charlie's mind noted. *Exactly like one Dad used to have.* The reek of cigarettes and skin oil from the snakelike man in the back with her nearly made her eyes water. She thought his name was either Skitter or Skeeter. Her heart wanted to pound out of her chest. She'd never been so scared.

The third guy, the one called Stone, had gone off on his own after giving the two guards instructions to keep Charlie and Nita locked up and unharmed.

They pulled out of the Feed Store parking lot where the blond had stopped to make the call to Yeager. The car accelerated smoothly down the rural two-lane blacktop, appearing as just another vehicle in the early morning farm-to-market traffic.

The blond man kept speaking as if they were on a sightseeing trip. "I don't know what kind of relationship you and this truck driver have—it was hard to tell from the newscasts—but he seemed a mite upset." When Charlie didn't say anything, he added, "Which is a good thing for you. Means he'll be motivated to get us our money."

"How we gonna make the exchange?" the lean man next to her said. "The woman for the money?"

"That's Mr. Stone's worry, Skeeter, my man."

"So what now, Harlan?" Skeeter spoke in a raspy, dry voice that scared her worse than if he'd yelled.

"Now?" Harlan asked. He paused at a flashing red light, turned on his blinker, and headed south. "Now we need to find us a place to hole up for a couple of days."

"That we do," the scarecrow rasped out, looking straight at her. "We need someplace real quiet, too."

He grinned, showing a lot of yellow teeth. His glittering reptilian eyes seemed to have the ability to see right through her clothes as he appraised her from head to foot, the weight of his gaze tracing her skin. She had to clamp her teeth together to keep them from chattering and bury white-knuckled fists in her armpits to stop the shakes.

CHAPTER 24

McAllen International Airport
McAllen, Texas

"WHAT ARE YOU SAYING?" Victor asked. "We have 'til Wednesday morning?"

"Yeah." Yeager took a deep breath and blew it out, staring at the wall without seeing it. "It's like this whole thing has been one big clusterfuck, all across the country. And now headed for Mexico."

"Man, you don't got no luck at all." Victor opened a drawer, dug out his laptop, and fired it up. "Except in choice of best friends, homes."

Victor spun the screen to show Yeager some aerial views of a ranch house surrounded by acres of scrub trees and brown fields.

"What's this?" Yeager asked.

"This, my ugly and unhappy friend," Victor said, tilting his chair back, "is the pictures I took of the place where they got your truck. It's a ranch north of Monterrey. I flew over early this morning, stuck my camera out the window, and did some recon."

"Holy shit, Por Que. Did they see you?"

Victor shrugged. "Is not like I hovered around, you know, sayin', *Look at me, I'm planning to raid your place and steal back my friend's truck.* No, I took one slow trip by, snapped some pictures, and kept on."

Yeager studied the pictures, flicking through the images. The place looked as though it might have been a horse ranch at one time. The enormous house, surrounded by a rail fence, had several

160

cross-fenced paddocks and corrals around the property. A long, narrow structure, stables maybe, stood about a Hail Mary pass away from the main house. Opposite the stables, maybe a hundred yards to the east, loomed another square barn-like building. In the yard in front of that building, parked nose to the north, sat a red Peterbilt with a plain trailer attached. Yeager's rig. He'd know it anywhere.

Two other buildings, narrow little add-ons to the barn, butted up against the bigger building at polar opposites, north and south. And behind the big barn lay a small airstrip.

"Yeah, no way is this Steven Buchanan's setup," Yeager said. "I wonder what happened to him. Think we could land a plane on this strip?"

"We could land, but it wouldn't be like, you know, a secret infiltration. See this guy?" Victor pointed at a tiny figure between the main house and the barn, a man with the unmistakable silhouette of an assault rifle slung over one shoulder. "A guard. Where there's one, there's a bunch."

"Like cockroaches. So we need to get in quiet, slip through the guards, start up a diesel engine, and drive the truck away without being noticed."

"Easy, dude," Victor said with a toothy grin. "We Marines, remember?"

"You think they have motion sensors?"

"I would, I had their kind of money. IR cameras, too."

Yeager continuing flicking through images on the screen, a sense of lost time making his throat tighten. *Law Number Five: Hurry carefully.* He found it hard to concentrate when he kept picturing Charlie being held captive by a bunch of thugs. He clenched his teeth until his jaw ached. He paused on an image of another ranch, not the target place. "What's this?"

"Is a cheep ranch."

Yeager blinked. "A cheap ranch?"

"Sí. A cheep ranch. With cheep. See?" He pointed at the screen. "There's the cheep herder leading the cheep from the pen to the fields."

"A sheep ranch?"

"Is what I said. I started clicking pictures too soon, thinking that was the place, but no. It's a cheep ranch about a klick north of the target."

A sheep ranch.

"Thoughts?" Yeager asked.

Victor shrugged. "I'm just the chopper driver, man. You the ninja stealth warrior. I say drop a coupla cluster bombs and blow the fuckin' refried beans outta the place."

"You got cluster bombs?"

"Sadly, no." Victor frowned then brightened. "Hand grenades, we got."

"How in the world did you get...? Never mind. Forget I asked. What else?"

"Sidearms of all kinds. A couple of .45s for you, 9-mils for me. M4s, MP5SDs, a bolt-action Winchester with scope, night-vision goggles, vests, miscellaneous shit like that. Suppressors for the MP5SDs, frangible 9-mil rounds. We also have some C4 and det cord. Been savin' that for an especial occasion, you know?" Victor clamped his hands behind his head. "And don't forget my secret weapon. I got a grade-A psychopath with a plane and wing-mounted .50-cal."

"Well." Yeager scratched behind his ear. "The fuck we worried about, then?"

"Is what I'm sayin'."

———⇒✳⇐———

Abandoned Convenience Store
East of Austin

They drove for most of the morning, crisscrossing country roads outside of Austin, while Harlan looked for the right place to hide out. Charlie's mind kept returning to David. What was he doing? What would he think when they found the bookstore empty and his mother missing?

Survive today, she told herself. *Survive today. David needs you alive.* A strange lethargy blanketed her in a cocoon of numbness. Against all odds, she dozed off for a few minutes.

Charlie jolted awake when the car turned off a paved road onto a crushed gravel parking lot of a country convenience store. The place was vacant and out of business, situated on the crossroads of a two-lane blacktop and a gravel road. The store was a metal building with two high front windows and a door atop cinderblock steps. Attached to one side via a covered walkway was a small frame house with busted windows and more dry rot than paint, a home for nothing more than spiders and snakes.

The morning clouds had burned off, leaving the rolling hills and grassy fields lit by a broiling sun. There wasn't much cover, only a scattering of trees, spaced too far apart.

"Feel like campin' out, ladies?" Harlan, the ever-chipper blond creep, popped the door of the Challenger. The muggy air blew away the cool interior air, but it also blew out the reek of the snaky bastard next to her.

Skeeter thumped the seat in front of him, pushing Nita to get out of the car as well. Then he crawled out, leaving Charlie mercifully alone in the car, giving her mind a chance to process. She needed to think, plan, and come up with a way out of her situation. There was no way those assholes were going to turn her loose. She'd seen their faces and learned their names, or at least the names they used.

And what the hell was up with Nita? The woman as much as admitted she knew about the shipment of concealed cash and that she somehow helped Steven with the plot. When had Nita gotten that close to Steven?

Inconsistencies and vague suspicions from her marriage came back to her, odd glances and unusual behavior when they were all together. She'd blown it off as casual flirtation at first. But given what she later learned about her husband's affairs, she really should have put two and two together.

But Nita was supposed to be my friend. When she got out of the current mess, she and Nita would have a long talk. *The bitch.*

Who am I kidding? No way am I getting out of this alive. She had to make a run for it.

Nita's purse lay in the passenger-side footwell. There should be a cell phone inside, but Charlie would have to climb over the seat to get it.

She checked her captors' positions. Harlan had disappeared

around the side of the store. Nita stood by the passenger door of the car, visibly shaking, though the day was hot. Skeeter, the freaky one, rested his rump on the fender in front of Nita, gray smoke rolling around his face from yet another cigarette. To get away, Charlie would have to lever the driver's seat forward, open the door, wiggle out, and hit the ground running.

They were somewhere in the area known as Hill Country, not far outside Austin, judging by the time on the dashboard clock, which showed it was only a little after noon. She craned her neck, looking for some sheltering woods, another farmhouse, anywhere she could hide. She saw nothing helpful, not even another car passing on the road.

She was in good shape for a foot chase. She ran three miles at a stretch during workouts. There was no way Mr. Chain Smoker would catch up with her.

But he could simply shoot her. And what about Nita? Could Charlie leave her? After what she had admitted to, or as much as admitted to? Nita appeared disconnected from reality, eyes fixed forward, head completely still. She hadn't moved much or spoken at all since they'd been taken hostage. Charlie tried to burn a hole in Nita's head with her stare. *Yeah, I dare you to meet my eye.*

If Charlie took off, maybe Nita would take advantage of the opportunity and run in the other direction. *Do I really care? They're going to shoot me anyway, once they get what they want.*

But Charlie's muscles were frozen. She sent signals from her brain to get started, to lift a hand, lean forward, do *something*. It was as if her lethargy had turned to paralysis. Moving her head to look around felt like shifting a cinder block. She kept having an unreasonable feeling that as long as she could huddle in the back of the car, she would be safe.

Harlan shouted something from behind the store, causing Skeeter to shift, moving the car.

"Naw, I ain't got no damn crowbar," Skeeter yelled.

That raspy voice broke the lock on her muscles, and she was able to move again. Fixing her eyes on Skeeter's back, she inched her left hand down and forward, reaching for the seat release. Skeeter stepped a couple of paces from the car, throwing his cigarette away.

Charlie crouched on the floor behind the driver's seat, coiling into a position that would allow her to jackrabbit out of the car. She stretched for the door handle, keeping her head down. If she looked at Skeeter again and saw his sinewy evil, she might lose her nerve entirely. Closing her right hand on the chrome handle, she took a couple of deep breaths and tensed her legs like a runner in starting blocks. She clenched the handle and hunched up, ready to bolt.

Movement. She looked up.

Harlan grinned down at her through the window. "Hey, girlfriend. Going somewhere?"

CHAPTER 25

McAllen International Airport
McAllen, Texas

YEAGER RATTLED THE ICE IN his Popeye's takeout soda cup, sucking the remaining watery slush of Dr Pepper. He and Victor were sitting outside the hangar after inhaling enough calories to keep them going for the night ahead. The sun painted the western horizon a dull orange, a last flare before the day died altogether.

Monday night. Seven p.m. Thirty-seven hours to go.

Three simple steps: get the truck back, get it across the border, and trade it for Charlie and her friend. But the number of things that could go wrong was astronomical. Stealing the truck back from a bunch of Mexican outlaws would take a superhuman application of stealth and luck.

"So let's say we get the truck out of the compound," Yeager said, "and the money's still on it. And it's not shot to shit. And we're not shot to shit. So I'm driving this thing up to the border crossing and I'm saying to the Customs guy, 'Hey, don't worry about the tons of money in the back. It's just...' What? What is it? Gas money?"

"Income tax."

Yeager snorted.

"Hey, man, Democrats in office, you know." Victor clapped him on the shoulder. "Don' worry about the border. I got that covered. Customs docs for every situation. We tell 'em you're hauling medical waste, and they won't even come within ten feet. Speakin' o' that..." He stood up. "I need to file some paperwork. Customs wants twenty-four-hour notice on anything coming in, including a manifest."

"Contents, cash. End user, kidnappers."

"Yeah, *esé*. I think I'll be a leetle more subtle than that. When you heading out?"

Yeager glanced at his watch. "Now." He heaved up and headed for his pickup, retrieved from his house earlier that afternoon, along with all his emergency cash.

He had over six hours to make a two-hour drive, but it was better to wait there than wait here. That way, there was room in the timetable for unexpected complications.

Besides, he needed to be moving. Sitting still, he continued to brood about Charlie.

Yeager would be crossing the border clean, no weapons and no gear except for a radio, and he would then go straight for the rally point. Victor would make a hop to Brownsville, top off the tanks, then head into the Gulf toward the oil rigs. He would drop down to wave-top level, dogleg right, and enter Mexican airspace slightly north of El Barril, Tamaulipas. If everything worked out, they'd hook up around midnight, two klicks north of the target.

As Yeager climbed into the pickup, Victor asked, "Have I mentioned I hate you for this plan? Have I said that yet?"

"About twenty times, amigo." Yeager cranked the engine of the '73 Ford.

All 351 cubic inches roared to life, blowing blue smoke from the tailpipe. The old power steering pump squealed in protest when he cranked the wheel around. Yeager made a wide circle and aimed the truck at the open gate next to the hanger. He wheeled left onto the main road.

Headed to Mexico.

Hold on, Charlie.

Hacienda Del Norte
Northern Mexico

DaSilva paced the flagstone patio behind the hacienda, a demitasse of espresso in one hand and a cell phone to his ear. "The situation is

under control," he told his boss. "Obviously, the Cruz brothers have
been after our shipment this entire time. Humberto attacked the
bookstore where the truck was sent, and his man stole the truck.
Somewhere along the route, he must have stopped and hidden the
cash. I have twenty-four men here: eight on active patrol, eight in
ready-reserve, and eight sleeping. I am sending ten more to collect
Oscar Cruz and bring him here. Once we know where the money is,
the entire force will descend on the location like locusts."

"Ricky, I trust you like no other," the boss said in his rich, satiny
voice. He had a velvet tongue for the only man alive who could
make DaSilva's sphincter clench. "If you say it is under control, then
it is under control. I will stand by until you have something more…
positive to report."

"Sí. I—"

The phone went dead. DaSilva resisted the urge to throw the
little device into the brush. It would not look right to have a temper
tantrum where the peons could see. Outwardly, he maintained an
air of calm detachment, but on the inside… he fumed.

Maybe he would ask for a new bed-warmer for the night. And
she would not get off as easily as the last.

<hr>

**Abandoned convenience store
East of Austin**

They locked Charlie and Nita in the beer cooler inside the
convenience store. Empty of all but some flattened cardboard
boxes, dust, and cobwebs, the cooler had glass doors on one side,
blocked by racks for drinks, and a large metal door at the other end.
Cut wires and thumb-sized holes indicated where the refrigeration
units had once been mounted.

The place stank with an old mildew smell of a refrigerator left
turned off too long. Moldy cardboard, spilled beer, and a faint
dead-animal reek completed the bouquet.

Their captors blocked the handles of the glass doors from the
outside with some loose lumber, so even if Charlie managed to

crawl through the drink racks, she'd be unable to get out. Then they did something to the metal door, locking it from the outside. Charlie knew that because she'd already tried to open it.

After they'd finished locking them in, their muffled voices came from the front of the store. Charlie nudged open a glass door as far as it could go, enabling her to hear more clearly.

"We got a good spot here," Harlan said. "The car's hidden in the shed, and the women are locked up. All we need do is wait it out. We can take turns guardin' the women until it's time for the swap."

"And how we gonna manage this here swap, college boy?"

"Well, calm down, dawg. Don't be gettin' up in my grill. Like I said, that's Stone's problem. No need to worry. Time comes, he'll have us a plan."

"Fuck." Skeeter sounded disgusted. "I'll take first turn guardin' the women."

"Naw, I need you with me, homie."

"What fer?"

"We're short on cash, for one thing. For another, we need to get us some campin' supplies. I figure to kill two birds with one 9-millimeter, so to speak. Find us a sporting goods store, load up on supplies and cash at the same time. You and I can take one of these Podunk stores here'n Mayberry RFD land. Right?"

Skeeter grunted. "You hear that?" His voice, loud against the door, startled her. He must have stepped up close. "You ladies have some time together in there. Be sweet, and we'll bring you a treat!"

"I have to pee," Charlie yelled back.

"Pee in the corner, sweetheart," Harlan said from farther away.

"Wait!" Nita shouted. The woman had been silent for so long, Charlie had all but forgotten her. "Wait. I need to tell you something."

"Save it, sweetie."

"It-It's about the money." Nita swallowed and glanced at Charlie with what seemed like a guilty expression.

"What about the money?" Harlan asked, sounding closer.

"I lied about the money," Nita blurted. She moved away from Charlie to stand near the door.

"What are you doing?" Charlie whispered.

Nita refused to look at her. Her eyes stayed fixed on the cooler door. "I need to talk to your boss. Let me out of here."

After a clink of the latch, Harlan swung the door open, hinges creaking, and stepped back. "This better be good, honey, or you're gonna wish you'd stayed locked up."

Nita stepped toward the door. "Don't worry." Her voice had gained strength, sounding much more poised and confident, as if she'd flipped a switch. "What I have to tell your boss is going to make him very happy. Take me to him."

"We'll see who gets taken where." Harlan pulled a cell phone from his hip pocket. "Let's give him a call and see if he wants what you're selling."

Nita nodded in Charlie's direction. "Not here. Let's go outside for a minute."

Harlan shrugged and gestured for her to walk out. He swung the cooler door closed behind her and relocked it. Charlie listened as their footsteps faded and another door squealed open and shut.

For two hours after that, nothing much happened. She'd tried yelling for help but realized her voice would give out long before anyone heard her. She explored her little cage, looking for a weapon or a means of escape, and found a bunch of nothing. The cardboard boxes were just that—cardboard. There was no loose metal, pipes, racks, or shelves she could fashion into a weapon. She eventually gave up and settled as far from the door as she could get, partly to keep all the available distance from anyone coming through it, but also because she'd peed near the threshold. If nothing else, they'd have to step in a pool of urine to get to her. Petty revenge, but it felt better than curling up and crying.

The cooler was stifling hot. Before long, her shirt stuck to her, and she had to keep wiping sweat from her face. And she was damned thirsty. She couldn't stop picturing all the bottles of cold Ozarka water in her fridge at home or going to Sam's Club and seeing cases of the stuff racked floor to ceiling. She tried to swallow, and her throat hurt.

What was Abel doing right this minute? Was he already making a suicide run to Mexico, trying to get his truck back? Somehow, she had no doubt that he would try it. Even in the short time she'd known him, she was sure of that much.

All she could do was sit there with her questions: Had David become concerned that his mom hadn't called or come to pick him up? And what in the world was Nita up to? How did she play into all this? Would the gang of misfit morons let her loose in exchange for the truck? How long would that take?

More importantly, how long do I have before Skeeter comes?

CHAPTER 26

Hacienda Del Norte
Northern Mexico

ENRIQUE DASILVA STROLLED TOWARD THE red Peterbilt parked near the converted barn, his shoes clicking across the blacktop behind the main house. The cartel had paved over the clay soil many years ago, when they first took over La Hacienda Del Norte. The parking lot, surrounded by the buildings of the hacienda, was as big as a football field. Light poles were spaced around the perimeter and down the middle of the concrete expanse, giving it the appearance of an empty mall parking lot. Having a panel truck or a semi rig loaded with hundreds of kilos of product get stuck in the mud would not make the bosses very happy.

Pedro walked up and said, "The men and I are ready to go, boss."

"Good." DaSilva waved a hand in dismissal. Having Oscar Cruz in hand would relieve a lot of his worries.

Pedro nodded and walked away.

A servant in a butler uniform emerged from the back door of the hacienda. "*Señor* Santos, the table is prepared. Would you care to dine?"

Santos looked a question at DaSilva.

"Yes, yes, yes." DaSilva waved again. "By all means, let us eat. I am starving." He glanced back at the Peterbilt. Its big, steel rims with their enormous lug nuts gleamed, reflecting the beams from the security lights. "*Señor* Yeager will have to find a new truck, hey? He will never see this one again."

Charlie began a third systematic search of her prison. She started at the door, carefully stepping around the puddle she'd made, which had steadfastly refused to dry. The cooler—and what a misnomer that was—seemed to trap all heat and humidity. Her T-shirt and cut-off jean shorts were sodden with sweat, and her thirst had become a living creature, screaming to be soothed. She would have licked condensation off the dirty walls if there was any. Even her urine had soaked into the concrete, taking away that option as well. But as hot and stuffy as the refrigerator was, it wasn't humid enough to condense the moisture out of the air.

Dry enough to suck it out of her body, however.

The door, ceiling, and back wall were made of pressed tin with little diamond shapes stamped into it. The joints were riveted together, and none were loose enough to pull apart or even to allow her to get her fingers into the crack. The door was solid and heavy. She must have jiggled the lock a dozen times, hoping that whatever they'd stuck in it would work loose and fall out.

She tried it again anyway. *Nothing.*

She leaned back against the door. To her left stood row after row of metal drink racks partitioned to hold singles, six packs, and cases of cold drinks. Beer, soda and... water. Picturing how water had once sat there on those racks nearly drove her crazy. Against all odds, she searched the racks again, in case she'd missed a bottle left behind by some careless employee when they cleaned out the store.

How many times had she gone into a convenience store and snagged a chilly bottle of Ozarka or Fiji Water and thought nothing of it? She could have cried at the thought of all the times she'd poured out the remainder of those partially consumed bottles.

"Shit, Charlie," she rasped, surprised at how hollow her voice sounded. "Get a grip on yourself. Concentrate. Use your brain and find a way out of here."

The floor was a concrete slab, clear and smooth from side to side. No loose bits or cracks she could exploit to dig out a rock big enough to clock one of the sons-a-bitches when they came through the door. The racks were sturdy and heavily made, put together with bolts, lock washers and 3/8th-inch nuts. And whoever assembled them had taken pride in his work because each and every nut was tightened as if it had been spot-welded.

Empty cardboard boxes had been slit open along the tops, flattened, and left on the floor. Charlie dug through the pile—again—moving the chunks of cardboard to search the floor underneath. All she uncovered was a flattened potato-chip bag. Empty.

Nothing else.

The light outside had grown dim, and it was hard to see. *C'mon, Charlie. Think, dammit!*

Crunching gravel sounded from outside, along with the sound of a car engine. She froze. Maybe it was the owner coming to check on his property, or a leasing agent, or best of all, a cop.

A door banged open. "You miss us, sweetie?" Harlan called out. He sounded way too happy.

Charlie's heart squeezed and threatened to stop altogether. A droplet of sweat fell from one eyelash when she hung her head. More moisture gone, she thought.

Footsteps.

Coming toward the cooler door.

Charlie hustled to the far side of her prison, rustling the cardboard strewn across the floor and nearly tripping in the dark. She huddled in the corner.

And waited.

Reynosa, Mexico
Mexico-Texas border

Yeager crossed the border into Reynosa without a fuss. The border guards on the Mexican side barely glanced at his passport. He could have carried an arsenal in-country, and they wouldn't have noticed.

He pushed through the crowded streets, vying with drivers who defied death to get a few feet ahead of each other. The buildings

174

were a random mix of primary colors and pastels, no two alike. Reynosa was a city of exhaust fumes and frying food, overlaid by Tejano music blaring from shops and cars.

He found Highway 40 without a problem, and once outside the city limits, he was able to build up some speed on the arrow-straight four-lane divided road.

Scrub brush and sand lined both sides. Without city lights, the night was dark as six feet up a miner's ass. The Ford's headlights were slightly crooked, with the right beam shooting a little farther ahead and lighting up a narrow tunnel of road. The terrain remained invisible outside the cone of light provided by his pickup or the occasional passing car. Yeager's eyes drooped. He yawned again and again from nerves and the aftereffects of three nights with little sleep.

Charlie. He couldn't go a minute without thinking about her. Mental images of her tied up in a dark basement, scared and alone, twisted at his nerves. Or worse, she could be raped by those guys. Or maybe she was already dead, her body lying in a drainage ditch somewhere. The parade of morbid pictures wouldn't stop.

He'd thought about running a bluff and trying to take the kidnappers with a fake truck, but if they examined the load before telling him where they'd hidden the women, everything could go bad in a hurry. If he and Victor could take one of the kidnappers alive... *All right, that's Plan B.*

An hour and a half out of Reynosa, Yeager passed the entrance to the target ranch. A rail fence marked the property on either side of a tall gate. The drive up to the modern, electrically operated, wrought-iron entrance was wide enough to accommodate an eighteen-wheeler. Mercury vapor lamps mounted on either side of the gate lit the approach. He spotted a CCTV camera and a speaker-box interface. The arch over the gate read La Hacienda del Norte in wrought-iron script.

A second later, he was past the place and swallowed up by the night again. He put on his blinker at the next crossroad and turned right. Sparse traffic became non-existent traffic. Following his GPS, he drove until he found a turn-off onto a rutted farm road, more of a goat track than a road. Easing the pickup off the shoulder and into the tracks, he jounced and rattled his way into the brush, high beams alternately stabbing the sky or wallowing across the ground.

He came to an abandoned farm after exactly three-point-four miles and pulled into the yard. When Yeager shut off the engine and the lights, it was like he'd turned off the world. There was no moon, and the wash of the Milky Way lent barely enough light to make out shapes in the darkness.

The door creaked when he clambered out of the truck. Yeager stretched his back, unzipped his fly, and watered a cholla cactus. The desert air had cooled, making him glad for his long-sleeved shirt and the T-shirt underneath.

The honking call of a long-eared owl came from his right, somewhere behind the broken-down farm building. Only three walls still stood, leaving the inside open to the sky. Not a single pane of unbroken glass remained in the entire structure. As far as he could tell, there was no human within miles of the place.

Inside the Ford, he stretched out and propped his head on the armrest. Straightening out his legs as much as possible, he plugged the tactical radio in his ear, adjusted the boom microphone, and turned on the belt unit. He fiddled with the volume and adjusted squelch until the static disappeared. Closing his eyes, he tried to clear his mind. If possible, he wanted to catnap before Victor showed up with the Huey.

After that, there wouldn't be another chance to sleep for some time to come. Or so he hoped.

CHAPTER 27

"**L**ucy! I'm hooome." Harlan pushed open the door, one hand on the butt of his pistol tucked in his waistband. The woman huddled in the far corner, a small shape in the darkness. Her eyes glittered in the reflected light.

"I brought you something, sweetie," Harlan said. He picked up the plastic grocery sack that he'd set by the door and tossed it inside.

One of the water bottles popped free of the bag and rolled toward her. He grinned to see her fixate on the spinning plastic bottle as it came to rest a fingertip out of her reach.

"See? Don't say I never gave you anything." He closed the door and relocked it with a wire peg-wall hook that he stuck through the latch.

Harlan found Skeeter by the store's checkout counter, rooting through the other plastic sacks. A shiny new Coleman lantern sat on the floor by the counter, turned down low. Skeeter opened a can of vienna sausages and dumped them on a paper plate with some saltines.

"See?" Harlan said. "Like campin'."

"You think the bitch was lying to Stone? About knowing where Buchanan kept all his money?"

"Who knows? Stone has her now. Up to him to find out what's up with all that. We stay here and keep an eye on Red there and await developments."

Skeeter grunted. "Await developments. Shit." He drew the last word into two syllables, *shee-it*. The lantern hissed, painting his face in a monochrome glare.

Harlan cracked open a can of Diet Pepsi and took a swig. "It's only a matter of time."

"So what happens now?" Skeeter asked.

"Now we take some turns getting some sleep. I'll set us up a camp in the house next door. I'll grab some shuteye then come and relieve you about midnight or so."

"I get first watch?"

Something coiled and dangerous in Skeeter's voice caught Harlan's attention. He stared at the leathery face of the older man for a beat then grinned. "Why sure, partner, you can take first watch. Remember: we need her alive for the switch."

"Oh, she'll stay alive. Fer a lot longer than she wants to, that's a shore thang, that is."

"I guess that means I won't get a wink of sleep over here for the next little while or so, huh?"

———————✦———————

Charlie had the bottle of water open before the door closed. She drank half of it before she could stop herself. Breathing heavily, she scooted over to the plastic sack and checked out the contents: candy bars, beef jerky, snack crackers, and three more bottles of water.

The haul looked as though Harlan had raided a convenience store and picked things at random. Nothing weapon-like, however. He hadn't accidentally stuck in a bazooka or even a knife.

Taking another mouthful of water, she held it as long as she could before swallowing. Capping the bottle was like closing the lid on Ali Baba's treasure. But there was no telling how long this ordeal might last. She needed to conserve her resources.

The men were talking, the murmur of their voices humming through the walls. A flickering glow gave her enough light to make out the bare outlines of her prison, but not much more. Like shadows on the back of a cave wall, shapes moved and shifted at the front of the store, where the pair of thugs huddled.

So what kind of deal did Nita make? What else did she know that would prove valuable to the kidnappers? Charlie hated herself

178

for not finding out what her so-called friend had been up to when she had the chance.

She picked up her sack of supplies, intending to move it to her favorite corner away from the door. In the dark, she stumbled on the pile of flattened cardboard boxes, sending them skidding away.

She froze.

Something metallic had jangled across the concrete floor.

**Deserted farmhouse
Northern Mexico**

"Red Ball One, Red Ball Two. Copy?"

Yeager jerked awake, banged his wrist on the steering wheel, and cursed. Blinking, he shook off the dream—something with lots of snakes and a supermarket—and tried to orient himself.

Truck.

Mexico. Dark outside.

"Red Ball One, Red Ball Two. Copy?"

Yeager keyed his mic. "Go for One."

"Thought I lost you, home boy," Por Que squawked. "You fall asleep?"

"No." Yeager struggled upright and switched on the Ford's headlights. "Wide awake."

The thump of rotors came from the east.

"Any trouble?" Yeager dug four road flares from a cardboard box on the floorboard.

"Negative. Smooth as a cheerleader's ass."

"How would you know?"

"Funny guy."

Yeager lit the flares and set them at the four points of the compass, spaced across the open lot of the farmhouse. They marked out a landing area of about fifty square yards square.

"Got your lights," Por Que said.

"All clear," Yeager reported. "No breeze."

"Roger that."

The whop-whop of rotors transformed from distant sound to physical pressure, thumping in Yeager's chest. The Vietnam-era chopper came in low over the scrub, running lights off, and settled in the center of the landing zone without a pause. Yeager shielded his eyes from the dust and sand kicked up by the rotors.

Victor cut the power, and the big engine wound down. Moments later, the short, muscular pilot pulled back the sliding door of the cargo bay and hopped down, carrying a heavy duffel. The flight helmet with the attached night vision goggles made him look like a bug-eyed monster from a bad sci-fi flick. He trotted over to Yeager, not bothering to duck under the rotors.

They shook hands and slapped shoulders. The first part of the mission had come together without a hitch. Some of the tension left Yeager's shoulders.

Victor pulled off the NVGs and blinked. "You ready, dude?"

"You bet. Let's get this party started."

They moved around the truck, and Yeager dropped the tailgate. Victor gently settled the heavy nylon duffel in the bed and unzipped the bag. Polymer and blue-steel gleamed in the weak starlight.

They unloaded the bags in silence, removing weapons, flak vests, harnesses, magazines, flashlights, ropes, and other gear. When they were finished, enough armaments to start a small war covered the bed of the old Ford.

Yeager's mouth thinned in a feral smile. *Start a war. Exactly what I plan to do.*

❊

Hacienda Del Norte
Northern Mexico

Luis Cordoña stared at the monitors in the security office of La Hacienda Del Norte. The view had not changed in the past hour, and his eyes had long since glazed over. Missing something big enough to be a problem wasn't a concern, anyway. The video analytic software was programmed to detect movement and send an alert to the call-up screen directly in front of him.

So instead of paying rigid attention to a total lack of activity, Luis turned his thoughts to Serena, one of the workers in the processing room. At a few days over sixteen, she had developed some nice curves. The seat of her jeans had begun to fill out, and her boobs bounced a little when she walked. Luis followed her with the pan/tilt/zoom camera in the warehouse whenever she was on duty at the same time he was.

So far, he had spoken to her only a couple of times. The workers lived in a small dorm adjacent to the main barn, for easy access to the processing facilities. Cameras in the hallways ensured that the workers didn't roam at night and go anywhere they shouldn't. Serena remained in her room after lights out, leaving Luis very little opportunity to run into her when he worked the night shift.

The call-up monitor, a twenty-seven-inch flat screen, sequenced through the views of thirty-two smaller monitors on the wall behind it. Each screen was labeled with the area it showed. PARKING 1 remained on the screen for eight seconds. Nothing moved. The static view of the diesel rig, the one that the big bosses were all in a big shit about, remained unchanged. With the extra guards and the shift supervisor almost peeing himself to look good for the boss, Luis resigned himself to a long delay in his campaign to meet little Serena.

A ding sounded from the console, and the monitor changed views, flashing the ALERT signal in small text at the bottom. The camera, mounted on a perimeter building, pointed into the barren fields to the north, labeled NORTH FIELD 2.

Protocol mandated that the monitoring guard notify the shift supervisor at every alert from the analytic software. The cameras had infrared capability and were good down to extreme low light. The picture at night was nowhere near daylight quality, having the characteristics of an old black-and-white television show, but a trained operator could still make good use of the system. The software tried to help by drawing colored lines around the shape it saw moving across the field of view.

In the case of NORTH FIELD 2, the camera was set to a wide-angle view, covering a lot of territory and making objects appear very small. Movement also confused the image processor to some extent, which meant the shape drawn by the software resembled an amoeba floating across a Petri dish more than it did a human or animal.

"Hey, boss," Luis called over his shoulder.

"What?" the shift supervisor, Marco Garza, asked. "What is it?"

"I can't tell," Luis said. He squinted at the monitor. "Moves like a deer, though."

The CCTV integrator had promised that the analytic software could be tweaked to eliminate animal shapes and only alert when human forms entered the picture, but Santos had overruled that. He wanted to know about every incursion, down to the squirrel level, into his domain. The end result was that the security staff spent a lot of time chasing mule deer, jackrabbits, and once even a wild horse off the property.

Garza spoke into his radio handset. "North Guard Post, this is Central. Copy?"

"Copy," the guard crackled back.

"Movement, North Field 2. Could be a deer. Investigate and report. Over."

"Roger."

Another alert came from the software as Antonio moved out from his position by the stables and headed across the field. The first object stilled, and the software caught up with it long enough to draw a complete line around it.

"Deer," Luis and Marco said simultaneously.

The IR camera feed was clearer, and the tiny form of a mule deer, head up, still as a rock, was easy to make out.

"Confirmed deer," Marco radioed.

"Roger. I'll send him off. Want some venison steaks tonight?"

"Negative. We don't want to be shooting any guns with the big boss here. It might make him wet himself, no?"

A double-click of breaking squelch signaled Antonio's acknowledgement. Luis tracked the guard's movement toward the mule deer, curious how long it would take to spook the deer into motion. The wildlife had to be chased off; otherwise, the CCTV system would keep targeting it as a threat.

"Move a little to your left, Antonio," Luis said over the radio.

"Roger."

The small figure of the guard on the screen adjusted course, and seconds later, the mule deer bounded away, heading back out of range.

"Mission accomplished, Tony," Marco said. "Return to post."

"Roger that."

Luis entered the series of commands to log the contact and reset the system. Marco returned to the trashy gossip magazine he'd been reading, and the security office routine returned to normal operation.

Luis yawned. *Maybe I should patrol the dorms. See if Serena needs any protection from rampaging mule deer.*

CHAPTER 28

Abandoned Convenience Store
East of Austin

KEETER DAVIS POPPED THE TOP on another can of vienna sausages and shook them onto his paper plate. Harlan had taken the Coleman lantern, but Skeeter had a chunky Maglite set on the ten-foot laminated counter that ran parallel to the front of the store.

Skeeter sat on the chipped and dirty surface, facing the interior of the store and eating with his fingers. He alternated sausages with bites of saltine crackers and swigs from a bottle of Maker's Mark.

When he looked over his left shoulder, he could see the store's boarded-over glass door. Over his right shoulder, a narrow window ran the length of the front wall a few feet from the ceiling. If he stood on the counter, he could see outside. It was a cinch that nobody could see in, so he didn't worry overmuch about being spotted.

The Maker's Mark, along the anticipation of putting his meat to Miss High Tone back there in the cooler, lit a warm glow in his belly. The gals from the rich side of town were the best. They didn't fight as much. Oh, they might scream and kick a little, pretend they didn't want it, but once they got into it, they settled down. The trophy bitches from the nice houses weren't getting a good sticking from their banker or lawyer hubbies, so when Skeeter came along, they had to be damn near grateful.

The redhead in the cooler was a real classy lady, but she also liked to fool around with the hired help. Look how she took up with that trucker. Oh yeah, she was really going to enjoy getting a taste of his meat.

A wash of headlights painted the wall of the store. Skeeter snagged the flashlight and killed it, dropping the store into darkness. Tires crunched the gravel of the parking lot, bringing with them a sound he didn't want to hear: a cop radio crackling and squawking.

Skeeter scrabbled to his knees on the counter, careful to keep his balance, and peeked up over the windowsill. A Texas Department of Public Safety squad car rolled to a stop in the middle of the parking lot, driver's side facing the store.

He slipped the Ruger Blackhawk .44 out of his waistband and kept his head still. The state trooper turned on a tiny light at the end of a flexible arm and started writing on a clipboard.

Another pair of headlights flashed across the window. Skeeter twitched.

The second trooper pulled up to park door-to-door with the first guy. It looked as though they wanted to have a palaver, two good old boys on night shift sharing some dirty jokes or talking about who they fucked last. They sure picked a hell of a time and place for it.

I hope to shit Harlan don't go nuts and start a shootout. That'd pretty much do it for the fucking I mean to do later on. Skeeter settled on his haunches, dropping below the sill. It didn't matter if the cops yakked it up outside for a few minutes. He could wait.

The redhead in the cooler wasn't going anywhere.

Deserted farmhouse
Northern Mexico

Yeager turned himself into a walking *Soldier of Fortune* advertisement. Black tactical pants bloused into jump boots, a black shirt, vest, harness, and ball cap. M4 Carbine, HK MP5SD with suppressor, a Wilson Combat .45 semi-automatic pistol, magazines for all of them, a K-bar combat knife, a Fairbairn stiletto, and assorted grenades. Camo paint striped his face, and he carried a radio with boom mike. *And a partridge in a pear tree.*

"Here we go," Victor said, "waddling off to war."

"No shit. Here, hold this." Yeager handed off his M4 and climbed into the driver's seat of the pickup.

Victor passed both rifles to Yeager, ran around to the passenger side, and heaved himself in with a grunt. The old pickup threatened not to fire, chugged away for a few nerve-racking seconds, then caught with a roar. Yeager slipped into low gear and rolled away from the farmhouse, lights out, bumping along the dirt track by starlight alone. The GPS glowed inside the cab, the muted voice saying: "Drive one-point-six miles."

Their first waypoint. One stop to make before the target. Time to get his game face on.

"Have I mentioned," Victor asked, "how much I don't like this plan?"

<hr />

The cops in front of the convenience store had been gabbing it up for a good thirty minutes. Skeeter was close to going outside and popping both of them in the head, to shut them up. *What in the hell could they be gossiping about that was so damn important? Shouldn't they be fighting crime or handing out speeding tickets?*

Skeeter pulled at his bourbon every now and again, the tip of his nose starting to go numb. He slid into that stage between sleepy and mean. "Y'all g'won," he muttered, peering through a gap in the butcher paper covering the door. "Git on home to the little wifey, give her a pokin'. Go eat a fuckin' donut."

"Aw no, Mr. Skeeter," he answered himself in a high falsetto voice. "We gotta sit our fat, lazy asses right'cheer in front of this here store and fuck up all yo' best-laid plans."

"If y'all don't leave," he muttered in his own voice, "I'm gonna taken this here pistol, and I'm gonna put a .44 cabiler... uh, caliber hole in yo' head. You heah me, boys?"

"Why, yessir, we be nothin' but stupid cops, don' know nothin' 'bout nothin'."

Skeeter carried on his two-sided conversation for a while longer, then got tired of it, and stretched out on the floor. He sucked at the Maker's Mark bottle. A dribble came out, and he held up the bottle to see the thing was nearly empty. "Well, shit. Who drunk my liquor?"

He tipped the last of the bourbon down his throat. "Well, fuck 'em if they's gittin' any mo'."

He closed his eyes, rested his head on the cool floor.

And passed out.

Hacienda Del Norte
Northern Mexico

Enrique DaSilva and Emilio Santos enjoyed their cigars and cognac in the library. Santos had promised him a choice of fresh, young bed-warmers, and with a big meal inside him, DaSilva relaxed and breathed the fumes from the palm-sized snifter.

The cartel troubleshooter felt a little better about getting the money back, since he knew who had taken it. The men were two hours away from the Cruz residence, expected to arrive there about one in the morning. They would capture Oscar Cruz, and he would give up the money.

Once DaSilva delivered the cash, his next step would be to track down those in his organization who had leaked the info to Cruz. Setting up a new route would take time and effort, but fortunately, that wasn't his problem. The logistics chief bore the weight of that effort.

DaSilva's job was to find people who needed to be found and to kill them.

Unnamed road
Northern Mexico

Yeager and Victor bounced around on the front bench seat of the pickup. The old truck's twin I-beam suspension transmitted every rut and bump in the dry mud track right up into their butts.

"A bumpy ride," Victor said, "but at least it's taking forever."

"You got a date?"

"Yeah. With a cheep."

They topped a rise and rolled over into a shallow valley. At the base of the valley, barely visible in the starlight, stood an adobe farmhouse with its accompanying outbuildings. The *cheep* ranch. Yeager aimed the truck directly for the dark and silent house. Brush raked the sides of the pickup, scratching and clawing.

The first dog started barking at one hundred yards out. It was joined in chorus by two others within seconds. By the time Yeager stopped in the farmyard, they were surrounded by a half dozen baying mutts barking and leaping around the pickup as if they'd discovered the doggie messiah. The light over the porch came on, and the door opened a crack.

Victor slipped out, slamming the door behind him. He rattled off something in Spanish, using a calming tone and holding his hands out to the sides. Dogs jumped and tangled around his ankles, trying hard to love him to death, all at once. Yeager looked at the puppy love and shook his head. "You have a way with animals, Por Que."

"Is why I'm your friend." Victor stepped to the open door of the farmhouse and spoke to someone inside, presumably the shepherd that he had photographed earlier that morning, or rather *yesterday* morning.

Cash changed hands. That eight hundred dollars was the last of Yeager's emergency stash. The shepherd came out, carrying a pump-action shotgun, happy with his newfound wealth and ready to be helpful. He led Victor to the stock pen, waving for Yeager to follow.

Yeager cranked the wheel around, gritting his teeth at the squeal from his power steering pump, which started the dogs to barking again, and bumped across the yard. With a three-point turn, he backed the Ford up to the gate of the sheep pen and cut the engine, which rattled for a few seconds before dying. The eager dogs continued to bark and circle, trying to get attention or food. As soon as he stepped out, one of the friendlier mutts planted both feet on his chest, nearly knocking him back into the truck.

"Some guard dog you are." Yeager ruffled the floppy ears and scratched the dog's neck. The black-and-tan long-haired dog had gray eyebrows and a frenetic tongue. He obviously agreed that he was a good dog indeed.

"You have made a friend, *Señor*," the shepherd said in Spanish. He stood eye to eye with Victor but was more Jupiter to Victor's Mars. *He hasn't missed many free tortilla Sundays at the local* taquería.

"What kind of dog is this?" Yeager asked.

The short man looked confused. "A black one, Señor."

"Ah. Gracias."

"Don't mind him," Victor told the shepherd. He circled one finger around his ear. "He is a gringo from Texas, you know?"

"Ah," the shepherd said, nodding. "I see."

"Shut up and load the sheep," Yeager told Victor.

"Yes, boss."

Over forty sheep blatted and scurried around in the pen like a dingy, fluffy pillow fight. Victor slipped through the gate and made a grab for the closest animal, only to fall flat on his face, cursing, when the fuzzy beast let out a bleat of terror and darted away.

Yeager and the shepherd laughed.

Victor scrambled to his feet. "You think this is so damn funny, you big German asshole, you come and do it."

"But, Por Que," Yeager said, "my people were blacksmiths in the old country. You have a sheep-raising heritage. This shit's in your blood."

"Fuck you, Yeager. This ain't funny no more."

"Depends on what side the fence you're standing on."

With the portly shepherd's assistance, they managed to corral and load twelve loud, obnoxious sheep into the back of Yeager's pickup. Afterward, all three men smelled of sheep dung and sweat.

"Pee-eew!" Victor said. "Did I tell you how much I hate this shit? I wasn't raised to deal with no animals, *esé*. Uh-uh, no way, Jose. Fuck, you better not say nothin' about this cheep bullshit ever, so help me God."

"Damn, Por Que." Yeager stood next to the tailgate. In the truck, the sheep milled around, confused and nervous. He reached out and patted the closest ewe. She rolled her eyes and bleated at him. "I think this chunky one here has her eye on you."

Victor crawled up into the passenger seat and pulled the groaning door shut with a bang. "Just drive the truck, *pendejo*. I can't believe I let you talk me into this."

Yeager shook hands with the farmer, who grinned and bobbed his head. Ever since he'd figured out the two heavily armed men at his door wanted to buy his sheep, rather than shoot him and steal them, the man had become very happy. The farmer followed him to the driver's side, as did the black dog and three other mutts, tongues lolling and tails wagging.

"*Vaya con Dios*," the farmer said, shaking Yeager's hand again.

"I hope He's with me, *amigo*," Yeager replied in Spanish. "I'm going to need all the help I can get." He opened the driver's door, and the black dog jumped into the cab and scrambled over to lick Victor's face.

"Gaah! Get off me, you stupid mutt. You wanna blow us all up?"

The dog sat down in the middle of the bench seat, tail wagging.

"Not this trip, buddy," Yeager said.

The farmer whistled, and the dog jumped down, tail between his legs.

Charlie would probably like a dog like that.

Yeager jumped in and slammed the door before any other animal could join the party. He started the truck and pulled out, followed by the pack of baying dogs. Yeager lifted a hand in parting, and the farmer waved back then called to his dogs, who peeled off one by one. At the lip of the rise, the black dog stopped and sat in the dirt, tail still wagging.

Yeager kept glancing in the rearview mirror.

The dog stayed there until Yeager lost sight of him in the darkness and the dust cloud trailing behind them.

CHAPTER 29

Abandoned Convenience Store
East of Austin

SOMETHING METALLIC HAD SKITTERED ACROSS the floor. Charlie was certain of it. The darkness was almost complete, so she didn't see what it was, but something had broken loose when she stumbled into the boxes. And metal might mean a weapon.

The cardboard crunched under her feet as she crept across the pile. She kept her head down, eyes wide open, soaking up every inch of floor and seeing nothing. Night outside and no lights but for the kidnapper's flashlight made her little convenience store prison as dark as a storm cellar.

When she reached the edge of the flattened boxes, she got down on her hands and knees. She swept the floor with her fingers, moving in short arcs from left to right and touching every inch, every millimeter of floor space. If she could see the floor, she would no doubt be disgusted with the dirt and grime she was picking up. She wasn't exactly prissy, but there were limits to how much filth she could tolerate without gagging. Or there used to be.

The floor was sticky and reeked of old beer. Her nose tickled from the dust she was stirring up, and she sneezed once, twice, then a third time. She wiped her nose on the hem of her T-shirt. *Ew. Try not to think about it. Stay alive, then you can have a nice bath and some clean clothes.*

She crawled another few inches forward and continued her search pattern. The cooler wasn't that big so the thing, whatever it was, couldn't have gone far. The flattened boxes were sort of in the middle in a big pile, as if somebody meant to come back and collect them but never did. So logically, the metal piece would be somewhere in the back third of the cooler.

It had been quiet out front for some time. Earlier, she thought she heard tires on the gravel in the parking lot, and maybe some radio chatter, but that had probably been wishful thinking. Since then, nothing.

No sooner had she thought about it than a noise from the store rattled the glass door of the freezer. She went completely still. At first, she thought it was an engine starting up, then her brain clicked in and she recognized the sound. Snoring.

Whoever was on guard up front was sawing logs as though he wanted to build his own tree house. Maybe that meant they'd gone to sleep and she would be left in peace for the night.

Don't count on it, Charlie. Keep looking.

Austin, Texas

John Stone lounged on his sofa, shiny pistol in one hand, highball glass full of bourbon, no ice, in the other. The woman, Nita Lutz, huddled on the chair across from him, wrists bound with a plastic tie. She managed to look vulnerable, intimidated, and worried at the same time as she projected animal sexuality. Her balloon tits puffed out between her arms. She looked at him kind of sideways, with a little-girl-lost look that was damn sexy.

John shifted and tucked Little John into a more comfortable position. "I'll give you one thing, Nita, my girl, you're a piece of work. That's for sure."

"How do you mean?" Her voice had dropped down a level, from Southern Fried Chicken to Smoky Chipotle Sauce.

"You been shaggin' your boss's husband all this time, and she doesn't know a thing about it. Mm-mm-mm. I admire that level of deceit. I truly do."

"He said he loved me," she murmured.

"Well, I'm sure he did. Say that, I mean. So where is he now, this lover boy of yours?"

She shrugged, and interesting things happened with her melons. "I couldn't say. He ran off with the truck, and that's the last I saw of him."

"But you know where he kept his money, the money he stole off all them rich widows and orphans who invested in his biotech scheme."

She nodded.

"And you're sharing this with me why?"

"To stay alive, of course."

"So your play is, you want to exchange this money for your life?"

"No."

"No?"

"Uh uh." Nita shook her head, letting her hair tumble around her face. *Damn.* The girl was good, no question about it. "No, I want something else."

"You do, huh?" Stone drained his glass and set it on the coffee table. "What might that be?"

A tiny flicker of a smile played around the edges of her lips. Stone had a strong feeling he knew how Adam had felt right before biting into that apple.

Her pink tongue stroked her lips. "What I want is a full partnership."

———⟫✳⟪———

Unnamed road
Northern Mexico

Victor fiddled with the GPS, inputting the coordinates they'd selected. He guided Yeager to a desert trail branching off the dirt road. It was more the memory of a trail than an actual road of any kind. Random stretches of tire marks in the dirt indicated that other people had driven that way in the past, maybe in goat carts.

Yeager downshifted and concentrated on missing the deepest ruts. He decided it was a good thing the ground was dry. Otherwise, they'd have bogged down to both axles.

"So this woman, Charlie. What's she look like?"

Yeager blurted, "Like a glass of fine wine," and was surprised at his own poetic language. "Sky-blue eyes and this thick mass of copper hair are the first things you notice. Delicate face. Like fine china, you know? The good stuff that you only use at Christmas. Waist about this big." He made an "OK" sign with his right hand and glanced at Victor. "But what you figure out later, man, is how double-tough she is. The way she faced down that guy in Arkansas. Then later, when they hit her place in force, there was no crying, no hysterics. I knew she'd have my back, you know?"

"Damn, dude." Victor whistled. "She got a sister?"

"Hah! Step carefully, amigo. Charlie carries a .41 Smith & Wesson."

"No kidding?" Victor looked out the window and shook his head. "Dang, man. You don' want her no more, you call me, right?"

"You got it, Por Que." Yeager smiled then frowned. He'd managed to block out thoughts of Charlie, but talking about her made it all rush back to his mind, churning the acid in his stomach.

The GPS voice spoke. "In point three miles, arrive at your destination."

"Almost showtime, buddy," Yeager said.

"Let's rock n' roll, dude."

━━━═╳═━━━

Hacienda Del Norte
Northern Mexico

"Hey, Luis," Marco Garza said as he stepped back into the control room. "I think your girlfriend is up at the big house, getting fucked by the bosses, you know."

"What?" Luis spun away from the monitors and glared at Marco. A bodybuilder type, the shift supervisor wore a burgundy polo shirt stretched over his chest, his biceps stressing the sleeves. Luis ground his teeth. "What do you mean?"

"I mean, you simple shit, that Ray up at the big house called me and had me bring three women from the worker's dorm. Serena didn't hide fast enough, so I picked her." Marco shrugged his massive shoulders and settled in his desk chair. He laced his fingers behind his head and leaned back. "He told me the head guy from Sinaloa, you know, the one with the gray suit, walks like a robot? Ray said that guy wanted some pussy tonight. Last night, he took one of the girls from the dorm. Fucked her and fucked her up, you know?"

Luis did know. He'd seen the girl shuffling around earlier, one eye puffy and black. She moved as though she was holding her insides together with her hands.

"Anyway," Marco said, "last I saw, Ray was stripping them down for their big night, you know? One of them gets to play with Mr. Big Shot tonight. Lucky girl, yes?"

"Yeah," Luis mumbled, eyes on the floor. "Of course."

"But don't worry, dickhead." Marco opened a drawer on his desk and dug out a hot rod magazine. "Maybe when he's done, you can have sloppy seconds, yes?"

Fucker. For the first time, Luis considered ways to frag the puffed-up asshole. Both the one in front of him and the one in the house.

Charlie had searched from the boxes to the back of the cooler wall, crawling over every square inch, while trying not to think of the things she was dragging her fingers through. She disconnected her mind and focused it on Abel Yeager instead. She loved those sad, brown puppy-dog eyes. All he had to do was look at her, and she could feel herself try to ovulate.

A snort and snuffle broke the rhythm of the snoring coming from the front of the store. Charlie froze and waited, but the snoring didn't resume. Instead, she heard several hacking coughs, then whoever it was—and it had to be Skeeter—hacked something up and spat.

Silence.

The snap of a lighter was followed by a small glow that lit her small prison for a brief moment. It didn't last long enough for her to look around and find the metal object she sought. Darkness returned. She couldn't even see the ember of the cigarette she knew

Skeeter was inhaling. But he was awake. And an awake Skeeter was a dangerous Skeeter.

Charlie resumed her search, thoughts of Yeager banished. Instead, she focused all her concentration on the sweep of her fingers across the floor. Back and forth, back and—

The middle finger of her left hand brushed something that shifted away. She froze, totally still, heart thumping in her ears so loudly nothing else penetrated.

Charlie walked her fingertips forward, not daring to breathe or move. Much sooner than she expected, given her luck so far, she felt a metal object lying flat against the floor. She closed her hand around it and sat up on her heels, clutching her prize tightly lest it get away.

She knew immediately what it was. Larger than a stick of gum, but shaped the same, it was a simple box cutter. She pushed on one end, and the razor tip extended from the other. Simple. Utilitarian. Tiny chip in the blade.

Testing the edge, she cut a small gash in her thumb and winced. But she was light-years better armed that she had been. Hell, Muslim terrorists had taken over passenger airplanes with box cutters.

Charlie shifted back to her pile of boxes and sat down. She contemplated how to employ her tiny weapon against her kidnappers.

Scuffing sounds came from the front of the store, and she focused on the glass doors. *However you do it, you better be ready. Because here he comes.*

CHAPTER 30

Hacienda Del Norte
Northern Mexico

T HE WHITEWASHED WOODEN FENCE RAN the full perimeter around the target ranch. The top rail was about chest high, with three more below it. Yeager examined it under the narrow beam of a penlight but found no obvious trip wires, photoelectric beams, or other alarm-triggering devices.

"Maybe they don't have any alarms," Victor murmured.

"Wouldn't that be nice."

The load of fuzzy animals shuffled around, bleating and thumping the truck bed with their small hooves. Their racket trampled all other sounds. Yeager couldn't tell whether anyone had heard their approach or not.

After a moment of crouching in the dark, he gave up listening and jogged to the pickup to grab a crowbar from behind the seat. As he returned to the fence line, Victor moved off to the right, all but invisible in his black tactical gear.

Starting at the fence's top rail, Yeager jammed the crowbar into the joint and pulled, breaking it loose. Working quickly and hurrying carefully, he jimmied the rails from one section of fence, creating a twelve-foot gap. He inspected the joints while removing the crosspieces and confirmed there were no hidden alarm wires. Apparently, the guards relied on defenses closer to the main buildings for intrusion protection.

"Ready for Operation Sheep Attack?" Yeager asked Victor, who slipped back once the fence was breached.

"That the best you could do? All day to think of a code name? How about Operation Pull the Wool? Or Shear Terror?" Victor sighed. "Hopeless. Don' never tell anyone I did this. Ever. Understand?"

"Time to break out the NVGs."

"Roger that."

They crossed to the pickup and grabbed their backpacks. Their surplus night vision goggles were old and the battery life was limited. Yeager prayed they'd last the night as he settled the goggles on his face and switched them on.

Kickoff time.

Luis didn't see the pictures on the security office monitors. Instead, images of Serena committing acts of unspeakable depravity with that white-haired, silk-suited bastard danced in his head. Dirty movies featuring the slender girl played on a continuous loop. The more he tried not to think about it, the more he did.

There is nothing you can do, Luis. You are a peon, a trained monkey, guarding the dope and money of the cartel. He is a rich man. A leader. One of the blessed chiefs of the Sinaloa cartel. And your life is worth less to him than a bag of dog shit. You are nothing but a thug with a gun.

With a gun...

Luis switched fantasies. Suddenly, he saw himself taking his AR15, cocking the bolt, and standing up. Marco would look up in surprise and die with a stupid look on his face, one bullet through the muscle magazine.

Then Luis would go through the rest of the house, systematically eliminating the other guards, like Rambo. *Pow! Pow! Pow!* He would clear each room, speed-changing mags, rolling across the floor, and firing upside down.

He would burst into the bedroom of the old bastard right as he was about to stick his aging, wrinkled cock into Serena's virgin treasure. Luis would laugh at the old man, the *troubleshooter*, and sneer as the rich man cowered, trying to hide his dick with his hands.

Luis would show no mercy for this... this cocksucker. He would shoot him dead and use a whole magazine on him. He would then comfort the terrified Serena, who would come into his arms and huddle her naked body against his—

An alert popped on the screen, breaking his train of thought. It took him a few seconds to react. North Field again.

"Hey, Marco. I think that deer is back."

"Call out the Army," Marco said blandly without even looking up.

"Very funny," Luis muttered. The squiggly shape on the screen finally resolved itself enough for him to identify it. "A sheep? How did a sheep get on the property?"

Marco yawned. "Tell Antonio I want lamb chops."

Luis keyed his radio. "North Guard Post, Central. Copy?"

A buzz of static came from the radio, then Antonio asked, "What now? Over."

"You have a sheep in the North Field. Lock and load. Marco wants lamb chops. Over."

"Lamb chops? Tell me he's not serious. He wants me to go out in the dark and shoot a sheep, yes?"

Marco looked up from his muscle magazine. "Tell him I will pull his head off at the neck if he fires a shot and bothers the people in the house. Walk up to the sheep and bash its head in."

Luis relayed Marco's instructions.

Nothing came back for long seconds, then as Luis was about to transmit again, Antonio spat out, "Roger."

Antonio appeared at the base of the screen, moving across the field in the general direction of the sheep. *This should be damn funny. I'll have to download a copy for the other guys and let them watch Antonio try to catch a sheep and kill it.*

ALERT. NORTH FIELD 2.

What the hell?

Luis's eyes bugged out. The alert was in the same area... for another woolly sheep. The animal stopped to nibble at whatever kind of plant sheep liked to eat. Luis had been raised in the city; he had no idea what sheep found tasty.

He opened his mouth to report but was interrupted by more alerts.

ALERT. NORTH FIELD 2.

ALERT. NORTH FIELD 1.

The screen became jumbled with shapes as it tried to track each one.

"Marco, look at this."

"What?"

"A whole flock of sheep has gotten loose in the north field. I count five... no, six sheep."

"Impossible. The software must be glitched up."

"Why is it impossible? We have one sheep. Why not a flock?"

"Idiot. Let me see."

ALERT. NORTH FIELD 2.

ALERT. EAST FIELD 4.

ALERT. NORTH FIELD 1.

"*Madre de Dios!*" Luis swore. "I have contacts all over the field. They're moving all around, and I can't see shit."

"Call the barracks. Get the reserve out into the field. We will have to drive these sheep back to where they came from and find out how they got in. What a goat fuck this is."

Luis couldn't resist. "You mean a sheep fuck, no?"

"Shut up, Luis, and come on. You're in this little roundup too."

"Should we call Santos?"

"Santos is busy fucking your girlfriend. I, for one, do not intend to disturb him to say we've been invaded by sheep."

Before the cooler door opened, Charlie had hidden the tiny box cutter under the lip of her cardboard mattress and assumed a position of innocent prisoner waiting patiently. She needn't have bothered posing.

The lean, hawk-faced Skeeter swaggered in, looking as though he couldn't care less what she'd been up to. Under-lit by a heavy flashlight, the planes and angles of his face reminded her of a demonic wooden carving. "Well, hello there, pretty lady," he rasped. "Miss me?"

The reek of cigarettes and booze followed him in and saturated the air. He set the flashlight by the door, pointed so that it shone directly in her eyes. "Now, missy, just so's you know, we're fixin' to have a little fun."

In the reflected backlight, his leer was unmistakable. Her heart, already slamming inside her chest, kicked into a stuttering trip-hammer. Brain fog threatened to claim her, and she fought it back. Fainting would not be a good thing.

She tried to think of something to say, some words her college-educated mind could produce to outwit this backward hillbilly asshole, but nothing came. Her mouth had gone dry and coppery. Words refused to form.

"I'll give you to know," Skeeter said as he unbuttoned his shirt, "that I didn't bring no gun in here with me, in case you got any ideas about maybe snaggin' it and shootin' your way out. I figger I can handle a skinny thing like you without no pistol, about any day of the week."

He shrugged out of his shirt, revealing a wiry but muscular upper body. He had cable-like arms, protruding collar bones, and small patch of grayish-white hair on his chest.

"You... you don't have to do this." Her words trickled out, barely audible.

Skeeter laughed, a crowing sound that kicked off a coughing fit. He hocked and spat in the corner. "Oh, lady. I most surely do. Start shuckin' your way out of them clothes."

Charlie remained glued in place by fear, no more able to move than a statue. Her puny little box cutter with its chipped blade was nothing but a hideous joke. How could she ever have thought she could fight this animal with a tiny bit of razor blade?

With two strides, he loomed over her. He whipped one hand around and slapped her face. The pain nearly blinded her. He grabbed her T-shirt at the hem and ripped it straight up and off her body in one jerk, wrenching her arms.

"Now, darlin'." His face grew even harder, if that was possible. "You get shut of them clothes and right quick. Otherwise..." The lean man pulled a folding knife from his pocket and snapped open the blade. Six inches of polished steel gleamed in the weak light. "Otherwise, I'll start by cuttin' a finger off. When I get done with fingers, I'll start on toes. Then maybe a nose. I don't need none-a those to do what I want."

He folded the knife and slid it back into his pocket. He worked his boots off, standing awkwardly but never taking his eyes off her, then peeled down his socks. He grinned, showing his yellowed teeth again. "The way I see it, you can lay back and enjoy this and come out with all your parts... or I can start cuttin' bits off and still get what I want."

He unbuckled his jeans and let them fall to the floor. He wore no underwear. His uncircumcised penis was semi-rigid already, bloated with blood. "Well, what's it gonna be? The easy way? Or the hard way?"

Her original plan, if it could be called a plan, had been to lure him in close, slash his eyes or throat, then rush past him and out the door. His sheer vicious, reptilian strength ruled that plan out.

Think, Charlie. You have to outwit this cracker bastard.

With shaking hands, she unsnapped the button on her shorts.

CHAPTER 31

Hacienda Del Norte
Northern Mexico

T HE PROBLEM WASN'T INFILTRATING PAST the guards in the dark. The problem was trying not to laugh. The dozen men running around with flashlights in the dark after a bunch of nervous, bleating sheep looked like a Laurel and Hardy, Three Stooges, and Charlie Chaplin flick rolled into a farce and served with a comedy.

Yeager and Victor belly-crawled through the scrub brush about a hundred yards to the east of the nearest guard. They kept low for a time, then alternately scrambled forward in bursts of speed, one covering the other.

After releasing the sheep, Yeager had slapped the boards back on the fence using a portable electric drill and some drywall screws. It wasn't perfect, but it would stand up to a distant inspection in the dark. Then he'd hurried back to the truck and driven it off into the brush, out of sight of the fence line. Recovering it would be a problem for another day.

In the meantime, Victor had tried to shoo the milling flock in the direction of the ranch house. The sheep weren't terribly inclined to run, and Victor's hisses and waving arms didn't excite them much. They seemed content to graze right there by the fence. He picked up pebbles and pegged them at one ewe after another. The ones he hit made a loud "Baaaaah" and trotted off a couple of steps, only to stop and graze again.

By the time Yeager came back from hiding the truck, he found a really pissed-off Victor dancing around in the dark like a madman, hissing "Shoo! Shoo!" Yeager hopped the fence at the exact same time that Victor fired a suppressed burst from his MP5, chewing and spraying dirt behind the sheep. The sheep didn't like the patter of the machine gun and being pelted with sprayed grit; they ambled in fits and starts toward the ranch house.

"Oh, finally, you little cheep fuckers," Victor whispered. "Now you run." He ripped off a couple of more bursts and got them moving a tad faster.

Yeager and Victor then hunkered down, waiting to make sure their flock needed no more encouragement. When the animals were well on their way, Yeager tapped Victor on the shoulder, and they moved to the left, duck-walking to a shallow arroyo, where they dropped to the ground and waited for the show to start, which didn't take long.

Flashlight beams probed the night like a laser show. Men ran about, tripped, and cursed, chasing wooly shapes that bleated and bounded away whenever someone came close.

Victor's body shook, tears wetting his face, from holding in the laughter. He rolled over onto his back and snickered quietly as he turned off his NVGs to conserve the battery. "Oh, man," he gasped. "I forgive you, big guy. That was better than the time you jacked up the back of Dixon's squad car back in McAllen then blew past him at a hundred 'n' ten."

Yeager grinned. "That was pretty good, wasn't it? Let's hope them ol' boys are all busy chasing sheep. Let's go."

They belly-crawled out of the arroyo. When all the activity was well behind them, they zipped forward in short bursts, angling for the building stuck onto the back of the big barn.

Yeager paused at twenty yards out, trying to become one with a clump of sage brush. Directly in front of him, a short sprint away, sodium vapor lights coated the red brick in a yellowish glow. The building had been grafted onto the side of the large barn, an obvious afterthought. No doors. The barn itself was no more than a plain steel building on steroids, big enough to hold anything from a fleet of tractors to a medium-sized aircraft. To his left, across a football field of open ground, were the adobe stables. His rig was parked between those two buildings, on a concrete apron.

Yeager flinched at the sharp crack of a rifle coming from the fields behind them. He heard another shot then another. The shooting escalated to a continuous crackle of small arms fire.

"Looks like somebody got tired of chasing sheep," Yeager said.

Victor's jaw fell open in horror. "Oh, man. That's wrong."

"See? I knew you liked her, too."

"We gonna sit here all night, makin' fun of my love life?" Victor got up on one knee, his MP5 tracking from left to right and back. "Or are we gonna move?"

"We're moving." Yeager dashed to the right corner of the brick building, weapons and gear slapping his body.

A guard appeared at the side of the building and caught Yeager flat-footed. The guard was all of nineteen or twenty years old, wearing a denim jacket, jeans, and cowboy boots. The kid held an AK47 against his shoulder. He ripped off a burst, a wide-eyed look of surprise reflected in the glow of the muzzle flash.

One round hit Yeager low on his left side, a glancing blow on his flak vest. The slug spun him a quarter-turn and knocked him to one knee. Another round burned his cheek. The rest sprayed skyward as the guard failed to control the muzzle's climb.

A stutter of fire from Victor's suppressed weapon drilled a three-round burst into the kid's chest. The shots flung the guy against the wall, dead before he dropped. The AK47 battered the concrete where his lifeless fingers dropped it.

"You dead, man?" Victor called out of the darkness.

"No." Yeager grunted and winced when he tried to take a deep breath. "Just stupid."

"And slow, dude. I seen mannequins run faster."

Yeager struggled to his feet and jogged to the corner of the brick building, where he took up position while Victor sprinted to join him. The smaller man checked the guard and then the far corner, covering their blindside.

Yeager squinted and peeked around the corner. "Clear. Nothing moving."

"Same."

The shooting from the fields had died out. If they were lucky, no one had noticed the burst from the late guard. With a little more luck, they had a few minutes before the remaining guards made it back from their sheep-killing mission.

"Luck," Yeager muttered. So far, they'd had bucketloads of luck. *But luck is a fickle bitch, bound to turn on you when you need her most.*

———✦———

Charlie stepped out of her panties, shaking so hard she had to brace herself by putting one hand against the wall. Her teeth chattered, and cold shivers racked her body. The temperature hadn't fallen—it was like a hothouse inside the dead refrigeration unit—but fear had turned her hands to ice cubes.

Skeeter leered and stroked his stiffening penis. The more she shivered, the more he seemed to enjoy it. "That's right, baby," he crowed. "Git nekkid, and git ready."

As if his voice had flipped a switch, the fear drained from her, and she knew what she had to do to survive. A rush of warmth replaced the chill and broke the paralysis that had seized her brain. Like an engine turning over on a cold morning, her mind cranked up and started moving again.

"Oh, honey," she said. "I'm really ready." She hardly recognized her own voice. The throaty, sexy quality came from a remote corner of her soul, one she hadn't known existed, a ruthless, diamond-hard kernel of instinct.

She thought of Yeager and his First Law: *Come home at the end of the day.* Now she understood what that meant.

Charlie sank to her knees on the cardboard mattress. "You're built like a horse. Come here and let me take care of that big boy."

Skeeter grinned. "I knew you rich bitches was all alike. You like a little slumming, huh? Get a real man for a change."

"Oh, yes." She bit her lip and regarded him from under lowered eyelashes. "Please. I didn't know how bad I needed it."

She thought she might have overplayed her hand, but Skeeter

was apparently oblivious to overacting. His erection stood out like a flagpole.

She glanced down at the edge of the cardboard, making sure her knees were positioned where they needed to be. When she looked up, he stood directly in front of her.

I see what needs to be done. And I will do it.

Hacienda Del Norte
Northern Mexico

Luis Cordoña did not follow Marco outside when he ran to take control of the sheep crisis. Instead, he remained behind, sulking and staring at the monitors.

The security room had one door that led outside and another that opened into the kitchen. The kitchen door was the one that held his attention.

Right behind that door, maybe not two dozen feet away, the rich and powerful cartel boss enjoyed the gift of Serena's naked body. He was probably using her cruelly, the disgusting pig, taking her virginity with no more thought than blowing his nose.

Luis fumed. Various scenarios ran through his head, all centered around taking his weapon of choice, an AR 15, and shooting the old fucker in the balls. Then, he would grab Serena, who was nude in every situation his mind conceived, and race from the hacienda, the cartel forces hot on his trail. Fortunately, Luis was smart enough to know he would not get very far. Undoubtedly, he would die in a hideous and painful way once they caught up to him, and Serena would die with him.

ALERT – WAREHOUSE 3

At first, he thought a sheep had evaded the line of death and was running across the concrete lot between the barn and stables. Then his eyes focused, and he shot up straight in his chair as if he'd been zapped in the ass by a Taser.

An armed commando had broken cover from the corner of the dormitory and raced across the empty lot, headed for the truck in the center of the picture. While Luis watched, mouth open, another one broke away from the same spot and followed the first. Both were dressed in black and loaded down with weapons and equipment.

Delta Force! We're being attacked by U.S. Special Forces. Luis jolted from his trance and followed protocol for an armed surprise attack. He flipped the cover from a red plastic button in the upper right of the security console. Big and flat and round, the button was meant to be pounded by an open hand. Luis slapped the alert button again and again, even though he knew once was enough.

Flood lights burst into life, turning the hacienda grounds as bright as a ball field during a night game. Klaxons wailed, screaming out a warbling cry. Emergency strobes and sirens activated in the barracks, waking the off-duty shift.

The two commandos on screen barely paused. They continued making for the truck. The lead man was almost at the cab.

Luis saw his duty very clearly. Marco and the ready reserve were out of position, scattered across the north fields. Six other guards were in various posts around the hacienda, none closer than he to the Special Forces troops attempting to steal cartel property. The off-duty force would take several minutes to respond, having to don clothes and sort out weapons.

It was up to Luis to save the day. He, and he alone, must make a stand and stop those sorry bastards who dared to invade his home, his property, his nation, and take what was not theirs.

Fumbling with a ring of keys he snatched from Marco's desk, Luis shoved out of his chair and ran to a locked room. After three tries, he found the right key and jerked open the steel door. Stored inside was part of the hacienda's selection of special weapons: claymore mines, hand grenades, M60 heavy machine guns. But most importantly, it held rocket-propelled grenade launchers.

Ignoring the shrieking alarm and the bright lights, Yeager opened the cab door and heaved himself inside. The bruise in his side reminded him he'd already been shot once tonight, and his body wasn't happy. His cheek burned and throbbed from sweat invading the long scratch where the second bullet had nearly taken off his head.

He dug his key out of his pants pocket and stabbed for the ignition switch, only to find it dangling loose and trailing a tangle of multi-colored wires. "Shit."

Victor climbed into the passenger seat. He grunted and flopped on the seat, rolled down his window and settled his M4 on the sill. The MP5 was strapped across his chest again. "Are we there yet?" Victor asked.

"Got a problem."

"No, thanks. I have enough of my own." Victor glanced at where Yeager was studying the spaghetti of loose wires. "Oh. That sucks."

"Lucky for you, I am a mechanical genius," Yeager said and bumped two wires together. The diesel cranked once then died. Yeager squeezed the wires together and twisted. The big engine started chugging. After a few revs, it fired up with a roar and a belch of black smoke from the twin exhausts over the cab. "Hah! See? No problem."

"Can we go?"

"Have you been to the bathroom?"

"Twice. In my pants."

Yeager revved the engine, praying for it to warm up faster than it liked. He slapped the shifter into first and babied the accelerator. As he slid out the clutch, the big truck jolted forward. The engine tried to stall but didn't. Then they were rolling.

Yeager slapped the wheel. "Next stop Texas."

CHAPTER 32

Austin, Texas

J OHN STONE LEANED BACK ON the sofa and considered Nita Lutz. *Partnership.* That was what she'd asked for. Stone didn't have much need for a partner, but she'd promised him a share of the three million dollars Buchanan had hidden in offshore accounts. For three mil, Stone could see his way to at least keeping her alive. Hell, her tits alone were worth a million or so.

"What you got to offer," he asked, "besides money? I mean, what else you bring to this here partnership?"

Damned if the woman didn't lick those full lips and make them look even puffier and more sexy. It was as if she could flip a damn switch.

"Well," she murmured, "Steven enjoyed the fringe benefits."

"All right then. Let's get to fringing."

<hr />

Skeeter felt the power thrumming through his cock as he stared down at the red-haired women on her knees in front of him. Smiling and licking her lips, she had a face like a model on a magazine cover. Her apple-sized tits sported the pinkest nipples he'd ever seen. She took him in her hand and stroked his dick with an up-and-down motion.

Man, that feels good. I knew it. One look and she can't get enough. It's all about the dick, when you got right down to it. "Yeah, baby!" he groaned. "That's what you know you want. Make Daddy Skeeter feel real good now, y'hear?"

"Hmmmmm."

The bitch was nearly purring, she wanted it so bad. She raised her head and licked her lips again. Skeeter grinned. *All alike. Down deep, they all wanted the dick.*

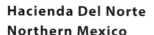

Hacienda Del Norte
Northern Mexico

The truck faced the exact opposite direction they needed it to go. Yeager cranked the wheel left, turning the rig in a big circle, which took him to the far north edge of the parking area.

So far, there had been no reaction to the alarm signal wailing into the night. His luck still held. *Law Number Seven: Never count on luck.* Yeager gunned the diesel through the last of the turn and lined it up on the gate at the far side of the compound. He speed-shifted and hit the accelerator, making the rig jump forward.

A lone figure dashed out of the house. The guard carried a tubular, awkward-looking weapon.

Yeager squinted. "What the hell?"

The guy stopped at fifty yards out and brought the weapon to his shoulder.

"RPG!" Victor screamed.

"Duck!" Yeager jerked to the left, but time—and luck—had run out.

A white flare and the projectile vomited a trail of smoke and burned a line straight at their front grill. With a shuddering bang, the grenade hit the right front quarter panel on the Peterbilt and exploded in a blossom of heat and pressure. The big truck jumped sideways, and the engine screamed as if mortally wounded. A chunk of the hood peeled back and smashed the already shattered windshield. The right front tire disintegrated in a shower of flaming rubber.

Yeager fought for control as the rig tried to jackknife and tip over at the same time. He fishtailed back and forth, blinded by the smoke and flame trailing over the hood. "I can't fuckin' see!" he shouted.

"This thing's done, man. Park it and let's bail."

A surge of panic hit Yeager in the gut. If he couldn't get the rig out of there with its load of cash, then he wouldn't have anything to trade for Charlie. Without the money, he would have to bluff and pray it worked.

He slammed his hands on the wheel, gunning the straining engine and trying to see through the black plumes of smoke billowing up from the engine compartment.

Too late, he saw the front doors of the big barn looming straight ahead.

<hr />

Enrique DaSilva jerked awake at the sound of the alarm siren shrieking. *An attack! Oscar Cruz? Or a new player? The shadowy figures behind the recent plague of attacks on the Sinaloa cartel's cash-smuggling operation?*

He threw off the covers and dressed in slacks and shoes, not bothering with socks. Grabbing his shirt off the back of a chair, he ran for the door. He paused only to retrieve his pistol from the dresser and tuck it in his waistband.

At the bottom of the stairs, he met Santos coming from a bedroom on the lower floor. Santos had pulled on pants and boots but wore no shirt. He carried a pistol in one hand and a walkie-talkie in the other.

"What is happening?" DaSilva demanded.

Santos glanced at him and held up a hand, asking for a moment. He clamped the radio to one ear, listening to a frantic voice spilling out between bursts of static. A boom from behind the house rattled the windows. DaSilva flinched and ducked.

"Someone is stealing the truck!" Santos shouted. He led the way toward the back of the house, running into the library. Light from outside flooded into the house, giving everything a silver coating. "For some reason, half my men are in the north field. If they live through this, I will kill them all."

They burst into the back garden in time to see a flaming diesel rig slam into the barn doors, rupturing the aluminum with a bang. The crashing boom rolled across the courtyard, followed by a shriek of rending metal as the truck ground to a halt, three quarters of its length buried in the barn.

DaSilva blinked. A single guard danced and capered in the lights of the parking lot, an expended grenade launcher lifted in the air above his head.

Yeager coughed and fought to keep his watery eyes open in the choking clouds of smoke and steam that swirled around in the cab of the truck. He'd taken a solid bang on the forehead when the rig hit the barn doors. Dizziness added to his misery. Victor kicked the passenger door, popping it open with a curse, and vaulted to the floor.

The truck had come to rest against a row of pallets filled with stacks of fifty-pound bags. Beyond the pallets, the remaining floor space was taken up with rows of low benches, each containing various sizes of bags, bins, scales, and other equipment. The walls were a brilliant white, adding to the appearance of a giant chemistry lab.

Yeager grabbed the fire extinguisher mounted on the bulkhead behind him and kicked his own door ajar. He climbed down more slowly than Victor had, wooziness threatening to spill him to the floor if he moved too fast. Using the extinguisher in short bursts, he worked his way around the front of the truck, snuffing the smoldering fire with clouds of chemical fire retardant.

With the threat of burning to death neutralized, he joined Victor crouched at the rear of the truck, aiming his M4 through the gap between the trailer and the wreck of the sliding metal barn door. The doors had been torn from their hinges, peeled back, and lay supported against the side of the trailer. That left a roughly triangular opening on each side of the trailer's rear wheels.

Victor fired a three-round burst as Yeager bellied up beside him.

The guard who had fired the rocket launcher dropped like a sack of flour.

"Take that, fucker," Victor muttered. He glanced at Yeager, the black camo paint on his face beaded with sweat. "Now what?"

"How many?"

"Guards?" Victor frowned. "Hell if I know. More than a squad, less than a regiment."

"Good. For a minute, I thought we might be outnumbered."

Victor laughed. "Hey, you remember that movie? The one with two guys, the outlaws? They're trapped by like a thousand Mexican troops, outnumbered with no escape. In the end, they run out into the square, and the movie ends, and you know they got shot to shit. You know that movie?"

"Butch Cassidy," Yeager said. "It was Bolivian troops."

"No, I'm pretty sure it was Mexicans. Anyway, I wanted to tell you: I never liked that movie."

"We're not gonna end up like that. We have several advantages that those guys didn't have."

"Like what?"

"Grenades for one. Modern assault rifles, C4." Yeager grinned. "And the natural fighting spirit of a United States Marine."

"Oorah. Looks like they're starting to get their shit together."

The ranch's guards, a ragged collection of cartel bravos in jeans and T-shirts and armed with a motley array of assault weapons, were reacting at last. One force grouped to their left, behind the hacienda's garden fence. Another collection of guards assembled at either end of the stables, over a hundred yards distant, at the far side of the flat concrete lot.

Yeager nodded. "If they try a frontal assault..."

"No shit," Victor said. "Even you couldn't kill 'em all."

"The flanking force worries me." Yeager peered through his weapon's sights. "A dozen or so behind semi-decent cover. They enfilade us while the other advances, we'll get chewed to shreds."

"Or they find another door and shoot our asses off."

"Cheery fucker, ain't you? Gimme that Winchester."

In his pack, Victor carried a disassembled bolt-action rifle equipped with scope. It took his practiced hands about thirty seconds to retrieve and assemble the rifle. "Here you go," he said. "Loaded, on safe. Five .308 Winchester, one in the chamber."

Yeager took the hunting rifle and sighted in on the group to the left. Mercifully, somebody cut off the siren, leaving ear-ringing silence. The distance was under a hundred fifty yards, a piece of cake for the .308. The 3x9 scope brought the assembled guard force into focus. *A gang of thugs is more like it.*

One man stood out, a chubby one with no shirt. Once Yeager focused on him, he could actually hear the man's voice as he yelled orders. He was speaking into a radio, shouting and gesturing at the force assembled by the stables. He looked pissed.

Yeager flipped off the safety with his thumb. He took a steadying breath, then another, achieving bone-to-ground lock from his knees through his elbows and into the rifle. On his third breath, he held halfway through the exhale and squeezed...

The rifle boomed and recoiled. When he regained the sight picture, the shirtless man was going down, blood spray still hanging in the air. Yeager couldn't see where the shot struck, but the look in the man's eyes registered as dead in his shoes.

The surrounding guards scattered and went to ground. Yeager glimpsed a white-haired man, older with a patrician face, his eyes wide with surprise. The man ducked back behind an archway on the hacienda's porch.

"One down," Yeager said.

"Oh, good," Victor muttered. "And here I thought we'd be hanging out all night, you know?"

Abandoned Convenience Store
East of Austin

Charlie took her mind to a blank place and blocked out the gamey smell of Skeeter's privates, the meaty feel of his penis, and the horrible voice he used to tell her how much he enjoyed her attention. His rambling, disconnected utterances in that Southern cracker voice encouraging her to get on with it had begun to make her ill. She stuck all that away in a corner of her mind and locked it down, refusing to think about it. For if she thought about it, she'd surely gag and vomit, losing her element of surprise.

Glancing up through her eyelashes, Charlie saw the thug's head thrown back. He was so totally focused on the pleasure that he had lost all concept of the need for defense.

Exactly how she needed him to be.

She held his penis with her left hand, working it gently up and down. Quietly, silently, she slipped the fingers of her right hand under the edge of the cardboard and felt for the box cutter.

Charlie gathered the small slip of metal into her right hand. Sliding her fingers along it, she made sure that the blade was fully extended, sharp edge up. Moving with such stealth took an effort of will greater than anything she'd ever done before. Forcing herself to remain calm and go slowly, she brought her right hand up near her left.

She forced calm into her hands and mind and thought through each move in advance.

"You little rich girls," Skeeter crowed, eyes closed, hips moving in time with her hand, "really know how to take care of a man, you kn—"

Charlie jerked the box cutter across the underside of Skeeter's penis, nearly severing it at the base. He let out a banshee howl of pure agony. His penis flopped like a snake chopped nearly in half.

He shrieked again and whipped a backhand across her face that sent her reeling across the flattened cardboard. The box knife skittered out of her hand. Through tears of pain, she kept sight of her tiny weapon, and using the momentum of the blow, she rolled in the same direction. She closed her hand on the thin tool and picked it up in one motion. She twisted to her feet.

Skeeter had gone from howling to grizzling in pain. A line of drool trailed from his mouth, and his eyes were closed. He held both hands over his groin, while blood slicked his flanks and drizzled over his knees.

She sucked air, panting as if she'd run a marathon, sweaty hair tangled across her forehead. The beast was wounded but not dead. If she stopped, he'd find the strength and resources to overcome his wound and kill her on the spot. Charlie reached deep into a well of animal ruthlessness.

He opened his eyes and focused such a look of pure rage on her that she nearly froze to the spot. He turned and stumbled toward his pile of clothing.

Where he'd left his knife.

Charlie jumped on his back and locked both ankles together around his waist, clinging to the skinny hoodlum with the strength of her legs. The wiry man reared back, slamming her against the wall of the cooler with a solid boom.

She grunted from the stunning force and lost her grip. Skeeter pivoted, slinging a fist around in a blurring arc. His fist smacked against the side of her head. Lights flashed, and a bolt of pain jolted through her skull.

Charlie may have blacked out for a moment. The next thing she knew, Skeeter was tottering toward her, one hand holding the bloody ruin of his groin, the other gripping his knife, blade up. She scrambled to her feet then dove left when he slashed at her.

"Goddamn bitch!" His words were so slurred, she could barely understand him. "Look what you did to me!"

He came at her again, and she kicked out, hitting a kneecap. He staggered back, giving her enough space for her to spring to her feet. She snagged his shirt off the floor and tossed it into his face. When he batted at it, she stepped in and kicked him in the groin, hard and fast, like punting a football.

He dropped to his knees. She ran around behind him, grabbed his head, and pulled his chin back. She dug the broken point of the box cutter into his windpipe with a gristly, cracking sound. Air whistled through the hole she'd made. With another savage jerk, she ripped the blade across his throat, feeling it tear as much as cut a jagged hole through his Adam's apple, releasing a hiss of air. Blood sprayed over her fingers.

Skeeter's clawed fingers scrabbled at her hands, pulling without effect. She continued sawing at his neck. Blood fountained across the wall of the cooler when she hit his carotid, spray-painting it with a hideous Rorschach pattern. Skeeter fell to his knees, his mouth open in a scream that failed to make it past the gaping hole in his throat. The effort added an aerosol mist to the pulsing stream from the severed artery.

He dropped to all fours then collapsed. The blood flow fell from a jet spray to a trickle, and the last breath shuddered out of his body.

CHAPTER 33

Austin, Texas

S TONE ZIPPED UP HIS PANTS and said, "Refill my drink, would you?"

"Sure, honey." Nita stood in front of him, apparently unfazed at being stark naked. She gave him a saucy grin and flounced over to the liquor cabinet, big round ass cheeks swaying.

"So let's talk about this here partnership," he said. "What's stopping me from taking your money and leaving you in a ditch somewhere?"

"Now, is that any way to talk to a woman who just gave you a blowjob?"

"Well, now, I admit, that there was enjoyable, but I can get that for a lot less money down by the courthouse. I even have some clients I can do some pro-boner work for, if you know what I mean."

Nita leaned over and trickled bourbon into his glass from the crystal decanter. She straightened and came around the table to plant one knee on the sofa beside him. It brought her tits directly to eye level, filling his vision in wide screen 3-D. *Or is that Double-D?*

Stone cleared his throat. "So what really happened to your buddy, Stevie Buchanan?"

"I killed him."

The meaning behind her words failed to register at first, and by the time they did, the bottle flashed in his peripheral vision. The heavy decanter smacked his skull with a *thunk* and sent rockets of pain exploding behind his eyes. The room tilted, and his vision filled with sparkles in the instant between the slam of the glass bottle and the start of the first wave of pain.

"Ahhh!" Stone sprawled, paralyzed, his system shocked. Through bleary eyes, he glimpsed the bitch rearing back for another shot.

"This partnership," she gritted out, "is now *over!*"

She swung again, and another flash of light blew up behind his eyes.

＊

Hacienda Del Norte
Northern Mexico

The hacienda guards had pulled their act together. Incoming fire sparked and zipped off the concrete floor of the barn. The metal walls popped as bullets slapped the thin aluminum, leaving round holes with jagged edges. Victor huddled behind the trailer's rear tires and fired in short, controlled bursts.

Yeager slid back into the shadows of the warehouse and worked the bolt on the Winchester, methodically aiming and firing until the magazine ran dry. "Out," he called.

Victor paused to shrug out of his pack and scoot it across the floor. "More in there. All the C4, too."

"How much you bring?"

"About twenty kilos."

"Holy..." Yeager shook his head. "Detonators?"

"In your bag." Victor ripped off another burst without bothering to look around.

"Gee, thanks," Yeager muttered, then louder, he said, "I'm going to check the perimeter and set up some surprises in case they try and flank us."

"Roger that." Another three-shot burst. "Better hurry 'cause I think they're working up to do something here."

Yeager scooted back and moved to his left until he was out of sight of the main door. Then he threaded his way around the line of pallets and deeper into the warehouse. *Or is it a lab?* He laid the hunting rifle on top of the closest pallet-load of sacks.

Six benches ran at right angles to the main entrance and crossed all the way to the back of the cavernous, remodeled barn. Yeager moved to the south wall first. A simple metal door had been cut in the middle of it. The door was locked from the other side, and Yeager didn't want to take the time to bust it open and investigate.

Going to one knee, he unzipped Victor's backpack and found ten square chunks of C4 plastic explosive, individually wrapped in cellophane. Beside those he found a full roll of silver duct tape and a roll of thin, flexible wire.

"Oh, bless you, my son," Yeager said. In his own bag, he found two different types of detonators: electrical remote controlled and mechanical ring pull. The mechanical type functioned like a hand grenade; when the ring was pulled, it went bang. And if it was stuck in a block of C4, that went bang, too.

Yeager taped one of the pliable bricks to the wall. The tape screeched off the roll in two long strips. He tied one end of a piece of wire to the ring on a mechanical detonator and inserted the pencil-thin device into the block of explosive. Taping the detonator down so that only the tip was exposed, he left the ring with its wire attachment dangling free.

Looping the roll of wire over the doorknob, he measured off a foot and cut the excess wire with his K-bar knife. Then, he secured it with a knot around the doorknob. A half inch of slack remained. If things worked according to plan, when somebody opened the door, the ring would jerk from the detonator, and the intruder's day would be ruined.

"How we doing up there?" he shouted toward the front.

Victor's voice came back over the smattering of gunfire from the outside, punctuated by his own short bursts of return fire. "Another day... in paradise... you know."

"I see two more doors need rigging!"

"Take... your time. I got nowhere else... I gotta be."

"How many?" DaSilva demanded.

"Two, at least, Don DaSilva," Gomez, the guard force leader, reported. "Two crashed into the barn, but there may be more."

DaSilva remained behind the solid adobe porch arch, while the guards hunkered behind the garden fence. Gomez had established discipline with cuffs and shouts, and the dozen or so men were holding their fire and awaiting orders. The other cadre of guards, situated around the stables, continued to trade sporadic fire with whoever was in the barn.

"Why are half our men out by the stables?" DaSilva asked, scowling at Gomez.

A lean, lanky man in his forties, Gomez had a dark Frankenstein face striped with a scar from his left eyebrow to his chin. Gomez looked away. "That... is unclear."

"Unclear? Clarify it!" DaSilva's anger burned in his stomach, and he clenched his pistol. He was very close to shooting someone, no matter who it was.

Gomez licked his lips. "Marco... um... Marco said they were tricked by a herd of... sheep in the field."

"Sheep! We are being attacked by sheep? What the fuck is going on?"

"I believe that the sheep were a diversion. To confuse our video cameras."

DaSilva thought about that. *How had the attacking force known about the hacienda's security? Did they have inside information? Did they believe the money was still in the truck?* Was there a mole inside the organization? If so, they had made a mistake. The truck held nothing but books. The idiots were trapped in the barn with no way out and for nothing!

"Gomez," he ordered, "send four men to the back of the barn. Make sure no one gets out."

"Sí, Don DaSilva."

"Take four more men and enter the barn through the barracks. Tell the idiot Marco to send four men around the north side and hold there. Make sure no one leaves through the dormitory. Have him maintain pressure and keep the cocksuckers pinned down with the men he keeps by the stables. You and your men take them in the flanks. The remaining four men will stay here with me."

Gomez bobbed his head. "Sí. It shall be done." He strode off, barking orders.

222

The two teams designated by the leader broke cover and scurried toward their new positions.

DaSilva took a deep breath and forced it out slowly. *Now it is time to find out who is fucking with us.*

Yeager skirted the benches in the rear of the barn and rigged the door leading to the airstrip in back. Next, he hustled over to repeat the procedure on the north side entrance, the one from the dormitories. If the dorms were occupied, he hoped the residents were smart enough to stay hunkered down and not come through that door to see what all the excitement was about.

He moved down the north wall, back toward the front. On the truck's passenger side, the barn door had folded back and nearly ripped loose from its hinges, leaving a triangular gap at the bottom. On the driver's side, the door had been shoved back, but it hugged the side of the trailer, leaving almost no gap. He couldn't see out, but more importantly, they couldn't see in. Yeager worked quickly to finish his final task then inspected the front of his rig. He still had a faint hope of driving the vehicle out and getting away.

The truck's nose was embedded in the middle of the line of pallets holding sacks of… *What? Cocaine?* If that was the case, he was looking at a hell of a lot of drugs. The plastic sacks reminded him of sand bags, stacked in neat squares, two dozen to a pallet.

The grille of the Peterbilt had knocked a half dozen bags loose and split one open. White powder had sprayed in an arc across the floor.

"Hey, Por Que!" he called out.

"What?"

"Enough dope here to light up LA."

"Just say no, dude. You wanna give me a hand here or what?"

Yeager used the stack of drugs as a barricade as he crouched and shuffled to the passenger side of the rig. He risked a quick look over the top, and his heart sank into his stomach.

The left side of the Peterbilt was pounded like bad steak. Because of the shredded front tire, the whole cab leaned sideways, resting on the steel rim. The cowling over the engine compartment had been blown open, revealing a severely wounded machine leaking fluids from several cracked or broken hoses, pipes, and joints.

The truck wasn't going anywhere for a long time, which meant he wouldn't be driving it back over the border and trading it to Harlan and his merry band.

Charlie...

<hr />

Abandoned Convenience Store
East of Austin

Charlie sat in the cooler for a long time, her mind in neutral. Nude. Butt getting numb from the cold, concrete floor. Staring at the dead man. One minute, she wanted to cry and never stop, then the next, she wanted to kick the corpse and spit on it. The rest of the time, all she could do was think of the horrible bubbling hiss when she'd cut open his windpipe and how the cartilage had felt under her hand when it parted.

When she finally moved, she didn't know how much time had passed. *Water.* She had to wash her hands before she did anything else. Using the remaining water in her open bottle and some from one of the new ones, she rinsed off her hands and doused her arms and legs. Red rivulets ran down to pool at her feet, spreading to join the thick blackened puddle leaking from Skeeter's gaping neck.

She didn't know which memory would haunt her more: having to take his reeking penis in her hand or trying to cut it off.

Or slicing the bastard's throat with a rusty box cutter. She shuddered. *At least I'll get to have a memory. And David will have a mother.*

She shook her hands and tried to squeegee the water from her arms and legs. Finally, she just pulled on her clothes, ignoring the dampness and the shivers of adrenaline reaction that racked her.

"Hold it together. Think of David." Simply hearing her own voice made her feel better. She was alive, and the sorry piece of shit who'd tried to rape her was dead.

"Fuck you, Skeeter," she told the corpse.

Remembering too many horror movies where the bad guy wasn't really dead, she skirted around him to the cooler door and stepped into the main store. The door clunked behind her, making her jump. She figured out how they'd locked her in, using a wire peg hook threaded through a ring meant for a padlock. Still feeling superstitious, as if Skeeter would come stumbling out of the cooler at any moment like an animated redneck zombie, Charlie secured the door with the peg hook.

"You're not coming after me, asshole," she muttered.

One down. One to go.

Hacienda Del Norte
Northern Mexico

The rattle of incoming fire increased from a few random pings to a full storm of copper-jacketed hail. The metal wall of the barn began to resemble a colander as the guard force by the stables started shooting in earnest. Bullets skipped and rang across the pavement and popped into the back of the trailer. Victor cursed when some hit the rear tires.

"Get back here!" Yeager yelled. Rounds impacted the sacks of cocaine that he sheltered behind. If the incoming bullets caused little puffs of cocaine to drift in the air, he'd be inhaling the stuff like some Cuban dope runner or a redneck Scarface. He snagged a paper dust mask off a nearby table and slipped it over his nose and mouth. He concentrated on providing covering fire while Victor scrambled back. The M4 kicked Yeager's shoulder in solid thumps as he targeted muzzle flashes, ducked, and moved to another position. *Fire, duck, repeat.*

Victor scooted around the line of pallets to his left, rolled, and came to rest with his back against the stack, breathing hard. "So now what, Jim Bowie?" He panted as if he'd run a marathon. "The Mexicans got us surrounded."

"I thought you were a Mexican," Yeager yelled. His voice sounded tinny over the ringing in his ears.

"Not today. Today I'm like, you know, one of the valiant defenders."

Yeager started to yell something back when God slapped his hand on the ground and a white-hot flash lit the inside of the warehouse.

———⟫✶⟪———

DaSilva crouched beside a bench, remaining out of the warehouse sniper's view. Santos getting shot right next to him—one second talking, the next flying backward—had stunned him. He had no wish to be killed from afar, without even a chance to shoot back. Killing like that... well, it was not something people did to DaSilva.

He grabbed a radio from one of the four men left with him and ordered Marco to increase the suppressing fire on the front of the barn. He hoped the attacking force would be pinned down while Gomez and the flankers took them by surprise.

The radio crackled in his hand. "Don DaSilva?" Gomez said.

"Yes?"

"We are in position."

"All units!" DaSilva barked. "Fire on the intruders. Gomez, go, go, go!"

A moment later, a mammoth thump blew out the barracks windows. Blooms of fire spewed glass and debris as far as the garden fence, bits spattering across the men huddled there.

DaSilva flinched and ducked, even though nothing came close to him behind the protection of the porch's adobe arches. "*Madre de Dios!*"

A trap. Gomez and his men had walked into a booby trap. Given the size of the explosion inside the barracks, there was no doubt that all of them were dead.

Damn. "You," he said, pointing at one of the men crouched nearby. DaSilva's ears were still ringing, and his voice sounded as if it came from a well. The man he picked was huge, built like a refrigerator. "What is your name?"

"Lopez."

"Lopez, take two others and follow Gomez. Their trap is sprung. They won't be expecting another attack from that direction."

Lopez and the other three exchanged doubtful looks. Nobody moved.

"Go!" DaSilva fired a bullet into the ground near the guard's foot.

Lopez stood slowly, moving like a much older man. He jerked his head at two of his *compadres,* and they all moved off, heads down, clearly unhappy.

Time for the frontal assault.

CHAPTER 34

SKEETER'S HANDGUN LAY NEXT TO a stack of metal shelving. The long-barreled Ruger Blackhawk was chambered for .44 magnums, a souped-up cowboy six-gun. Charlie checked the load by flipping open the gate on the side, setting the hammer to half-cock, and spinning the cylinder. There were six fat cartridges, one in every chamber.

Her dad owned one exactly like it. He used it because the Ruger had a transfer bar that prevented misfire by making sure the hammer couldn't strike the firing pin unless the trigger was pulled. Charlie was finally glad she'd sat through all the hours of gun tutoring. "Thanks, Dad," she whispered.

Everything felt surreal. Cotton wool packed her brain. Her thoughts came at random and slipped away without leaving any lasting impression. Except for two: David and Abel. She needed to reach Abel before he got himself killed going after that money.

Charlie went through the open door leading from the convenience store to the wood-frame house where Harlan had said he was going to set up camp. Twenty feet across a covered, screened walkway, she moved through another open door and into the house. The room she entered had once been a kitchen, but all that was left was a shell of drywall and cabinets with no doors. A dim glow came from yet another doorway that had nothing left but the frame.

She tiptoed over to that one and peeped into a living area. Hissing, yellow light emanated from a Coleman lantern turned to its lowest setting. Two sleeping bags lay on either side of the lantern. Harlan slept in the closest one.

She kicked his foot.

He jerked awake. After a couple of blinks, his eyes focused then widened in surprise. "Hey," he said. "Hey."

"Put your hands—"

Harlan came up, hard and fast, a glint of blue steel in his right hand.

She shot him once in the chest.

She cocked the single-action revolver and shot him again.

He thumped to the floor, his Hawaiian shirt blossoming with reddening flowers.

Charlie looked for a cell phone.

Hacienda Del Norte
Northern Mexico

Yeager stared at the ceiling of the barn, stunned. He blinked and worked his jaw, his ears whining a high-pitched tone that drowned out all other sound. Then he remembered he was in a firefight and struggled to a sitting position behind the wall of cocaine-filled sandbags.

Victor was on all fours, shaking his head like a dog. Smoke and dust fogged the air on the south side of the barn, where the barracks door used to be. There was nothing left but a massive hole torn in the wall. Yeager hoped the dust in the air wasn't filled with cocaine.

"Por Que!" Yeager yelled. "Por Que! Victor!"

Victor looked up and nodded. "I'm good," he mouthed.

"Left flank," Yeager said, pointing to the smoking new hole.

Victor nodded again. "Hey, stupido. Next time, don' use so much C4."

Yeager smiled and gave him a thumbs-up.

"What's the plan?" Victor asked, scooting over to sit with his back against the pallet of dope.

"The plan? Kill all these sonsabitches so we can get out of here with the money."

"Kill 'em all? Tha's your plan?"

"How else are we gettin' outta here with the cash?"

Victor shook his head. Yeager peered over the top of his improvised barricade, trying to see through the gap in the barn door. Bullets pinged sporadically through the metal sides of the building or thumped into the dope bags, more annoying than threatening. His pants pocket buzzed, and he jerked in surprise before he realized it was his cell phone ringing. He dug it out and looked at the Caller ID. *Blocked.*

Victor's eyebrows arched. "You're answering the phone in the middle of a firefight?"

"It might be the kidnappers." He thumbed the button. "Yeager here."

"Abel?"

The voice was faint and hard to hear through the crackle of static and the ringing in his ears, but he recognized it instantly. "Charlie? Is that you? Are you okay?"

"Marco?" DaSilva keyed the mike as if he wanted to crush it. "Marco, do you hear me?"

"Marco here."

"We are done fucking around with these guys. You and your men will hit the barn on my command. Get them ready."

There was a long pause, long enough that DaSilva almost keyed the mike to repeat his orders. He stared at the stables, willing the nightshift commander to answer him.

"Don DaSilva…" Marco said, then the radio crackled to silence.

"Listen to me," DaSilva said, enunciating each word with care. "We will kill the lights in the courtyard. Your north group will swing wide north, and your south group will swing wide south, like a claw. That way, you will approach the barn out of sight of those inside, further hidden by darkness. At the door, toss in grenades then rush in." He couldn't help but add, "Wait for the grenades to explode before you go in."

"*Sí*, Don DaSilva."

"Move when the lights go out."

"*Sí*."

DaSilva pointed at the single guard still with him. "Get the lights." The man nodded and rushed off, crouched low to minimize his profile. He disappeared into the hacienda.

DaSilva scratched his cheek with the front sight of his pistol and stared at the triangular gap where the trailer of the diesel rig protruded from their drug processing building. *Not long. Not long at all.*

"You mean we don' have to stay?" Victor asked.

Yeager shook his head, staring at his silent phone, still unable to believe it. "She got away. Somehow, she got away. The bad guys are dead."

A bullet hit the bag next to Yeager's head in the same instant that Victor yelled, "Tangos!" and started firing.

Yeager ducked and rolled, coming up in a different position and using one of the workbenches as a shield. Three men fanned out from the hole in the barracks doorway, two going right, one left.

Yeager snapped a three-round burst at the two on the right and missed. One ducked behind another bench, while the other crouched and tried to bring his weapon to bear. Yeager's next burst took the second guy center mass, sending the guard crashing back into the wall.

Victor traded shots with the guy behind the bench, and Yeager looked for the guard on the left. Not seeing him, Yeager crabbed sideways, deeper into the warehouse, keeping low.

"Por Que?" he called.

"Yeah?"

"You work on getting Extraction Plan B into action. I'll take care of these guys."

"You got it. Plan B comin' up."

Then the lights went out.

Charlie sat on the front porch of the abandoned house and waited for the police to arrive. She didn't know where she was, so she'd described the place to the dispatcher as best she could. She told them about Nita being taken to see John Stone, and the dispatcher said she would send somebody to investigate.

"Sit tight," the woman said. "Help is on the way."

Help. She'd killed two men. She was going to need lots of help. They'd kidnapped her, planned to kill her, and sexually assaulted her. But after killing Skeeter, she could have walked away. She could have taken the road out front either left or right and headed for the nearest house.

Shooting Harlan had been an act of pure selfish rage and a desire for vengeance. The law didn't take kindly to that type of thing. She would likely be arrested and might have to defend herself in a murder trial. Maybe she would hire that guy who'd represented Abel. He seemed very good.

Whatever. She couldn't work up a pinch of regret for exterminating those two assholes.

She picked up the late Harlan's cell phone and dialed Tomas's number. It was pretty late, and she would be waking them up, but that was unavoidable.

She was going to talk to her son, no matter what.

———◆———

Yeager pulled the NVGs back down over his eyes, and the inside of the barn turned from pitch black to monochrome green. The guard on the right was holding his weapon over the top of the bench and spraying bullets in Victor's general direction, showing only his hands and keeping his head down.

"Frag out!" Yeager pulled the pin on a fragmentation grenade, counted off two Mississippis in his head, then lobbed it over the guard's head.

The indiscriminate fire paused. The guy was probably staring into the darkness and wondering what had landed behind him. Yeager ducked, covered his ears, and clenched his eyes shut.

Crack!

Even with his eyes closed, Yeager saw the flash, and he felt the thump in his chest. He peeked over his makeshift barricade and assessed his target. Heavy damage had been done to the wall, and an arm was lying across the bench.

One down. He low-crawled down the aisle, eyes and ears straining for evidence of the other guy's whereabouts. He paused three-fourths of the way to the end. The back wall of the warehouse was about twenty feet away. The man who had peeled right had ducked behind the first row of benches and dropped out of sight. Two aisles separated Yeager from the first row.

So he's either one or two aisles over. Or somewhere along the back, between the benches and the wall. Yeager crawled forward on elbows and knees, making as little noise as possible. Not that it mattered much. Victor was calling on the radio in between bursts of suppressing fire as he tried to keep the guards out front from getting too rambunctious. Incoming rounds still pinged and popped, hitting walls, floors, ceiling, and light fixtures. *And if the other guy's hearing is as fucked up as mine—*

The guard flew around the corner of the workbench, tripped over Yeager's prone body, and went sprawling. The M4 cradled in Yeager's arm cracked him in the cheek when the guard kicked it. The guy ended up sprawled on top of Yeager, his own weapon clattering down the aisle.

Stunned by the blow to his face, Yeager twisted under the guard. He groped for his weapon's grip, dragging it from under his body.

The guard was huge. Yeager had seen smaller offensive tackles in the NFL. And the guy was quick, too. Before Yeager could get properly oriented, the enormous guard twisted with a wrestler's speed and slapped the M4 out of Yeager's hands. He punched Yeager in the face, sending his NVGs flying. Lights flashed twice: once with the punch, next when his head bounced off the hard floor.

Yeager didn't see the second punch coming. He managed to get his hands up enough to partially block the big fist before it crashed into his nose. There was a reason getting hit in the nose ended most fights right away. The pain was excruciating.

Had the giant landed that punch squarely, Yeager would have been down for the count. Even so, lights flashed in his brain for the third time in as many seconds.

The heavy guard straddled Yeager's waist, pinning him to the ground. He cocked his massive right fist. The position held Yeager like a bug on a board, but it also left his attacker's family jewels wide open.

Doubling his fists together, Yeager hammered the guard's crotch. Once. Twice. A third time—mustering all the passion and anger he could generate. When the big man doubled over and groaned, Yeager tried rolling out from under him. His opponent protected his groin while struggling to keep Yeager pinned. They twisted and writhed, wrestling for position. Everything Yeager tried resulted in a lot of nothing.

The guard grinned at him through stained teeth. He managed to get both hands around Yeager's neck, and he began to squeeze. Yeager's vision darkened almost at once, and he strained his neck tight to keep from getting his larynx crushed.

Enough of this shit. Yeager fumbled past the big man's leg, found the butt of his Wilson Combat .45, and popped the safety strap. The pistol was cocked and locked, which meant it was only a matter of...

...disengaging the thumb safety...

...and...

Boom!

The 185-grain jacketed hollow point slammed into the guy with the power of a freight train. It took him under the ribs and must have blown through heart and lungs. Blood sprayed from his mouth, splattering Yeager's face.

"Get off," Yeager gasped then shot the big sonofabitch twice more.

With the ponderous grace of a redwood, the guard toppled left and thumped onto the concrete floor with a wet smack. Wheezing and scrubbing his face with a shirt sleeve, Yeager tossed the guard's leg aside and rolled onto all fours. From there, it was a matter of willpower to push himself upright. He stood for two seconds until a wave of dizziness made him drop back to one knee. When the blackness at the edges of his vision passed, he struggled up again.

"See, that wasn't so bad," he muttered. "Now let's try walking."

Yeager weaved through the tables to the pallets. He found

Victor with his back against the barricade, like a man taking a break from a hard day's work, without a care in the world.

Except for the blood streaming down his cheek.

DaSilva strode toward the barn, approaching the men crouched against the wall to the right of the gaping door. Sounds of fighting inside the building had died, but no one had come out. That meant Lopez had either failed or succeeded and died in the attempt, but DaSilva wouldn't have bet on the latter result.

With a half dozen men on the right and another half dozen on the left, there was nowhere for the infiltrators to hide. Instead of feeding his men into the battle a little at a time, allowing the tiny number of defenders an even fight, he would flood them with a full dozen men and five from the rear as well.

He had dispatched the man who had killed the lights with an RPG to blow open the rear door so that team could enter without setting off any traps. The explosion in back would be the signal to move.

"Marco?" he barked. "Who is Marco?"

A young man with a goatee, shaved head, and bodybuilder arms stood up and raised his hand like a schoolboy. "I am."

"When the back door blows, all your men will charge the gap. We will overwhelm the intruders with numbers."

Marco smiled and bobbed his head.

"Any minute now," DaSilva said. "Get your men ready."

CHAPTER 35

Over northern Mexico

C UJO HUMMED "DOCK OF THE Bay" and adjusted for a slight crosswind with a gentle nudge of the rudder pedal. His single-engine Cessna buzzed over the rough terrain of the Mexican desert at fifty feet off the deck. Running without lights and guided by a GPS, dead reckoning, and divine influence, he scanned between instruments and terrain.

He loved flying, especially night flying. Even better, he loved combat flying. Piloting his tiny plane into a firefight, in the dark, over enemy territory—well, kind of enemy territory—made him maybe the happiest man in the world. Even if he sometimes had difficulty with the real world, and struggled to remember his birth name—David Milton Quattlebaum III—he could fly anything with wings or rotors and fly it better than anyone he knew.

On hold at the tiny airfield, Cujo chewed his nails and almost prayed that Victor and Abel's mission would go sideways so they could call in a Plan B Dust-off. So when Victor called, Cujo was in the air before the call terminated.

At one mile out, Cujo brought the Cessna into a gentle climb, gaining some altitude to assess the situation. He overflew the target at five hundred feet and took a long look out the right hand window.

He spotted the barn immediately. The moon had risen, three-quarters full, and gave plenty of light for his NVGs to make out the men clustered on either side of Abel's truck, which looked as though it had mated with the barn. Fifty yards beyond the barn, an airstrip ran north to south. His job was to find the airstrip and land.

Abel and Victor would hightail it overland and jump into the plane, then they would all fly off into the wild, black yonder.

From behind the barn, a green streak of light burned across his view. A bloom of fire temporarily whited out his goggles. Seconds later, a detonation on the ground rocked the plane.

"Looks like Plan A turned to shit." He grinned and almost bounced in his seat.

"Victor!" Yeager felt for a pulse, found it, and breathed a short prayer. He slapped his friend's cheek, trying to bring him around. "Por Que! Wake up, buddy. Time to go."

Victor's eyes cracked open, seeming bleary and unfocused. "Wha' happened?"

"They shot you in the head. It bounced off."

"Well," Victor mumbled, "tha's okay, then." His eyes sagged closed again.

"C'mon, man. No sleeping on the job. We gotta get moving."

Yeager looped Victor's arm around his neck and hoisted his friend to his feet. They stumbled toward the back of the barn, down the same aisle where Yeager had felled Goliath. The giant was still down. Yeager smiled at that, pretty sure he wasn't up for a rematch with the big son of a bitch.

He headed for the back door, willing his legs to move faster. Victor's feet bumped along, more hindrance than help. Yeager was on the verge of picking him up and carrying him when the back door blew up. The explosion knocked him on his ass, and he took Victor down with him.

"Aw, fuck me, not again." If he said it aloud, he couldn't tell it over the ringing in his ears.

"Less C4," Victor mumbled then closed his eyes again.

Men piled through the smoking gap. Yeager's M4 lay a dozen feet away, but he still had his MP5 strapped across his chest. Snapping it up, he ripped off a sustained burst, completely ignoring fire discipline and Sergeant Masterson's wise advice. He simply needed to get lots of rounds downrange to make the bastards cringe and wet their shorts.

The guards dove for cover down the back aisle. Without shouting a warning—after all, the only other friendly in the area was right next to him—Yeager tossed two grenades, one left and one right. They blew almost simultaneously.

Shrieks of pain and fear erupted, dimly heard through the ringing in his ears. Yeager swapped magazines, letting the spent one clatter to the floor. He struggled up and chugged forward, breath rasping in his throat and arms swinging for momentum. He had to follow up the grenade attack before the enemy recovered their wits.

At the end of the bench, he had a choice: go right or left. He went left.

And dropped, hit in the back by a sledgehammer blow.

<hr />

Cujo banked hard left with one hand on the yoke. With his other hand, he worked the latch on the window and slid it open. Night air blew in, cool but not too cold.

Perfect, in fact.

Reaching out the window, he grabbed a lanyard and pulled. The catches released, and the clamshell cover he'd fashioned to look like an external fuel tank came free, peeling apart to fall away. He laughed and pumped his fist when the .50-cal was revealed.

Lining up the Cessna to pass north to south across the mouth of the barn, where the men were clustered on either side of the trailer, took only seconds. He trimmed out the plane, steadied the yoke, and dove.

The little aircraft dropped like the proverbial rock. Cujo made a slight correction, and the five or six men at the back of the truck looked up. Their faces grew in his forward windscreen until he could almost make out individual expressions. He poised his feet on the rudders, ready to compensate for the recoil, and reached for the second lanyard he'd installed. This one trailed overhead, like an engineer's whistle on a locomotive, and was attached to the machine gun's trigger. With a tug, he triggered the .50-cal at three hundred feet away. Three hundred feet became one hundred, then fifty, then nothing, all within a few seconds.

The little plane shuddered and bucked and tried to crab sideways in the air. Cujo danced on the rudders and twisted the yoke, fighting to hold it straight. A line of slugs as big as a man's thumb walked across the tarmac and ripped through the half dozen men. The Browning M2 mounted under his wing fired over five hundred rounds per minute with a muzzle velocity approaching three thousand feet per second. The guards were shredded like paper dolls.

Flashing overhead low enough that his wheels almost hit the top of Abel's trailer, Cujo applied power, and fought for altitude. He winced. Abel's trailer had taken a considerable number of hits as the plane jerked and wobbled under the heavy recoil. Cujo had pretty much managed to rip it to shit.

"Oops. Sorry, Abel." He pulled up and banked to the right to set up another pass.

DaSilva stared, mouth open, at the small plane as it climbed over the roof of the hacienda, making a sweeping turn to the right. He froze, forgetting the pistol in his hand, as stupefied as the men around him.

The men from the other side of the trailer, who'd taken position at its rear in order to assault the inside of the barn, littered the ground like so much chopped meat, some moaning and twisting in agony.

DaSilva shook his head, eyes still fixed on the plane as it banked back to the left. *An airplane? Where'd they get an airplane? What now? Was he coming back? Yes! Yes, he was!* "Bastard!" DaSilva screamed, spittle flying.

With a third of his assault force wiped out in one pass, he had been reduced to six men, plus the ones from the back, who had to be engaged with the enemy. The choice was simple: stay outside and be slaughtered like pigs or enter the barn and kill the foot soldiers. If the foot soldiers were dead, the plane wouldn't matter.

With one last glance at the Cessna as it lined up for another pass, DaSilva slapped Marco on the back. "Go! Go! Go!" he shouted, shoving the muscle-bound guard. DaSilva tried to get under cover by sheer force of will.

Marco grunted and motioned to his men. They hit the gap between the trailer and door, pouring into the barn and firing blindly as they ran.

<hr>

The bullet that hit Yeager in the back had enough impact to break a rib and knock him flat on his face. Yeager had been shot before and more than once while wearing body armor. He'd never grown to enjoy the experience. A small projectile traveling at a multiple of the speed of sound imparted a tremendous amount of kinetic energy when it struck a target. Yeager likened it to being kicked by a very large pissed-off horse.

He blacked out for a few seconds then came back to his senses in a rush, completely aware of his surroundings and the impending danger. He'd fallen forward, so the shooter was behind him, probably taking aim to shoot him in the ass and claim a glorious kill in the name of drug traffickers everywhere. He jerked and rolled to his right, bringing the MP5 up in one motion. Acquiring the target took a nanosecond.

A bald-headed guard with a goatee knelt nearby, blood dribbling from his nose. Armed with a semi-automatic pistol, the guard twisted to bring his weapon up, even as Yeager brought the MP5 to bear. The guard fired, and the bullet whipped past Yeager's head, close enough for him to feel the heat.

Yeager triggered a burst, the suppressed MP5 sounding more like a sewing machine than an automatic weapon. The rounds hit the guard in the center of his chest and slapped him backward. He didn't move again.

Yeager swiveled his head, checking the remaining guards. He confirmed they were all out of the fight, either dead or too wounded to care. Slinging the MP5, Yeager jogged back over to Victor and hoisted his friend onto his feet.

"Time to go?" Victor mumbled.

"Yep. Time to go, buddy."

He helped Victor through the gaping hole in the back wall of the warehouse and headed into the night. The breeze chilled his exposed skin and felt wonderful after the smoke and death of the enclosed barn.

He had no time to enjoy it. More guards stormed the barn and started spewing rounds everywhere. Some bullets zipped through the thin metal walls and kicked up dust near his feet or whizzed past with an angry whine.

"Won't take 'em long to figure out which way we went," Yeager said. "We need to make the airstrip and hope that crazy bastard has the plane ready."

"Yes, Mama."

Yeager couldn't tell if Victor was that out of it or being his usual smartass self. "C'mon, buddy. Let's move it."

CHAPTER 36

ENRIQUE DASILVA FOLLOWED HIS MEN into the converted barn and gaped at the destruction, a great hole in the side and one in the back. Workbenches torn up and equipment shattered. Product had leaked all over the floor from burst sacks.

Incredible. "Fan out," he ordered, waving his pistol. "Search the room. Find out where they went." But DaSilva had a pretty good idea where the pair had gone, considering they had a plane at their disposal.

He jogged to the hole in the back wall where the door used to be. "There," he shouted, jabbing a finger.

Two figures huddled together, one obviously wounded, making for the airstrip. It was a long shot for a pistol, but DaSilva attempted it anyway, venting his anger by emptying the fourteen-round magazine at the retreating pair. They fell, disappearing from view. Were they wounded, or taking cover?

"To me!" DaSilva dropped his empty magazine and inserted a new one. He toggled the slide release to chamber a round. "Come. Let us finish this."

"Condor One, Red Ball here. Over." Yeager crouched in a shallow depression, the airstrip a few feet behind him.

Victor lay beside him. He was starting to come around and was not happy about it. "Ow! My fucking head." He reached up to touch the gash where a bullet had creased his scalp and hissed in pain. "Man, this shit sucks."

Yeager nodded and clicked to transmit again. "Condor One, Red Ball. Do you read? Over."

"I gotcha, Red Ball," Cujo voice crackled in his ear. "You about ready to come home? Over."

"Roger that. Quit fucking around and get down here. Out."

Yeager took inventory of his remaining weapons. He changed mags on the MP5 and put the partially spent one back in its pouch. The full one in the weapon was his last. He did the same to his .45. Plenty of ammo there, forty-two cartridges in six clips, plus two grenades.

Victor had his sidearm, a Beretta 92, and four grenades. The Beretta used a high-capacity magazine, and he carried six more like it, adding up to almost a hundred rounds of 9-millimeter. But the remaining guards carried assault rifles and could fire at greater range and accuracy.

"We're gonna have to see the whites of their eyes before we fire," Yeager said.

"Who're you? George Washington?"

"No." Yeager shifted to ease the pressure on his bruised ribs. "I'm one beat-up, tired, Marine ex-truck driver stuck in a firefight in the Mexican desert"—he keyed the transmit button—"waiting for a crazy sumbitch in a Cessna to land his fucking plane so I can go home."

Cujo's voice crackled through the small speaker. "I'm comin'. Keep your panties on." The drone of the plane's engine changed pitch as Cujo leveled it out for approach.

"I hope he can see to land," Victor muttered.

"Pray."

So far, the enemy troops had kept their heads down, except for that initial smattering of pistol fire. Several men—Yeager couldn't be sure how many—had deployed into the field and taken up positions about fifty yards away.

The Cessna touched down about a quarter of the way down the runway. The brakes squealed, and the little plane fishtailed as Cujo reversed prop and tried to bring the aircraft to a halt.

One guard popped up like a gopher, rushed forward, and fired his weapon, then dropped back to the ground. Then the others did the same. Through luck or skill, they all advanced at random times, making it hard to target any single individual.

When none of the fire came near Yeager's position, he risked a look over the rim of the shallow ditch. The guards, instead of firing at him and Victor, were targeting the Cessna. One lucky hit would disable their ride home. NVGs on, Yeager rose to one knee and fired short, controlled bursts at everything he saw moving. He didn't think he made any clean kills, but it slowed the advance somewhat.

"Red Ball One, Condor. Over."

Yeager slid back down and keyed his mike. "Go."

"Where are you?"

"Get stopped and ready for takeoff. We'll come to you. Over."

"Roger that. I'm ready now."

Yeager watched as the Cessna completed a turn at the end of the runway. That would be a long run for two sore and aching Marines, but it beat waiting for a bullet. "You up for this, Por Que?"

"Oh, hell yes."

Yeager snapped out the pins of his last two grenades and chucked both of them in the general direction of the oncoming security detail. Victor did the same with all four of his. Six loud *cracks* fired off in rapid succession, but neither looked back to gauge the effectiveness of the grenade barrage.

They pelted down the runway, legs and arms pumping at full speed. But they still ran about as fast as a kiddie car.

Victor clapped his hand to the back of his right leg and went down. Yeager leaned down, grabbed his stocky friend around the torso, and heaved him over his shoulder with a grunt. He kept running.

Ducking under the wing of the plane, Yeager found the door already open. He dumped Victor into the right front seat then clambered over him to get in the back.

Before Yeager's butt met the seat, the plane shuddered into motion. The single-engine Cessna growled as Cujo applied maximum throttle and then some. A hole starred the window next to Yeager's head, the bullet passing somewhere in front of him.

"We're taking fire!" the pilot yelled.

"Well, no shit, Cujo," Yeager said.

Yeager shoved the window and forced it to slide open a few inches. Sticking the nose of his Wilson .45 outside, he fired at the muzzle flashes, emptying the pistol in seconds. The volume of incoming fire tripled. "Take off!"

"Working on it!" Cujo shouted.

The engine shrieked, taxed to its upper limit, as the shaggy-haired pilot worked the controls. Another bullet hit the window, and shards of glass flew and cut Cujo's neck.

"Goddammit!"

Hail-like thumps hit the Cessna at increasingly short intervals. Another bullet came through the fuselage and hit Yeager in the chest. Its force spent, the round delivered a small punch and bounced off his vest.

"I've been shot again!" Yeager said.

"You win, dude." Victor worked on trying to get a bandage around his leg.

Yeager clenched his hands on the seat in front of him and willed the plane off the ground. After another thump, something *popped!* in the aircraft's body.

"Shit!" Cujo yelled. "My rudder control's gone to shit. Hold on!" Before the last word was out of his mouth, he eased back on the stick, and the Cessna nosed up and into the air.

"Wooo hooo!" Victor yelled and clapped a bloody hand on Cujo's shoulder. "You did it, man!"

Cujo grinned like a kid at Christmas. "You want to go back and strafe 'em again?"

"Oh, hell no."

Yeager let his body be pushed back into his seat by gravity as the plane climbed higher. "Do me a favor," he said.

Cujo nodded. "Sure, dude. Anything."

"When you get up to about a thousand feet or so, circle back over the ranch."

"Okay." Cujo glanced back at Yeager, his eyebrows coming together in a frown. "Why?"

"Something I gotta do."

The Cessna climbed higher, and Yeager's body let him know how it felt about the night's work. There didn't seem to be a square inch that didn't ache, from his toes to his hair.

Charlie. He smiled. She was worth every bit of it.

His thoughts drifted, and he jerked when Cujo shouted, "We're here!"

"Bank it in a spiral to the right, directly over the barn. Por Que's gonna want to see this."

"See what?" Victor asked.

Below, someone had turned about half the lights back on. A couple of tiny figures milled around the back of his truck, looking in the open door of the trailer. He didn't see anybody else in the vicinity; not that it would have mattered if he had.

Taking out a small device similar in size and function to a garage door opener, Yeager flipped up the safety cover and pressed the white button in the middle of the little black box. A half second later, the fourteen kilos of C4 that he had planted under the diesel tanks of his Peterbilt cooked off.

An enormous fireball mushroomed through the roof of the barn and billowed out of the doors. The two cartel people by the truck were first knocked down then turned into human candles. Chunks of metal roofing spiraled into the sky and fell back to earth a long way from where they'd started.

"Holy Mother of God," Victor breathed.

Yeager chuckled. "Looks like I'm out of the trucking business, huh?"

"No shit, man."

The flames soon engulfed the length of the truck trailer and spread to the surrounding warehouse. Within minutes, the entire building was belching fire and smoke.

"Damn, man," Victor said with awe. "Do you know how much money and dope you just destroyed?"

"No. And I don't give a rat's ass." Yeager leaned back and closed his eyes. "Take us home, Cujo."

CHAPTER 37

Austin, Texas

ITA HAD WANTED TO BE naked when she bashed in John Stone's head because washing blood off skin was easier than getting it out of her clothes. Earlier, with Steven, she'd ruined a perfectly good pillow by firing a .380 bullet through it.

She washed her hands in the kitchen sink and cleaned the crystal decanter she'd used as a mace, removing her fingerprints. She found a spot of blood on one breast and another on her abs, both of which she wiped off with a dish towel.

Using the towel, she opened cupboards until she found a plastic tub of disinfectant cleaning wipes. She opened the lid and pulled out several sheets of moist towelettes. Her reflection in the window over the kitchen sink caught her attention, and she gave herself a quick, wicked little grin like a girl who'd made off with the whole cookie jar, her parents none the wiser.

Slipping back into the living room on bare feet, she used the cleaning wipes on Stone's flaccid penis, removing all traces of her saliva. She inspected his body and the area surrounding it. Finding two of her long black hairs nestled in his curly pubic hair, she plucked them out and tucked them into her purse. If there were more lying around, she'd couldn't find them. What she needed was a good vacuum cleaner, but she'd have to risk it.

Besides, she planned to be long gone before anyone came looking.

With the dishtowel, Nita wiped over everything she could think of having touched then trotted back to the kitchen. She pulled a black trash bag from the same cabinet where she'd found the wipes and threw the dishtowel inside it.

Back in the living room, she added the plastic ties they'd used on her wrists to the bag then took a quick look around for anything else that needed to go. All she wanted to do was obscure the trail as much as possible and make it a tad bit harder for the cops to put her at the scene of the crime.

She could reasonably argue self-defense, given the kidnapping. But explaining Steven's dead body in her apartment would be harder. *Oh, well.*

So many things to do, so little time. She had to rent a U-Haul and swing by the bookstore. In the warehouse waited twenty-nine cardboard boxes full of cash. Getting the money separated from the books and packed away in the shelves with the store receipts had taken three hours on Saturday night. It would only take thirty minutes, tops, to load them in the U-Haul and zip out of there.

When Steven had told her to leave the money and that they'd go back later and get it, she saw the road ahead as if revealed by the hand of God. *Why share when she didn't have to?* So she'd unloaded the cash but left the skids of books on the truck for Charlie. Her redheaded friend would offload the pallets and never know the real treasure had been inside them.

After that, all Nita had to do was get rid of Steven, which had made her horny as hell for some reason, then load up the money. Unfortunately, she'd stopped by the store to measure what size truck she needed before heading to the U-Haul place, and the morons had shown up.

Satisfied with her preparations, Nita dressed quickly. She sat on the hearth to pull on her socks and shoes. Stone's glassy eyes appeared to be staring right at her, one slightly askew from the dent in the side of his head.

Standing, she removed Steven's flash drive from her pocket and cupped it in her palm. His twelve million on top of the cash in the boxes would take her a long way away from any potential prosecution. She would be deep into Mexico within twenty-four hours and in Argentina by the end of the week.

It was too bad about Charlie. No way the two numbskulls would let her live. *Call the cops after I get across the border? Yeah. Maybe.*

"You should have told me you had partners, Stevie." Nita kicked Stone's heavy coffee table and sent his bourbon glass tipping over the side to spill on the hardwood floor. "Oh well, live and learn."

She tossed the thumb drive in the air, caught it, and slipped it back in her pocket. *Time to get the hell out of here.*

Stone's pants lay in a tangled wad around his ankles. Nita dug in a pocket and found a ring of keys, one of which looked like it might match the Jag sitting in the front driveway.

"Thank you, Mr. Stone. This might be worth one blowjob."

She skipped to the front door, trash bag in one hand, keys in the other. She wrapped the plastic bag around her hand and opened the door, stepped out, and pulled it closed behind her.

"Freeze! Police!"

A flashlight pinned her shadow to the door. Nita jumped and sucked in a quick breath. Two cops flanked her, guns drawn.

Baja Peninsula, Mexico

In a heavily guarded estate in Baja, Mexico, a man held his phone in one hand while the other hand fiddled with a letter opener on his desk, spinning it in circles. "Enrique..." His tone was like that of a parent disappointed with a child's report card. "This is very distressing news. Everything is gone? The product and the facility?"

"*Sí.*"

"The truck?"

"Totally destroyed, Señor."

"The money?"

"Missing. We don't know where it is."

"Do we know who has done this thing to us?"

"Not yet," DaSilva said. "Oscar Cruz is being brought here now for questioning about the cash. But his people could not mount an attack of this scale. DEA? CIA maybe? It has to be agents of the United States, no? I will find out. Trust me."

"I do trust you, Enrique. That is why you have the position of importance that you do. However, your performance in this matter has been... less than favorable."

Silence on the other end of the line. The man spun the letter opener and let it build. After fifteen seconds passed, he said, "Find out who did this, Enrique. Make them suffer as they have made us suffer. Your position of trust with me depends upon it."

The man from Baja ended the connection.

Luis Cordoña found himself face down on the asphalt of the courtyard with a splitting headache. He brought one shaking hand up to feel his forehead and nearly screamed with the pain. A jagged wound tracked up from above his left eye to his hairline. Blood and grit caked the wound, and it throbbed with a hammering thud with every heartbeat.

Struggling to a sitting position took almost everything he had, and trying not to puke took the rest. When his eyes focused, they nearly fell out of their sockets.

The courtyard had turned into Hell. Flames totally engulfed the barn and the trailer. The outbuildings were burning as well. Tendrils of fire shot into the air, launching sparks into the night sky.

Dead men lay everywhere. The empty rocket launcher had a dent from a bullet notched into one side. *A ricochet must have come off the launcher and hit my head.*

Motion to his right caught his eye, and he saw a vision. An angel in a white gown drifted toward him from the house. Then she came closer, and he realized it was Serena, wearing nothing but a sheet and looking stunned.

Luis found the courage and strength to get to his feet. "Here, Serena. Come here."

She walked over to him, almond eyes wide, mouth open in wonder. "What happened?"

"We were attacked."

"I want to go home." The girl shivered, and her teeth started chattering.

Luis gathered her in his arms and held her close. "We will go. I will take care of you. Do not worry, little one."

"You there!" The silver-haired big shot looked a little chewed up. He was much less intimidating with his clothes blackened and dirty and his hair blown in every direction.

Serena stiffened in his arms. "That man," she whispered, "h-he hurt m-me."

"You there," the big shot repeated, demanding and arrogant. "Let go of the puta and come help. We must find out who did this."

"Sí, Señor," Luis said and let go of the trembling Serena. "Wait here a moment, my sweet," he whispered to her.

"Come on," the big shot snapped. "We have a lot to do. First we must—"

Luis pulled his old Army .45 from its holster and shot the silver-haired man until the magazine ran dry and the slide locked back.

Serena fell back into his arms, and Luis waited until her shivering stopped. He took her to one of the hacienda's many cars. He drove away, turning east toward the orange thread of sunrise painting the horizon, planning to never look back.

Yeager plugged a finger in one ear and pressed the phone hard against the other one. "Hey."

The plane rocked and bounced with turbulence, the flight characteristics skewed by the big .50-cal mounted on the wing and a number of whistling holes in the fuselage.

"Hey, yourself." Charlie's voice was distant, crackling and broken.

"I thought I'd failed, and you'd—I thought I'd lost you. How'd you get away? Did they hurt you?"

The pause lasted too long.

"Charlie, what happened? Are you okay?" he asked.

The plane rattled and bumped. Victor cursed.

Yeager shot him a hard look and whispered, "Be quiet."

Victor slanted a pained look, but said nothing.

The phone whined and popped with static. "Talk to me, Charlie. Are you okay?"

"Yeah. Yeah. I'm okay."

Even with the background noise, Yeager could hear an undercurrent in her voice that was anything but okay. Shouting into a phone wouldn't help. A solid chunk of ice settled in his belly. "All right. But if they hurt you..."

"I can't... I can't talk about it right now."

"Okay. All right. How's David?"

"Shook up, but he's fine."

Yeager waited. When Charlie didn't continue, he said, "So I'll see you soon?"

"Yeah. Let me... let me get myself together. Look, I have to go. The cops want to ask me some more questions."

"I'll call you when I land."

"Okay. Yeah," Charlie said. "Call me then."

EPILOGUE

THEY LEFT HIM THERE. THAT surprised him very much. Not as much as the devastation surrounding him, of course, but he was still shocked that they just left him.

The sun was an orange ball in the morning sky, and already the day was very hot. Oscar Cruz wandered into a downstairs bathroom of the Hacienda Del Norte and relieved himself. He used the marble washbasin to run water over his battered face, cooling the soreness. His captors had not been gentle when they pulled him from his bed. His ribs still ached from the beating they had delivered.

When they had arrived at the hacienda, they found nothing but the dead, including a silver-haired man Oscar assumed was the boss. His two captors had shouted at each other, paced around, and shouted some more. Their eyes bulged, and the fear-sweat drenched the pair of them. Eventually, they had just shoved him to the ground and left.

Very surprising.

Oscar was alone with the dead. He returned to the rear courtyard and examined the former boss—if that was who he was. He found a wallet with a black Amex card, a huge wad of cash, and not much else. Very bizarre.

Looking up, Oscar froze, mouth open. The burnt-out hulk of a trailer protruded from the shell of a barn. Smoke spiraled up, and the reek of charred chemicals made his eyes water. The truck and barn were fused in a blackened mass. He could make out no words anywhere on the vehicle to say where it had come from or why it was stuck in the hacienda's barn.

The only building left standing was the stables. Curious, Oscar went to see if there was anyone alive in there who could tell him what had happened.

———✥———

Yeager pushed through the terminal exit doors at Austin's Bergstrom Airport. He spotted Charlie, and an immense weight lifted from his chest. They hugged, and he clung to her slender body the way a drowning man clutches a life preserver. An island in the river of flowing passengers, Yeager held fast and let the darkness fade away.

"We missed the Pinewood Derby," Charlie murmured into his chest. "I thought David would be upset, but he said, 'Maybe Mr. Yeager could help me build a really fast car next year.'"

Yeager's throat clenched, and no words formed in his head.

"What do you say, Mr. Yeager? Do you want to stick around and help us build a car?"

Yeager squeezed his eyes shut. "You have any bookstore jobs for an ex-trucker?"

Charlie leaned back so he could see her wicked smile. "I think we could find a position for you. What do you say, truck-drivin' man? Want to go home and submit your application?"

"Yes," he whispered. He cleared his throat and tried again, louder, with confidence. "Yes, Charlie, I do."

"Okay then." She took his hand and led him to the exit. "Let's go home."

ABOUT THE AUTHOR

Scott Bell has over 25 years of experience protecting the assets of retail companies. He holds a degree in Criminal Justice from North Texas State University. With the kids grown and time on his hands, Scott turned back to his first love—writing. His short stories have been published in The Western Online, Cast of Wonders, and in the anthology, Desolation. When he's not writing, Scott is on the eternal quest to answer the question: What would John Wayne do?

43917331R00160

Made in the USA
Lexington, KY
03 July 2019